Liza scowled. "Dear Cordelia's publicist has gone to Maine for two weeks."

Kristin dropped into the chair beside her desk. "Ouch. No interview, no new job. What are you going to do?"

"I could, ah, meet him somehow. Then I could— charm the guy. He's single. I'm single. We meet *accidentally*. One thing leads to another. Soon he's putty in my hands and *wants* to help me out."

"Let me make sure I have this straight. Liza Dunnigan, the woman who until quite recently referred to herself as practical and predictable, is going to beguile Jack Graham, eligible man about Chicago, commonly referred to as a player?"

Liza lifted her chin. "You think I can't? Seems to me the only way to catch a player is to get in the game."

"This new Liza is really beginning to surprise me."

She wasn't the only one.

Liza could almost hear her brain lecturing: Who are you kidding? You never put the moves on guys.

She shoved the thought away. This was her chance to prove she was more than just a woman who never broke the rules, more than just a woman who did everything exactly the way she was supposed to.

She wasn't going to blow it now.

Dear Reader,

I've always liked advice columns. They're like a window into other people's lives, a glimpse of their loves and hates, their disappointments and dreams. Very often, people write to ask about relationships and how to tell if what they have is what they really want.

Who hasn't, at one time or another, wondered what their life would be like *if only...*? Who hasn't, at one time or another, wished they could throw aside their present life and turn themselves into someone new?

That's just where Liza Dunnigan is. Tired of being labeled as *practical and predictable*, fed up with dead-end relationships, she's determined to change her life—and nothing is going to get in her way. Enter Jack Graham, a handsome man-about-town who doesn't believe in true love—even though he writes an advice column for the lovelorn. Jack, too, is trying to change his life and the last thing he needs is a woman on a mission.

Put these two together, mix in one old basset hound and some quirky neighbors, and it's welcome to Coldwater, Maine, in January, temperature 10 degrees and rapidly heating up.

I love to hear from readers. Please feel free to contact me at my Web site at www.pamelaford.net. Or write me at P.O. Box 327, Grafton, WI 53024.

Pamela Ford

DEAR CORDELIA
Pamela Ford

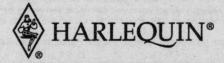

TORONTO • NEW YORK • LONDON
AMSTERDAM • PARIS • SYDNEY • HAMBURG
STOCKHOLM • ATHENS • TOKYO • MILAN • MADRID
PRAGUE • WARSAW • BUDAPEST • AUCKLAND

ISBN 0-373-78036-2

DEAR CORDELIA

Copyright © 2005 by Pamela Ford.

Books by Pamela Ford

HARLEQUIN SUPERROMANCE
1247—OH BABY!

Don't miss any of our special offers. Write to us at the
following address for information on our newest releases.

Harlequin Reader Service
U.S.: 3010 Walden Ave., P.O. Box 1325, Buffalo, NY 14269
Canadian: P.O. Box 609, Fort Erie, Ont. L2A 5X3

To Vicki, Donna, Mary, Kathy Z. and Denise
for years of great camaraderie, critique and chocolate.
And to Kathy J., who brought us together
and set us on the right path.

Dear Cordelia,
Freud had it all wrong. He should have asked: What do men want? Why is it that saying the L word practically gives men hives? Why does the merest hint of the word *commitment* catapult men into flight? Why will a man relentlessly pursue a woman, only to change his mind about her once she yields to his advances? I'm beginning to believe men think of women as they do fishing trips. Catch and release. Thank goodness it's January—the lakes are frozen over just like my heart.
Shivering in Chicago

Dear Shivering,
Things could be worse. You could still be dating a commitmentphobe. At least now you're free to find the right guy. In the famous words of Mae West, "A woman has to love a bad

man once or twice in her life to be thankful for a good one." Don't give up yet. Cordy predicts that if you let the ice in your heart melt a little, you'll soon land the keeper you've been looking for.

Cordelia

CHAPTER ONE

LIZA DUNNIGAN flipped through the papers in her in-box and grimaced at the work that lay ahead of her. An article on twenty different easy-to-make tortilla treats, a story featuring Super Bowl menus guaranteed to score a touchdown, and a third piece, tentatively titled "Waffle Mania." Ugh.

Seven years of quick easy dishes and happy holiday entertaining and cool low-carb cooking and blah, blah, blah. Enough! She'd been working in the same job at the *Chicago Sentinel* since the day she'd graduated college—the small, private girls' school her parents had insisted she attend when she'd really wanted to go to the University of Wisconsin with its wild parties and blue jeans and Big Ten football games. Instead, it had been sherry with the dean, charcoal blazers, plaid skirts and discussions of Thomas Hardy.

Well, no more.

She glanced up as one of her food-section co-workers slid into the chair next to her desk. Kristin Coulter, every man's dream woman—tall, thin, blond, blue-eyed. She wore clothing effortlessly, making everything she put on look like a *Vogue* cover. Good thing she was as nice a person as was ever born. Because it kind of made her hard to despise.

"You look different today," Kristin said.

Liza looked down at herself. "Plain navy suit. White cotton blouse. Low-heeled pumps. I don't think so." She reached behind her back to give a quick reroll to the waistband of her skirt. Kristin probably never had to roll up her waistband to make her skirt length fashionable. *Probably because Kristin had the good sense to buy new clothes when styles changed.* Liza was a bit taken aback that such a thought popped into her mind. Until this moment, she'd always considered Kristin's attention to fashion a frivolous waste of money.

"Not your clothes," Kristin was saying. "Your face. Seven years together in the food section and I can tell these things. You're hiding something."

Liza grinned.

"I knew it! What is it?"

She glanced at her watch with its slim, black leather band. *How very mundane.* "In half an hour I'm going upstairs for an interview—"

"You're leaving the food section?" Kristin gaped at her.

A tiny thrill ran through Liza at the fact her announcement came as such a shock. Kristin's reaction was reinforcement of just how predictable she'd become. It was definitely time to put her new plan into action. As of today, her motto was, *Throw caution to the wind.*

Kristin leaned forward and waggled a finger at her. "This has something to do with Greg, doesn't it?"

Jeez. "No. It's about me. I'm twenty-nine years old, in a rut twenty feet deep and a mile wide."

Kristin pushed herself up, put her hands on her hips and faced Liza, eyes twinkling. "It's about Greg."

Liza exhaled in defeat. "Fine. If it makes you feel better, I admit, Greg is the catalyst. But all he did was open my eyes. When he called me 'practical and predictable,' it made me realize just how boring I really am."

"Honey, that was months ago. Just because he dumped you doesn't mean he's right. The world could use a few more practical people."

"Let it be someone other than me. *I* am changing my life."

"Because of Greg."

"No. Because of me. All my life I've followed the rules, taken the safe route even when I didn't want to. And what has it gotten me? Don't answer that. It's too late for sales pitches about yesterday's life. I've thought about this for months. It is *time* to shake things up. I'm going after the kind of job I've always wanted, the kind of job I should have applied for years ago."

"You're leaving the food section," Kristin repeated, almost dumbfounded.

"Cross your fingers," Liza said airily. "There's an opening upstairs for an investigative reporter and I'm going for it. With any luck, I'll soon be saying goodbye meatballs and hello mystery."

FORTY-FIVE MINUTES later she was seated across a large beat-up metal desk from Bill Klein, managing editor, a paunchy and wrinkled middle-aged man who looked as if he had left investigative reporting behind years ago. While his desktop was virtually empty, fat manila files and stacks of paper covered almost every other flat surface in the room. Behind him, fish burbled and swam across his black computer screen.

He hadn't cracked a smile since the interview began, hadn't seemed impressed by her résumé. And now, it was painfully clear, as she watched his bald head bent over her portfolio of sample articles, that he wasn't impressed by her writing either.

"You've been with the food section for seven years," he said in a monotone. "Tell me about that."

Liza cleared her throat. The job-hunting book she'd read said to sell yourself, make your experience match the skills needed for the job. Food—investigative reporting. Now *there* was a match if she'd ever seen one.

"I get story ideas from almost anywhere. I might read something that will inspire a concept for a series. Or a meal in a restaurant will trigger an idea. Then my first step is—" she paused for emphasis "—*research and investigation.* I'll look into the history of a certain dish or the uses of a particular spice. I dig in, search to find the truth and expose it to—"

A loud screech from the interoffice buzzer on his telephone stopped her midsentence.

Mr. Klein sighed and picked up the phone. "Yes?"

Liza shifted in her seat so she could look through the glass wall behind her at the newsroom, awash in activity. She could picture herself there, phone squeezed between shoulder and ear as she typed the finishing touches of a gripping exposé into the computer. Her heart beat a little faster. This was where the action was, the excitement, the pulse of the newspaper. She had to get this job. She just had to. This was about as far from predictable as you could get.

After a long pause, Klein said, "You tell him the deadline is nine o'clock. If he's not finished by then, the story doesn't go in. It's not a big enough scoop to hold the presses. Got that? And Mary, hold my calls, I'm doing an interview right now."

He banged the phone onto the base and shook his head. "Sorry. We're using a freelancer until we can fill this position. The guy doesn't understand the meaning of the word *deadline*."

Liza nodded. "I've never missed a deadline in the food section. I'd bring that same conscientiousness to investigative reporting. A reporter needs to know when the story is finished.

I guess it's sort of an intuitive thing." An intuitive thing? Oh, please, she needed to learn when to quit talking.

He raised an eyebrow. "Tell me, does this intuition thing help out when you can't get anyone to confirm information on the record that someone has slipped you off the record?"

A thrill of excitement rushed through her. Never once in all her years on the food section had anyone ever had to go off the record to answer her questions. *Off the record.* The very thought made her all the more determined to get the job. She sat up straighter.

"I guess…intuition would help me choose just the right persuasive argument to get the original source to go on the record. Or even help me decide whether I can push that person to give me names of people to contact who could confirm the information."

She leaned forward and felt the waistband at the back of her skirt unroll a bit. "Mr. Klein, I think I could do a good job for you and I'd do whatever needs to be done to—make sure I do just that." Babbling, babbling.

He drew a long slow breath and sat back in his chair. "I'm sure you work hard—"

"And I can even work harder—"

"But this isn't an entry-level job. You've no experience in this type of journalism. And you're used to the pace of the food section—we've got tight deadlines. We'll get breaking news late in the afternoon and you'd have to investigate it and submit your story in a few hours."

He closed her portfolio and shoved it gently toward her.

"I can do that. If you look at the back of my portfolio there are some stories I wrote for my college newspaper. They're much more investigative. I didn't start writing about food until I graduated." Her words tumbled out in a desperate rush. "My goal was always to write about something more meaningful, something more important to life than food." She felt her dream slip away with her prattling. "Not that food isn't important to life…"

"I need someone who can hit the ground running. I'm sorry." He stood, signaling the interview's end.

Liza stared at him dumbly. It was over? Her one chance to break out, change her life, prove to herself that she wasn't so predictable after all? Defeated, she lifted her portfolio off his desk and stood to shake his hand.

"Thank you for talking with me," she said.

He pulled open the office door and stepped back to let her pass, then followed her out. For a brief heart-stopping moment she thought he wanted to talk with her further, then she realized his attention was focused on a young man heading across the newsroom in their direction.

"Are you getting anywhere on the interview with Dear Cordelia?" Mr. Klein asked when the reporter neared.

Liza hesitated, curious. Dear Cordelia, the advice columnist? She bent over a nearby drinking fountain, letting the water run over her lips, swallowing every now and then so it looked as if she was actually taking a drink— a very long one. The back of her waistband unrolled a little more.

"Nope," came the reply. "Can't get near her. What a recluse. Her publicist says she doesn't want publicity. Just wants to be left alone to write her column and help people find *true love*. So what does she need a publicist for?"

"True love for me would happen on the day she finally grants us an interview."

"Well, at this rate, we won't have it by Valentine's Day… And you know I'll be off for two weeks—"

"Yeah, yeah. Hell, let it rest until you're back from your honeymoon."

Still bent over the water fountain, Liza tipped her head slightly and watched Mr. Klein step back into his office. She straightened and dabbed at the water that trickled over her lower lip to her chin. Reaching one hand behind her back, she surreptitiously rerolled her waistband so her skirt length was even all around.

So, he wanted an interview with Dear Cordelia, the purveyor of advice about romance and marriage, the author of the bestselling *Dear Cordelia's Authoritative Guide to Finding Love and Keeping It.*

Well, well. This certainly presented possibilities. The practical, predictable person would go back to her office and write a story on the many uses of the lowly tortilla. Right. And Mr. Klein had already made it clear she belonged in the food section—not in investigative reporting. Uh-huh. She knew where her place was, where her skills were valued.

Before she could second-guess herself, she spun on her heel and marched back into his office. "Mr. Klein?"

He raised his head; surprise flickered across his face.

"I couldn't help overhearing the conversation you just had...about Dear Cordelia?"

He stared at her, silent, and a heat wave of mortification swept over her. She pushed forward.

"I love her column. I've been reading it for years."

He lifted an eyebrow.

"What I'm trying to say is... I'd like to— I could— I mean— How about letting me try to get the interview for you?" The words rushed out of her, not at all professional like the book advised. "I could do it on spec, to show you my investigative abilities, while that other reporter is on vacation. If I don't succeed, he can take over where I've left off."

The corners of his mouth twitched, the first sign all morning that she'd made any type of impression on him at all. Great. He was going to laugh at her.

"What about your responsibilities for the food section?"

Oh. "Well...vacation," she blurted out. "The new year just started. I could—I've got two weeks—I could take them off now to track down Dear Cordelia and get the interview." She mentally winced. Showing desperation was a definite no-no in the job-hunting book.

He steepled his fingers. "I've been trying to get an interview with Dear Cordelia for ten years now. She's never, by the way, given an interview to anyone anywhere. In all my years of reporting, this is the only story I never got. I've assigned a dozen reporters at various times to get an interview with Cordelia. And everyone has failed."

Her heart dropped into her stomach.

"In other words, Liza Dunnigan, what makes you think you can succeed where nobody else could?"

Because this is the most impulsive thing I've ever done in my life and if I don't try, then Greg is right about me. "Because I want this interview as much as you do," she said. "Because if I succeed, we agree that you'll hire me to fill the investigative-reporter opening, which is really what I want." Good Lord, did she just say what she heard herself say?

A slow grin slid across his face. He threw back his head and laughed. "Kid, you just might have what it takes."

"I know I can do it." She gripped the handle of her portfolio tightly to keep her hands from shaking at the enormity of her lie. Any moment the ceiling was going to open and a lightning bolt would shoot down from above and take her out.

Close the sale, the book said. *Ask for the job.* "Do we have a deal?"

"Oh, what the hell." He reached a hand across the desk and she grasped it with her own. "Deal. Let's go get the file so you can get up to speed on the first lady of the lovelorn, Dear Cordelia."

"YOU'VE GOT TO BE kidding me." Jack Graham shifted the telephone to his other ear and spun his chair round so he could stare out the window at the gray, blustery January afternoon. Today was one of those days that earned Chicago the nickname the Windy City. "The caretaker kicked off before the dog?"

"Happened yesterday morning," Dorothy Cooper, his grandmother's neighbor, said with precision. "Heart attack right after church in the parking lot. Like the good Lord just didn't want Billy to leave, wanted to call him home right then and there. I'll go feed C.J. and let her out, but you know I can't bring her over here. I have allergies…and at my age even allergies can be dangerous."

Jack nodded to himself. Just what he needed—one more damn thing to take care of.

Halfway across the country, in Maine, no less. *Happy Monday.* He sighed.

As a publicist, he always had one fire or another to put out. And on top of his regular work, later this week he had an appointment with a wide receiver for the Chicago Bears who wanted to talk about Jack becoming his agent. Representing this guy would be a huge step toward realizing a dream he'd had since college.

Except, the dog's caretaker had died.

And now—hold the presses, stop the train— he had to drop everything and go to Maine to arrange for a new caretaker for his grandmother's basset hound.

"Jack? Did you say something? Speak up— I don't hear so well anymore. What do you want me to do? You'll be coming out, won't you?" Dorothy asked.

Guilt washed through him; his grandmother had loved that dog. She'd taken it in as a mangy, moth-eaten stray and given it a home—just like she'd done over the years with so many other dogs and cats, and a little boy named Jack. Before she died three years ago, she'd set up a trust fund to cover the cost of a caretaker, to allow C.J. to live out the rest of her days in her home. "Uh, yeah. Can you keep taking care of

C.J. for a few days? I've gotta clear my calendar, then I'll get out there as soon as I can."

"At some point, Billy's daughter's gonna want to get in there and get his stuff."

"Maybe she'll want the job," he said hopefully.

"Hmmph. I know you always *see* her when you come back. And it's none of my business who you hire, but she's got all those boys—four of 'em—"

"Right. Forget I said it. Just let her in if she wants to pick up his things before I get there." He paused, thinking.

It had been hard enough to find the guy who took the job three years ago. Now who the hell was going to want to take care of a fat, old, shedding, slobbering basset hound that had one bulging eye from glaucoma?

"You know it might speed things up," he said. "Can you put an ad in the classifieds for me? Something like… Live-in caretaker needed for twelve-year-old basset hound. Single person preferred. If interested, leave message at…" He paused. "You wouldn't want to do some interviews, would— Oh, never mind. Put in my grandmother's phone number. I'll set up appointments once I get there."

Jack's new secretary stepped into the room

and dropped a note on his desk, all the while smiling prettily in her clingy little sweater and short skirt. He grinned back at her. She might be a bit light on gray matter, but she sure improved the office scenery. Maybe he should take her with him to Maine to interview candidates. They could call it a business retreat.

He watched the young woman stroll gracefully from his office and he shook his head. Not a good idea. Years ago, he'd given himself a rule to live by—never fraternize with employees. Too much risk that the woman would learn more about him than he needed her to know. If that ever happened, he stood to lose way too much—his income, his lifestyle, his reputation, his future.

It crossed his mind that if the temptation got too great he could always fire the girl. He chuckled. Then she'd be fair game.

He finished up the call with Dorothy and set the phone back in its cradle as he scanned the note. A reporter from the *Chicago Sentinel* had called asking for an interview with Cordelia. This was the third call from that guy in as many weeks. And he was just one of many reporters who had called.

"Not gonna happen," he muttered, crumbling

the paper into a ball and tossing it in his garbage can. The month before Valentine's Day always brought out the most requests for interviews with Cordelia. As Cordelia's publicist, all the requests came to him. After years of turning them down, he'd have thought the media would accept that Cordy just didn't give interviews. Instead, the clamor seemed to be increasing.

"The worst thing you can do is run from the media," he said aloud, repeating the advice he typically gave other clients. Unfortunately, that advice didn't help in this situation at all.

Because Cordelia didn't exist.

He'd started the damn column himself in a local shopper paper as a way to make extra money in college. His grandmother's dog, Cordelia Jane, had provided his nom de plume. Dear Cordelia had been a short-term financial solution—not a career plan.

Except, then the column had taken off. A bestselling book had followed. With success came the need to make sure no one discovered Cordelia was a man. So he appointed himself Cordelia's publicist and became a roadblock to the media.

And shoved his dream of being a sports agent into a dark corner.

Until now.

After ten years as Cordelia, he'd finally begun to go after his original goal. In the last year, he'd become the agent for a couple of up-and-coming athletes. Now he just had to build his clientele until he was doing well enough that Cordy could retire. He couldn't risk the truth ever getting out; it would ruin his chances of success. What big-time athlete would want to be represented by a guy who wrote a column for the lovelorn?

He shoved himself out of his chair and walked over to the window to watch Mother Nature try to make it snow. In order to go to Maine, he'd have to reschedule his appointment with that pro-football player. Hell. His future postponed once again.

It wasn't as if he couldn't easily run his business via cell phone from Maine for a week or two. His primary business was writing the column anyway and he was way behind, due to the fact that he was putting so much energy into building himself a sports agenting business. At least in Maine he'd have no excuses not to get the column written.

Exhaling slowly, he headed out of his office to tell his secretary to book him a flight.

"HE'S OUT for two weeks?" Liza heard her voice rise several notches. She clutched the file on Dear Cordelia that Mr. Klein had given her.

"Well, he might be back sooner, but it's too early to tell." Jack Graham's secretary sounded very young. "Unless it's an emergency, you'll have to call back then."

Liza would have stammered if only she could think of something to say. The man she needed to get to had gone out of town during the two weeks she had to get to him?

"This *is* an emergency—in a sense," she said, wondering exactly what type of emergency she could invent to find out where Graham had gone. She kept talking, spewing out the first idea that came to mind. "You see, I'm on the class-re-union committee and I need to talk to Jack as soon as possible. He volunteered to, ah—"

"Oh my gosh, what a coincidence. Are you calling from Coldwater?"

Coldwater? Coldwater, where? What was the right answer? She gambled. "Yes, I am."

The secretary laughed. "I don't think he'll mind if I tell you—that's where he is too. He flew out this morning. Go knock on his grandma's door and you can talk to him in person."

"Really? Oh, that's great." *Coldwater? Cold-*

water, where? "I can't wait to see him again," she said, stalling. "You're sure I can find him at his grandma's?"

"Absolutely," the secretary said firmly in her very young voice.

"Okay. I guess I'll run over there right now."

"You'd better wait a little. He flew into Bangor and rented a car. He's probably not there yet."

Liza breathed a mental sigh of relief. Bangor? There could only be one Bangor. In Maine. Voicing her thanks, she hung up the phone and ran an Internet search just to be sure.

Three minutes later, she dropped her head into her hands as reality hit her smack in the face. Jack Graham had gone halfway across the country. To Coldwater, Maine.

This was unbelievable. At this rate, she would be trapped in the food section forever. A desperate breath slid out of her.

She had two weeks off. And she had two choices. Either give up on the story right now or go to Coldwater herself.

She lifted her head and stared at her Word of the Day desk calendar. Today was the day she'd thought to make her first contact with Jack Graham by setting up an appointment for next week. So much for advance planning.

Now the only way she'd get this assignment done would be to track Graham down in Coldwater—admittedly one of the more impractical ideas that had ever popped into her head.

She mentally checked off all the reasons she shouldn't go to Maine. She didn't have the money for the trip, she'd never *ever* done a real investigative job like this, and there was no guarantee she would connect with the man even if she went to Coldwater.

Her gaze landed on her desk calendar again. Word of the Day: Myopic. 1: affected by near-sightedness 2: lacking in foresight or discernment: limited in outlook.

Yeah, well, that certainly fit. If she were the superstitious type, she might be able to interpret this as a sign she should definitely go to Maine.

Or not.

If only she had more guts.

"What's the matter?" Kristin strolled up to her desk. "You've got two weeks off for a trial run of your dream job. Why the long face?"

Liza scowled. "Dear Cordy's publicist has gone to Coldwater. Maine. For two weeks."

Kristin dropped into the chair beside her desk. "Ouch. No interview—no new job."

"What would you think if I follow him there?"

"And then what? Chase him around town and ask for Dear Cordelia's phone number?"

Oh. "I could, ah, meet him, somehow. Then I could—charm the guy. He's single. I'm single. We meet, *accidentally.* Over a few days we meet again, have dinner, go to a movie. One thing leads to another. Soon, he's putty in my hands and *wants* to help me out."

Kristin winced. "Let me make sure I have this straight. Liza Dunnigan, the woman who until quite recently referred to herself as practical and predictable, is going to beguile Jack Graham, eligible man about Chicago, commonly referred to as a player?"

Liza lifted her chin. "You think I can't? Seems to me the only way to catch a player is to get in the game."

"This new Liza is really beginning to surprise me."

She wasn't the only one.

Liza exhaled slowly. She could almost hear the pragmatic side of her brain lecturing: *Who are you kidding? You never put the moves on guys.*

She shoved the thought away. This was her chance, her one chance to prove she was more than just a woman who never broke the rules, more than just a woman who did everything exactly the way she was supposed to.

She wasn't going to blow it now.

CHAPTER TWO

JACK STARED across the dining-room table at the woman he was interviewing for the care-taker's job. She'd seemed promising on the phone, and even more perfect once he saw her—tall, leggy, big green eyes and long, wavy red hair. Definitely his kind of woman.

Except, the more she opened her mouth, the more this third candidate was looking like strike three.

He'd been heartened to find four phone messages when he arrived in Coldwater, four people interested in living in his grandmother's house and taking care of an old basset hound. It was certainly more than he'd expected for a town of only two thousand four hundred people. When he'd called each of them back and explained the situation, all four had remained interested. That was another good sign.

Which brought him to today and the interviews. Billy had died a week ago and Jack needed to find someone soon. He'd already imposed on Dorothy long enough, and he didn't like the idea of leaving the dog to live alone in the house any longer than she already had. One of these candidates had to work out or he was going to have to start searching all over again.

Things weren't looking promising, however. Candidate number one had been a chain-smoker. Even an hour later, he could still smell the smoke. And candidate number two had spent most of the interview talking about remodeling the house. He let his gaze drift around the 1920s home. Tall windows filled the rooms with sunlight. Wide oak crown moldings and baseboards framed the ceilings and honey oak floors, which were set off by old Oriental rugs. Nothing wrong with this old place—it was comfortable, lived in. *Homey.*

Plus, it came completely furnished—from the furniture to the dishes to the linens. This was the perfect situation for…someone. All he had to do was find that person. And candidate number three was not looking like the winner.

"You have two cats?" he asked. He looked in confusion at his notes from the telephone calls. "Did you mention that on the phone?"

She shook her head and her red hair rippled around her face. "You asked if I had any other pets. And I don't. I have two sisters. They just happen to be cats in this life."

O-kay. Definitely strike three. Jack nodded and scratched her comments on the paper next to her name. "I'll just mark that down here." He looked at her a moment, debating whether to ask one more question. He knew he really should end the interview, but, what the heck? "Any…brothers?"

"Three."

He knew it. "Cats too?"

The woman leaned forward eagerly. "One actually was born a human in this life. But the other two are birds. Isn't that interesting?"

"Extremely."

"Because my sisters were born cats and my brothers were born birds. And you know, cats are predators toward birds, so it can create some real problems."

Jack stared at her, fascinated and dumbfounded at the same time. "Especially at family dinners, I would imagine."

"You have no idea. I'm starting to wonder whether we should all go in together for counseling."

Jack nodded. "Where are your bird—ah—brothers?"

"Oh, they live with me."

Of course. He looked at his watch, then tapped it with his finger for emphasis. "We've gone a little long," he said. "So, we'll have to wrap it up—I've got another interview in just a few minutes. Thanks for coming." He stood, still talking so she couldn't try to keep the conversation going. "It's been great meeting you. I've got your number… I'll give you a call once I've made a decision."

He walked her to the door and watched as she drove away, two cats sleeping in the rear window—must be her sisters. He shook his head. He'd lied just to get her out of here—the next candidate wasn't due for another half hour.

C.J. lay on her side sleeping in a patch of sunshine on the hardwood floor. He sat beside the old basset hound and ran a hand over her head and plump body, over the black-and-tan patches of short silky hair dotted with flakes of dandruff. She thumped her tail on the floor. Jack petted the dog's flabby underbelly.

"Poor dog. You wouldn't be so bad except for that eye," he said. "Maybe an eye patch would help—you'd look sort of dashing." He rubbed C.J.'s graying muzzle and she slurped his hand with a sloppy kiss. This dog was all gentleness. "Aw, you good old pupper. Don't worry. I'll find someone to take care of you. Someone normal. Someone who likes you just the way you are."

He frowned at the dandruff and brushed it away. No need to have too many obvious flaws for the next interviewee to see. He hoped she was halfway decent, because if she wasn't, he was in trouble.

Now that he thought about it, after the last woman, the first two didn't seem so bad anymore. Maybe he'd better quit being so picky. After all, the dog didn't care if there was cigarette smoke in the house. And if someone wanted to redecorate a little and paint the walls, well, truth be told, they were looking pretty dinged up anyway. Search him how that had happened. Billy had lived here alone.

Jack leaned back against the wall, thinking. He'd probably been too businesslike. Not very inviting. As soon as he learned something he didn't like about a candidate—like cigarette smoking—he'd ruled them out for the job.

He could almost hear his grandmother now, admonishing him not to forget the human aspect, not to overlook connecting as a person. He'd do that in this last interview. He'd be more open-minded, more friendly, more willing to compromise.

The doorbell chimed and he glanced at his watch. Fifteen minutes early—a good sign. He appreciated promptness. He pushed himself to his feet and shuffled through the papers on the table to find his notes on the next interviewee. First name: Elizabeth. Nice classic name; he only hoped she was as nice a person.

LIZA STOOD on the front porch of the large bungalow that used to belong to Jack Graham's grandmother. She pressed the buzzer and stared at the door knocker engraved with the name *Graham.* Shifting nervously, she tugged at the collar of her short down jacket and sucked in a breath of cold winter air to calm the pounding of her heart. This investigative-reporting stuff took nerves of steel.

She was about to put into action the plan she and Kristin had concocted. Using the newspaper's resources, they'd gone searching for any information they could find about Jack's grandmother. It hadn't taken them long to learn she'd died three years ago. From that, they'd speculated, since the house had probably been sitting empty all this time, Jack must have gone home to put it on the market.

Granted, it was a little odd that three years had passed before he finally decided to sell. But some people took longer to grieve than others—maybe he'd needed to hold on to the house until he had some sort of closure after her death. Or maybe he was selling to get closure. She shook her head. Who cared? The key thing was, she had found a means to meet him.

And, she was dressed to catch him.

Kristin had taken her on a clothes-shopping spree like she'd never been on before. Out had gone the mantra she'd heard from her mother all her life: *classic shows class.* And in had come a new one: *fashion before comfort.* She'd never had so many pieces of clothing that were fashionable—and formfitting—in her life. A finger of cool air slid across her lower back and she reached under her jacket to tug her sweater down over the waistband of her new low-rise jeans.

After a long minute of waiting, she took hold of the knocker and pounded it four times. Twenty degrees outside and her palms were sweating. She hoped he didn't want to shake hands.

She blinked hard a couple of times as though the action would clear the panic, the sense of what-on-earth-am-I-doing from her brain. Every muscle in her arms and legs was tight. She squeezed her hands into fists and slowly opened her fingers in an effort to calm herself.

All she had to say when he came to the door was that she'd heard his house was going on the market and she was interested in buying it. Didn't matter if it was true, all it did was create an opportunity for her to meet him. And meeting him was the first important step to getting an interview with Dear Cordelia.

With any luck, Jack would invite her inside to give her a tour of the house. But just in case he didn't, she and Kristin had brainstormed some other ways to get her foot in the door, so to speak. Car trouble, needing directions, or frostbitten fingers—which was why she wasn't wearing mittens right now. She blew on her fingers. If the guy didn't hurry up and answer the door soon, she *would* have frostbite.

Exhaling slowly, she watched her breath drift away like a piece of steamy lace. She scrunched her shoulders up and down a couple of times to generate some heat. What if he wasn't home? Just as she was about to give up, the heavy front door swung open. Jack Graham stood in the doorway in blue jeans, a ski sweater and thick rag-wool socks without shoes.

Her stomach flopped. In photographs he was always moderately good-looking in that posed sort of gee-I'm-self-assured way. In person, he was—she had to hold herself back from gulping—ruggedly handsome. Tall. Light brown hair, casually mussed. Ice-blue eyes.

What had ever made her think she could seduce Jack Graham into arranging an interview with Dear Cordelia for her? Men like him never gave women like her a second glance. Failure lodged a knot in her throat so big she couldn't speak. Maybe she could just tell him, sorry wrong number, and run back to her car, back to her job, *back to her predictable life.*

And then, he grinned—oh God, what a grin, no wonder he was a player—and reached out to shake her hand. No man should be allowed to have a grin like that.

"Hi. I'm Jack Graham. Come on in." He stepped back to let her enter the house.

Whatever. Maybe these new clothes brought out an allure she didn't even know she had. She swallowed the lump and drew a breath—short and shaky, but at least she was breathing. No sense in passing out right after she'd made it through the door. She had no idea why he was inviting her in, but she was darn well going to make the most of it.

"I'm Liza. I'm here about the house," she said, mentally cringing at how she'd boiled down her carefully prepared statement to five cryptic words.

"Liza." He smiled like he knew her already. "I know. Good to meet you."

He knew? She tried not to gape. Maybe she and Kristin had been right—maybe the house really was for sale. Maybe they had hit the jackpot with their advance planning. "Sure. I mean, good to meet you too."

He motioned at an old-fashioned coat tree in the corner. "You can hang your jacket there, then have a seat at the dining-room table. Give me just a minute—I was going to get a Coke. Would you like one?" He lay another incredible smile on her that warmed her to the toes of her oh-so-stylish boots. She wasn't sure she could even answer the man—no guy who ever looked like him ever smiled at her like that.

Wow. More maybes filled her mind. Maybe this was going to be easier than she'd expected. Maybe, now that she was an investigative reporter—with hot new clothes—she really did have some sort of aura that men found attractive. Maybe she'd been settling for guys like Greg, when, all along she could have had guys like *Jack Graham.* The thought made her dizzy.

She settled into one of the dining-room chairs and tried to strike an appealing, open, seductive, friendly, trustworthy pose. Cordelia's book had said body language was so important. She shifted to the right and then left, crossed her legs and uncrossed them, leaned an elbow on the table, then two elbows, then neither. She was still working out the details when Jack set a glass of Coke in front of her on the lace tablecloth and dropped into the opposite seat.

She straightened and slid her hands into her lap, praying Jack hadn't noticed her extensive posturing. The warmth of a faint blush crept up her cheeks and she willed her embarrassment to go away.

Ice popped in her glass and startled them both. Liza grinned sheepishly.

Jack laughed. "I'll start. That's C.J. She was my grandmother's dog." He pointed at a rolypoly basset hound napping in the sun under a big window, her floppy ears like open wings on the hardwood floor.

At the sound of her name, C.J. roused herself

and ambled over to say hello. Liza reached a hand down and patted the dog's head. "Hi, C.J.," she said.

"I guess it's safe to assume you like dogs."

"Ah, yeah, actually, I do." Her eyes widened at the sight of C.J.'s bulging eye. She glanced up at Jack.

"She has glaucoma," he said. "My grandmother didn't notice it coming on and now she's blind in that eye. The vet says it doesn't hurt, so we just leave it alone… I know it's ugly, but she's a really good dog."

"She has the most woeful expression." Liza ran a hand down C.J.'s neck, then turned her attention back to Jack. This was certainly an interesting home tour—soda at the dining-room table and a discussion about the dog's glaucoma. Well, as long as she was inside the house and actually talking with Jack Graham, she wouldn't complain. She was already much further along than she had hoped to be fifteen minutes ago.

She searched for something to say. "How old is she?"

"Twelve. Probably not too many years left."

C.J. ambled over to her water dish in the corner and began to drink. With each lap of her tongue, water slobbered out the sides of her mouth and splattered onto the hardwood floor.

Jack frowned. "Bassets are sort of naturally sloppy. When she drinks, it can get pretty messy. I hope that doesn't bother you."

Bother her? Why would she care whether his grandmother's dog was a sloppy drinker? She was buying the house not the basset hound.

He seemed a little fixated on the dog. Maybe he was really struggling with letting go. She could imagine all the emotions he must be feeling about selling his grandmother's house. C.J. might be his last remaining connection with her. That was probably why all he'd done was talk about the dog so far—and not show her around the house. Maybe she should try to get the conversation back on track.

"I really like this house, the big front porch. Lots of curb appeal. Is there much of a backyard?" she asked as chirpily as she dared without sounding like a ditz.

He nodded. "Enough for a dog. You'll have to mow the grass and rake." He glanced out the window. "And shovel. The only other thing is…it's important you clean the gutters out in the fall and make sure the downspouts are attached. Since it's such an old house, it's good to keep water away from the foundation—to prevent leaks in the basement."

Jack Graham might be an eligible man about Chicago, but he definitely had some weird quirks. Was the guy going to come back and make sure the new owner kept up the maintenance on this place? She nodded and smiled weakly. "Do you mind if I look around a little?"

"Sure." He eyed her closely, as though appraising her in some way, but didn't make a move to stand. "Do you live nearby now?"

She drew a breath for courage and shook her head. "Not yet. I'm joining the staff of the Maine Culinary Institute over in Orono." She swallowed hard and let the lies keep flowing. "I've always wanted to live in a small town and decided this is the perfect opportunity."

"That won't be a bad commute at all." He nodded. "You'd have time to let C.J. out or go for a walk. We walk every day. She's getting slower but she still gets around."

What was going on here? Her brain started to race. Maybe he wasn't selling after all—maybe he was renting. But that didn't sound right, because he kept talking about the dog. He wouldn't be expecting a renter to take his grandmother's dog, would he? Jeez, the way he was talking, it almost sounded as if he was planning to live here with her. Was he moving to Coldwater and looking for a roommate? Or maybe the guy kept a woman in every port—and she would be the one in Coldwater.

She cast a sideways glance at him. This whole thing was giving her the creeps. He'd been way too friendly at the door—what had that been all about anyway? When he invited her in, she'd been optimistic about getting to know him, but now, his bizarre behavior was erasing any appeal the guy had. Although, as she thought of it, the alternative—a return to the food section—held even less appeal.

She really had to pull it together. Jack Graham was probably nothing compared to the types of people she would deal with once she became an investigative reporter. She'd better get used to it now. Besides, she didn't have a choice. He was the gatekeeper to Dear Cordelia.

"I love walking. In fact—" She jumped to her feet. "How about if you walk me around the inside of the house—I'd love to see more of it."

He stood. "Sure."

The doorbell chimed and Jack tossed her an apologetic look before striding across the room to open the door. She could hear the low mur-

mur of conversation, and a minute later Jack stepped aside to allow a blond-haired young woman wearing torn blue jeans into the room. His face was the picture of confusion. "Are you here for the dog?" he said to Liza.

"I'm here for the house."

"I know," he said. "But the dog goes with the house. You can't have one without the other."

Now, *this* was a new home-sales twist. Or rental twist. Or girl-in-every-port twist. *Whatever.* "Oh." She nodded as if she understood what was going on even though she had no idea at all.

Jack squinted at her. "I'm a little mixed up. Did you call me on the phone?"

"No. I just knocked on the front door."

"And your name is—"

"Liza."

"Isn't that short for Elizabeth?" There was definite exasperation in his voice.

"No—I'm not an Elizabeth. My mother didn't like nicknames—said they were pointless. I'm just plain Liza." *Babbling, stop babbling.*

He turned his attention to the teenager. "You're the Elizabeth who called me."

She nodded and looked around the room. "This place is awesome. How many bedrooms does it have? I have three roommates." She peeked into the door to the kitchen. "Awesome, this place is great. There's so much room, maybe we could get another roommate. Does the furniture stay? 'Cause I have a couch already, but mine isn't as nice as this one, but I could put mine on the front porch—"

"And the dog?" There was no mistaking the lack of patience in Jack's voice.

"Oh yeah, the dog will be fine." The girl bent over C.J. and gave a little wave. "Hi, puppy. Wake up! We like dogs—all of us do."

C.J. opened her eyes and clambered to her feet. The girl jumped back. "*Eeowww.* What's wrong with his eye?"

Jack looked weary. "Elizabeth...the position has been filled."

The girl straightened and made an exaggerated sad face. "It has? Already? Are you sure?"

"I'm sure. Thanks for coming. I'll be in touch if the other person doesn't work out."

The girl looked around the room, up the walls and across the ceiling as she made her way to the front door. "Okay, well, keep us in mind, 'cause we really would, um, take good care of that old dog."

Jack shut the door and turned to face Liza, his

expression sheepish. "I'm sorry. When you said your name was Liza, I just assumed it was short for Elizabeth. I had no idea you weren't the person who called—"

"The dog comes with the house?"

He nodded. "More like the house comes with the dog."

"How does that get written into a sales contract?"

"Sales contract? I'm not selling the house—I'm looking for a caretaker for the dog."

Liza looked at C.J. and the dog wagged her tail.

"Oh. I thought you were selling." You mean, this guy was normal? That is, as normal as someone could be who was looking for a caretaker to live with a dog? That revelation did wonders for his appeal. Not to mention those blue eyes…

"I thought you were applying for the job." He did that grin again, the one that made her start to think about things other than investigative reporting. Her stomach flopped and she smiled back at him.

"So you're looking for someone to stay here and take care of the dog?"

He nodded. "It's in my grandmother's will. C.J. gets to stay in the house, with a caretaker, until she dies. The man who had the job passed away last week." His face got a hopeful look. "You wouldn't, by any chance, be interested in being a caretaker instead of a home owner?"

Her mind raced—if she took the job, he'd have no reason to stay in Coldwater. He'd go back to Chicago. She could follow him there, but then she'd have to find a way to meet up with him again. And then she'd have to get him to believe a story about how she'd suddenly decided she didn't want the job at the Culinary Institute after all. Any halfway-intelligent person would think the whole thing smelled.

On the other hand, if she turned down the job, he'd just hire someone else and he'd still go back to Chicago. She cocked her head to look at him. Somehow she had to slow this down, drag it out, keep him in Coldwater until she got what she wanted from him.

"I might be interested. Do I have to decide today?" She looked up into his eyes.

He shrugged. "Not really. Although the sooner the better. I really need to get this settled."

"Because I—I'd have to think about it. The responsibility and all. I wasn't planning to have a dog." She looked at C.J. as though considering the idea. "So the caretaker lives here…free?

Utilities included? In exchange for taking care of C.J.?"

"That about covers it. Shovel the sidewalks, mow the lawn, rake the leaves."

She nodded. Well, she may not have gotten a date with Jack Graham, but this had the potential to be even better. She could take her time making a decision, string him along until she got the connection she needed to Dear Cordelia. She couldn't wait to get back to the inn and call Kristin to tell her everything that had happened.

A loud knocking at the front door drew their attention.

"Another candidate?" Liza asked.

Jack rolled his eyes. "There aren't any more."

He crossed the room but the door opened before he got to it. A tall, slender woman with short, blond-streaked hair stepped toward them, smiling at Jack like someone who knew him well. "Welcome back, stranger," she said, opening her arms.

"Connie. How are you?" Jack reached out and the two embraced, their mouths meeting for a kiss that was definitely more than platonic.

What was this? A firsthand look at *a woman in every port?* Hmm. Connie could cause a little trouble in the "beguile Jack to get information about Cordelia" department. Then again, maybe not. If she remembered the Chicago rumor mill correctly, Jack had been known to juggle multiple women.

Liza watched, fascinated, as the two pulled back slightly to have a soft conversation. All Jack's focus was on Connie and all hers was on him, both of them seemingly oblivious to anything around them. She felt a twinge of envy, wished that just once in her life a guy would make her feel like nothing in the world mattered except her.

Suddenly, four children piled through the doorway, their vision obscured by cardboard boxes upside down on each of their heads, their arms laden with other empty boxes. They charged into the room, blindly banging into one another and falling to the floor, laughing hysterically. The smallest dropped the box in his hands, pulled the one off his head and threw it, giggling when it hit the window. He looked to both sides, then charged into the dining room and hurled himself onto the floor beside C.J. The dog rolled to her feet and ambled away with the kid crawling and wiggling across the floor behind her, repeatedly calling her name.

Liza felt dazed. Four boys. She'd never seen so much chaos in one spot.

Finally even Jack and Connie couldn't ignore the turmoil any longer. Connie stepped away from Jack and clapped her hands. "Boys! That's enough!" She turned her attention back to Jack. "I thought we'd better pack up some of my dad's things and take them to Goodwill." She glanced behind him, her gaze lighting on Liza for the first time. Liza could have sworn the woman's eyes narrowed. "Unless you're busy."

Boxes slid across the floor, smacking into the walls and furniture as the boys tumbled into one another. One of the boys slid into Jack's leg, almost knocking him over.

"I'm just interviewing candidates to be the caretaker," Jack said.

Connie's eyes grew round. "Interviews? I was thinking maybe I would take over Daddy's job. This house would be fine for me and the boys—"

"Uh yeah, how old are they now?" Jack took a step back.

"Well, you can see they're getting big. Eleven, ten, nine, and Jake over there's seven."

"Wow. And you want to be C.J.'s caretaker, too, huh?" He turned and looked at Jake who was once again writhing across the floor on his belly in pursuit of C.J. The dog lumbered into the kitchen.

"The boys got to know C.J. while Daddy was caretaker. They were over here all the time. Won't be like anything's changed for her."

"So that's what happened to the walls," Jack muttered.

"What?" Connie asked.

"Calls," Jack said hastily. "Just thinking about all the calls I have to return." He caught Liza's eyes with his own and she knew he was begging her to say that she would take the job. But much as she wanted to help, she couldn't. As soon as she said yes, he'd be flying back to Chicago. And she couldn't let that happen yet.

Connie took a step toward Jack and smiled, tilting her chin down a little and looking up at him flirtatiously. "Shoot, Jack, this'd be perfect. Anytime you want to come home to visit, you can stay here with us."

Jack nodded and raised one hand. "The thing is, I didn't know you were interested… and I've already offered the job already to Miss—uh—uh—Liza—"

"Dunnigan," she said.

"Miss Dunnigan."

Connie stepped around him and looked from one to the other, her smile fading. The boys stopped jostling one another and fell silent, as if suddenly aware of a change in the room's tone.

"You're going to be the caretaker?" Connie asked.

Liza felt a prickle at the back of her neck. Poor C.J. didn't deserve to live with this woman and her four hellions. She opened her mouth to retort yes and stopped herself just in time. "I haven't decided yet," she said with decisiveness.

Connie's mouth went tight.

"Connie, why don't you get started with the packing," Jack said in a pacifying voice. He slung an arm around her shoulder and walked her toward the staircase. "No matter who gets the job, we'll still have to move your dad's things. I'll give you a call later, and we'll get together."

Connie smiled up at him and nodded. "Come on, boys." She headed up the stairs with the brigade behind her, five sets of feet clomping in military precision.

When they were gone, Jack turned to Liza. "Sorry about that. I've known Connie since high school."

"So I gathered."

He cleared his throat. "Yeah…those kids would probably give C.J. a stroke. If you take this job, it would make my life a whole lot easier."

She actually felt sorry for him. But what kind of investigative reporter would she be if she let emotion rule her decisions? She tried to smile as nicely as possible. "I just need some time to think about it. Why don't you give me your number and I'll let you know," she said with much more self-assurance than she felt.

CHAPTER THREE

LATE THAT AFTERNOON, Jack looked at the sheet of paper on which Liza had scratched her phone number and the place where she was staying—the historic Belleview Inn. The woman had excellent taste. The inn regularly landed among the top magazine picks for "discerning travelers."

What a stroke of luck that she wanted to move to the area. Why anyone would want the slow pace of Coldwater was beyond him. But the fact that she did made her all the more perfect for the job. Besides that, she seemed *normal,* which was a key requirement. Plus, she liked dogs and hadn't seemed put off by C.J.'s many…imperfections. And she was relatively attractive in an understated sort of way.

Now, *that* was critical. Probably one of the dog's most important criteria—that the new caretaker be cute. He shook his head. *His* criteria maybe, if he were a dog.

Liza was no raving beauty, but there was

something about her that intrigued him. Maybe it was the way her brown eyes sparkled when she spoke, or the way her short dark hair framed her face in tousled waves. There had been a moment when they were standing in the living room, when he'd almost reached a hand up just to touch those waves. And then Connie—and chaos—had come in the door.

He hoped Liza didn't take too long to reach a decision about the job. Because if things didn't work out with her, it was back to the drawing board for him. Either that, or it was Connie and her four bulls. Good thing he didn't have a china shop.

Maybe when Liza said she needed time to think about the offer, what she really meant was that she was uncomfortable taking care of someone else's dog. Especially a dog with bizarre medical issues. Somehow he needed to show her that C.J. was one of those dogs who grows on you so much that soon you don't even notice things like her eye or her drooling or her dandruff…

He looked at the dog. "And the only way she's going to realize that is if she gets to know you. Hell, C.J.," he muttered. "Could you turn on the charm a little?"

Liza Dunnigan sure seemed right for the job. Now he just had to convince her of it. And the sooner it happened, the better. He needed to get back to Chicago, back to his life, back to his meeting with that pro wide receiver.

He wished he could tell his grandmother about his progress with the new business. Suddenly, as he looked around the room, all he saw were memories of her. His gaze stopped at the small table by the window where she had done her crossword puzzles. He could picture her there even now, taking a break from the exercise bike she'd stuck in the middle of the living room so she wouldn't have any excuse not to ride it. He grinned. And still, she'd found excuses.

He drew a long slow breath and exhaled. God, sometimes he really missed her. Every now and then something triggered a memory and he would get this deep ache inside, a longing to see her just one more time.

Suddenly the house felt closed in, confining. He'd been indoors all day, interviewing candidates since just after noon. He needed to get outside, refresh in the icy air.

"Hey, Ceej, want to go for a walk?"

Five minutes later, he and the dog were crunching along the snow-covered sidewalk in the rapidly falling winter dusk. His breath curled white in the chill air and he hunched his shoulders against the cold.

"Jack! Jack Graham!"

His grandmother's neighbor waved at him from her front steps. Dorothy Cooper wiped her hands on her apron and pulled her heavy sweater close to her neck. He raised a hand in greeting and turned up the walk to her porch.

"How did the interviews go? Did you find someone to look after our dear C.J.?" Dorothy asked.

"Well, I'm—"

"I couldn't help but notice them coming and going all afternoon. That last one seemed awfully young—"

"In her late teens—"

"But the one before her looked like a nice girl. And pretty, too. Not too pretty like some of those ones you date, but the kind of pretty a man should come home to. Did you give her the job?"

Jack held in a laugh. The last few years of her life, his grandmother, Dorothy and another neighbor, Margaret Sanderson, seemed to devote a lot of their energy to matching him up with a *nice girl*. They weren't impressed that he dated all sorts of *women* in Chicago. In fact, that seemed to make them all the more determined to find him a wife in Coldwater.

"She's thinking about it so cross your fingers," he said. "Seems nice—you'd like her for a neighbor."

Dorothy narrowed her eyes. "I would?"

Jack nodded. "Pretty easy to talk to."

"You don't say." She set her arms akimbo and looked at him for a long moment. "When's she going to decide by?"

"Tomorrow, hopefully. But I'm not sure. If she turns me down, I'm going to be a broken man."

Another gray-haired woman popped her head out the front door. "Hello, Jack. Have you hired someone yet?"

"Hi, Margaret, not yet."

"One looks promising. Says she's easy to talk to," Dorothy said with a knowing nod.

Margaret stepped out onto the porch. "She is? Which one? Not that last girl—"

Jack held in a laugh. "No, the one before. That last one seemed awfully young—"

"That's what Dorothy and I said!"

"I was just going to tell Jack, maybe he should think about staying on. Do his business from

Coldwater—then he could take care of Cordelia himself." Dorothy nodded at Margaret.

"Ladies, you know I get claustrophobic if I stay here too long. It's too small a town."

Dorothy snorted. "It's all in your frame of mind. Now, if you were coming home every night to a pretty thing like that girl—what's her name?"

"Liza."

"If you were coming home to Liza, you wouldn't even notice where you were living."

Jack laughed again. The ladies had apparently decided to drop all pretense of subtlety in their quest to marry him off.

Dorothy shivered. "We'd better get inside before we turn into blocks of ice. What I really came out here for was to invite you to supper with us tonight."

"Oh, thanks. I figured I'd just hit a restaurant."

"No, no, no," Margaret said. "We'll be eating at six. You just come on over when you're ready."

"Okay. Thanks." Jack flipped up the back of his jacket collar to keep the wind off his neck and continued down the sidewalk. When he left the house, he'd intended only to take a walk. But now, as he and C.J. strolled along, as lights began to appear in windows of homes along the way, he knew he was purposely taking a path that would lead him past the inn where Liza Dunnigan was staying.

Nothing wrong with an *accidental* meeting. Give her a chance to see C.J. actually moving around, let her see that C.J. could be fun. He glanced down at the dog. Well, okay, fun might be stretching it a bit.

As he neared the inn, he thought about slowing his pace, then realized if he and his overweight basset hound went much slower they would be standing still. He walked past the inn and nonchalantly tried to peer into the windows. Reaching the end of the block, he paused, crossed the street and retraced his steps, albeit on the other side of the street. Hmm. That accomplished nothing.

He stopped at the end of the block and looked back. He supposed he could walk the distance again—it was dark, after all, and unlikely that anyone would notice him making the repeat tour. If that didn't result in an accidental meeting with Liza, well, at least he'd tried.

LIZA TURNED UP the volume on her cell phone as she crossed her cozy French country room in the Belleview Inn. She sank into the window seat overlooking the street. "So what do you think I should do?" she asked Kristin.

"Do? Nothing. Don't do a thing. Don't say yes, don't say no."

"But—"

"You have to keep him in Coldwater till you find out where Cordelia is. Otherwise you're screwed. You can't just follow him to Chicago and start asking questions. How will you explain that you're there?"

"I quit the Culinary Institute?" Liza asked.

"Right. And you went back to the newspaper job you told him you hate."

"Oh, yeah. Not to mention I said my dream was to live in a small town."

Kristin snorted. "No red flags here. Jeez, Liza. You show up in Chicago and Jack Graham's gonna run from you as fast as he can. You have to keep him in Coldwater."

"It seems so dishonest." Liza nervously pushed her hair back from her face.

"Welcome to investigative reporting. How do you think those famous guys get all those great stories?"

"Research, contacts?"

"Liza, you said it yourself ten minutes ago. If you accept the job, he's going to leave town.

If you turn down the job, he'll offer it to someone else and still leave town. The common denominator is that Jack Graham wants to leave town. Your job, then—"

"I know, I know. Is to make sure he stays in town. And the only way to do that—"

"Is to string him along about the job." Kristin sounded resolute.

Liza hesitated. "He might get a little upset when I ultimately turn down the job after all this stringing along."

"Cross that bridge another day. If you want this story, you don't have a choice. So what are you going to say when you call him back tomorrow? Practice it on me."

Liza sighed. She really hoped he didn't hate her at the end of all this. He might be a guy who got every woman he ever wanted, but he also seemed like a decent enough human being. She cleared her throat and began her spiel. "Jack, I'm really interested in the job, but I'd like to get to know C.J. better before making a decision. Would it be all right if I spent the next week or so getting to know the dog? I could visit at your house and take her for walks." She groaned. "I sound fake."

"No, you don't. You're fine. Just don't forget

to say something about how you're concerned about her health and want to talk to the vet."

"Oh yeah."

"And that you want to talk to a groomer about her dandruff and drooling—"

"With all these contingencies, he's going to start thinking I'm too difficult. Better quit or he'll take back his offer and I won't even have a chance." Liza leaned her head against the wall and stretched her legs out on the window seat.

"Okay! I'm done! So, is he as gorgeous in person as he is in pictures?"

"More. You would die if you saw his smile in real life." Liza gazed out the window at the narrow snow-covered street.

"I see. Is he smiling a lot? At you?" Kristin asked, teasing.

"You wouldn't believe how quiet this place is compared to Chicago."

"Oh, smooth. Nice transition."

Liza laughed. "I'm serious. This street could be a postcard from a hundred years ago. Picture this—it's night, snowing, big white flakes are falling on stately old homes, not a soul in sight except a guy walking his dog."

She paused, then drew in a sharp breath as the guy and the dog moved under a street lamp. She jumped to her feet. "Kristin! It's him!" She ducked behind the floral drape, holding the edge out with one hand to keep herself hidden, then peeked out to make sure she was right. "Ohmygosh. Jack Graham! He's walking his dog right down my street!"

"Do something!"

"Do something? Like what? Chase him down the street and ask for an interview with Dear Cordelia?"

"Get out there! Hurry up! Pretend you're on your way to dinner and invite him to join you!"

"But I ate already."

"*Liiiza!* Go! You make it an accidental meeting."

"Okay okay."

Kristin's words came fast and furious. "Now, be interested in him. Smile. Look into his eyes. Touch his arm. Laugh lightly. Ask questions. Act a little coy, a little mysterious. Okay?"

Okay? Nerves jumped in Liza's stomach. This was uncharted territory for her. "I don't know if I can do this."

"You can. Just think of going back to the food section."

"Right. Available but mysterious. Got it. Call you later." She dashed into the bathroom to see if she looked all right. Jeez, her makeup could use a touch-up and her hair was a wavy mess, but she didn't have a choice right now. He'd be gone in another minute and her chance would be gone with him.

Available but mysterious. How did one act like that? The fact that she didn't have a clue was probably the reason why men weren't falling all over themselves to go out with her.

She grabbed her jacket off the chair, shoved her feet into her boots and ran into the hall. Greg had called her *predictable.* The door banged shut behind her and she quickly locked it before running down the stairs and out onto the sidewalk. Any way you spun it, *predictable* was not a synonym for *mysterious.* Didn't mean she couldn't do it, just meant she'd better figure out how—quick.

Jack had just passed the inn. Thank goodness basset hounds had such short legs—they didn't get anywhere fast. She stared after them for a moment, gathering her courage before finally calling out his name. "Jack?"

He turned. In the light of the street lamp, she could see surprise flit across his face. "Hi." He shifted the leash to his other hand. "What are you doing here?"

"I'm staying here," she said, looking up at the inn.

"I'm kidding." He grinned. "C.J. and I thought we'd get some fresh air."

"It *is* a nice night." She felt dumb.

He nodded. "Are you off somewhere—or would you like to join us?"

She tilted her head, let a small smile touch her lips, and hoped she looked sort of mysterious—and not sickly. "I was going to get some dinner, but I guess I could walk a little first." She fell into step beside him and pulled on her gloves. "It's so quiet here. I'm used to a lot more noise."

"Me too. Where are you from?"

She hesitated, debating whether to lie and deciding against it. The closer she stayed to the truth, the less likely she would get caught. "Chicago."

"Really? Me too. And now you want to move here?"

She nodded and smiled. "I love it here. The small-town feel. Knowing your neighbors. Getting away from all the city noise and dirt. I've always wanted to live in a small town—this is just completing a dream for me." She was surprised at how easily the lie rolled out of her. Well, she would do whatever it took to get the information she needed.

"What did you do in Chicago?"

Her heart began to pound. This answer could blow everything. "I was a writer. For the food section of the newspaper." She tried to sound as nonchalant as possible.

"The *Sentinel?*" There was definite shock in his voice and she could sense him mentally pull back. If she didn't play this right, their budding friendship could end right now.

"That's the one. Newspaper work is pretty dull. I'm not cut out for it—all that research and investigative stuff—bo*rr*ing."

"That's why you're switching jobs."

"Right." She smiled at him and prayed he didn't ask any more questions. "What do you do?"

"Nothing too exciting. I'm a publicist, small firm—just me and a part-time secretary."

"It's a lot more exciting than writing about food. Do you work for anyone famous?" She held her breath, hoping she didn't sound too much like an actress in a B movie and praying she had just pushed them into a discussion about Dear Cordelia.

He hesitated. "Oh, mostly small companies, some public service…"

"Anyone *I* might have heard of?"

He paused, as though weighing his answer. Finally he said, "Oh, I don't know. Everyone's famous somewhere. Where were you going to eat?"

Whoa. Guess he didn't want to tell her he worked for Cordelia. Kind of odd. After all, it wasn't as though it was a secret. "I thought I'd wander downtown, maybe stop at that little coffee shop and get a sandwich. Unless you have a better recommendation."

He slanted a sideways look at her and she got the distinct impression he was debating something in his mind. "Ah, I might. My grandmother's neighbors invited me to dinner tonight. I'm heading over there once I drop C.J. at home. You want to join us?"

Liza's heart skipped a beat. Jack Graham, a man certifiably worth drooling over, had just asked her for a date. Sort of. Regardless, it was exactly the kind of *in* she had been hoping for. Kristin's words came back to her: *Act a little coy, a little mysterious.* "Oh, I couldn't impose…what would your neighbors think?"

"They won't care. Believe me—they'll be happy to see you. Besides, they might be *your* new neighbors. You can get the lowdown on the neighborhood. Demographics, crime rate, that kind of stuff."

Liza scrunched up her face. "Okay, but you go in and ask first—and make sure they aren't just trying to be nice."

"Deal."

Fifteen minutes later, Liza found herself being ushered into the house by a short, round, gray-haired woman. "My goodness, don't you have a second thought about eating with us," Dorothy said. "We're thrilled to have you. We saw you arrive for the interview today and knew you'd be good for the job. Told Jack that right away, isn't that right, Jack?"

He nodded, a wry smile on his face.

"Thank you." Liza grinned. The warmth of the house was a welcome change from the rapidly falling outside temperature. She shoved her gloves into her pocket just as another older woman hurried out of the kitchen.

"Hello, hello. I'm Margaret. So nice of you to join us. I'm Jack's neighbor from the other side. Or used to be. Dorothy and I decided to move in together when our husbands died. Now, don't you waste any time. Take your coats off and come right into the kitchen, the food's ready."

Dorothy nodded. "Margaret's sort of bossy."

Margaret popped her hands onto her hips. "And Dorothy's sort of a busybody."

Dorothy rolled her eyes. "But we've been neighbors practically forever—"

"So they overlook that sort of thing." Jack tossed his jacket over the banister.

Liza swallowed a laugh and followed the two women into the kitchen. She couldn't have asked for things to be going more smoothly than this. Before long, she and Jack would be friends—and she'd find a way to get him to talk about Dear Cordelia.

"We're having chicken and dumplings, I hope you like them. Jack loved them when he was young—used to finagle a dinner invitation from my boys whenever I made them," Dorothy said. She set a platter on the kitchen table and hustled back to the stove, while Margaret laid out another place setting.

Jack looked chagrined. "You knew that?"

Dorothy scooped steaming broccoli into a serving bowl and set it on the table. "Don't you think for a minute I minded one bit. You were just like one of my own."

"Yeah, I remember the spankings."

"Oh, I didn't spank you but once."

"Once was enough." Jack slashed the air with one hand.

Margaret laughed. "And well deserved it was too."

Dorothy smiled at Liza and shook her head. "We'd just had the house repainted. There were four of them—Jack, my two boys and Margaret's son. They had to be about nine years old—decided they wanted to be painters too. So they took old gallons of paint from the basement. By the time we caught them, the side of the garage was a mishmash of different colors. Those boys together were a handful, let me tell you."

Jack leaned forward and said in a stage whisper, "And she doesn't know the half of it."

Dorothy joined them at the table. "And I don't want to know. As long as you all made it safely to adulthood, there's no point fretting over what mischief you got into then."

"Amen." Margaret nodded her head. "Fill your plates, everyone. Don't let the food get cold."

Liza put a dinner roll on her plate and passed the basket to Jack. "Where are the other boys now?"

"They're all over. My Dan's in Boston, Will's in Atlanta and Margaret's son is down in Portsmouth. But they were all home for Christmas." Dorothy smiled at Jack. "Even Jack."

"And we didn't get into any trouble, either," he said around a mouthful of dumpling.

"Thank goodness," Margaret said. "Back in the old days, I was worried all the time."

Jack rolled his eyes. "Ladies, everyone gets into trouble when they're young." He nodded at Liza. "Tell her. What kind of trouble did you get into as a kid?"

Trouble? She *never* got into trouble. She shrugged. "Oh, I don't know."

"Come on, Liza, help me out here."

She grimaced. "I—I never really got into trouble."

A laugh burst out of Jack. "Oh come on. *Everyone's* done something. Out with it. I don't believe you were a Goody Two-shoes."

She stared at him, could feel the heat rising in her face. That's exactly what she'd been. She hadn't broken away from always doing the right thing—the proper thing—until two weeks ago. If her parents knew she was in Maine, lying about why she was here, and trying to use some guy to get to Dear Cordelia, they'd be mortified.

She forced away the guilt. It was about time they got mortified about something she was doing. They'd probably had the easiest job of raising a child in the entire western hemisphere. She was done living the life they insisted she lead; now she was going for what *she* wanted.

"Liza, everyone's done something. You didn't have to get caught, just had to do it. Come on, your secret's safe with us." Jack leaned forward, elbows on the table, a fork in one hand with a piece of broccoli speared on the tines, his eyes dancing. "What was it? Toilet-papering houses, stolen cigarettes smoked behind the garage, tomatoes thrown at passing cars on dark summer nights—"

"That's what happened to all my tomatoes?" Margaret glared at him.

Jack opened his eyes wide, the picture of innocence. "Not *all* your tomatoes. We took evenly from every garden on the block."

Margaret clucked her tongue and continued to eat. Jack turned his attention back to Liza.

She shook her head. "I led a dull life. An only child, born to parents who thought they'd never have any children. I think from birth on, my every outfit matched perfectly. I was—"

"The little princess." Jack looked as if he felt sorry for her.

"It wasn't that bad. You can't miss what you

never knew," she lied as she meticulously buttered her dinner roll and hoped the subject would change.

He shook his head and, for a moment, she saw a flash of sadness in his eyes. "Yes, you can," he said softly.

Margaret cleared her throat. "Now, now, none of this. We each make the best of what life has given us." She turned to Liza. "So, tell me, dear, do you have a boyfriend?"

Liza dropped her knife with a clatter onto her plate at the sudden reminder of Greg's unceremonious end to their relationship five months ago. This was not the change of subject she'd hoped for. She moved her knife to the edge of her plate. "Sorry. No. No, I don't."

"Jack isn't dating anyone right now either." Dorothy refilled her water glass.

"Dorothy, leave the poor girl alone," Margaret said.

A wry smile crossed Jack's lips. "They've taken over where my grandmother left off. Bound and determined to get me settled down."

"Single men are always lonely," Dorothy said. Margaret nodded in agreement.

Liza held in a laugh. If these two only knew how lonely Jack *wasn't* back in Chicago. And based on the welcome he got from Connie, it didn't look as if he would be lonely in Cold-water either.

Margaret waved her fork. "Jack, you know, I've been thinking. If Liza were to take the job and move into the house… Well, I don't mean to overstep here, but—"

"It's never stopped you before." He grinned.

"You really should have the walls painted."

"Thanks, Margaret. It has crossed my mind." Jack looked at Liza. "Remember, she's bossy, just in case you become her neighbor."

Dorothy frowned. "I have to agree with Mar-garet. The place is getting dreary, and some of those colors—"

"And remember, *she's* a busybody." Jack leaned forward. "The colors didn't seem to bother Billy."

Dorothy ignored him. "The colors are dated—don't you think, Liza?"

"Oh, I didn't pay any attention." She quickly stabbed a piece of chicken and popped it into her mouth in an attempt to stay out of the conversation.

"You didn't notice the harvest gold in the dining room?" Dorothy looked appalled.

"Oh, well, that, that was a little—"

"And the avocado green in the kitchen?" Margaret added.

"And the rust orange in the front hall, and the pea green in the living room?" Dorothy sighed.

Liza gave up. "Okay, I noticed."

"But did it bother you?" Jack asked.

"Not if I'm not going to live there," she said, hedging.

Margaret set her elbows on the table. "The house really needs refreshing."

"Is your nephew out of work again?" Jack asked.

Margaret looked offended.

Jack winced. "Sorry."

"Oh, for goodness' sakes," Dorothy said. "Of course he is. That boy's spent a lifetime getting by on good looks—and Margaret's said it herself a hundred times. But that doesn't mean your grandmother's house couldn't benefit from freshening up. And Davey could use the money."

Jack groaned.

"The whole place would be done in a couple of days. You could help him out if you want," Margaret said.

Jack looked at Liza and rolled his eyes. "Dave and I did some painting after college, while we were job hunting. I learned pretty fast I wasn't a natural at it."

"Good thing you got into publicity then," Liza said, hoping to nudge the discussion to Jack's work.

He grinned. "Especially since I wasn't trying to break into it. My goal back then was to become a sports agent." He shook his head.

"Really? That happened to me too. Here I am writing in the food section—or was, I mean, before I left—" Liza stopped, mortified at her mistake. She'd almost blown her cover story. "Anyway, what I always wanted to do was work in a culinary school."

"And now you're going to," Jack said.

Liza nodded, anxious to change the subject once more. "You seem to have done well in publicity."

"I'd say he has. Dear Cordelia is his main client," Dorothy said with a proud smile.

"No kidding! Really?" Now, *this* was a coup. Who would have guessed the ladies would help her out? She raised her eyebrows at Jack.

"She helps pay the bills." He forked some broccoli into his mouth and chewed slowly.

"What's she like?"

"Old, crabby, *private.*"

The two women nodded.

"Do you know her, too?" Liza asked.

"You could say we do," Dorothy said.

Liza furrowed her forehead, and her mind began to work. These ladies knew Dear Cordelia? If she couldn't get what she needed from Jack, maybe she could make a connection through Dorothy and Margaret.

"What she means is that we feel like we know her because of Jack's working for her all these years," Margaret said.

"You don't need to interpret for me. I know how to speak for myself," Dorothy said irritably.

"I never said you didn't."

"Is Dave available to paint right away? I did notice the walls looked a little beat up." Jack smiled brightly.

Liza mentally groaned. Something didn't seem right about the ladies' answer, and now Jack had just made another quick switch away from Dear Cordelia. This guy was determined not to talk.

"I'm sure he is. I'll call—he could probably start tomorrow if you get the paint."

"Tell him to pick up a nice off-white," Jack said as he spooned another dumpling onto his plate.

"That would be safest," Liza said.

"Predictable," Margaret added.

Liza blanched. How quickly she fell back into old habits.

"It's not that important," Jack said.

"Well, then go with colors. Your grandmother had color in every room." Margaret gestured grandly with one hand.

"Look, ladies, I'm willing to help Dave out here, but let's not get carried away. I don't feel like picking out paint—"

"Liza can help you." Dorothy looked at Liza. "Can't you, dear?"

Jack looked at Liza and shook his head. "I'm sorry. Years ago they escaped from an asylum. They were harmless, so no one ever turned them in. But they're getting worse as they get older. It may be time to call the head administrator."

"Oh, Jack, stop that nonsense. Liza, can you help him?" Margaret asked.

Liza sat up straighter. Of course. Whatever it took to get close to the guy. Dear Cordelia, here she came. "I'd love to."

Jack's mouth dropped open but not a word came out.

Margaret clapped her hands together. "Perfect. I'll call Davey!"

Jack raised his hands, then let them drop in

defeat. "And they wonder why I don't visit more often?"

He looked at Liza and for the first time she noticed how long his lashes were, how the skin crinkled in the corners of his eyes when he smiled, how a lock of hair kept falling onto his forehead…and how much she wanted to reach over and brush it to the side.

She jerked her eyes from him and focused on her plate of food. She came to Coldwater to get information, and instead, she was falling for the mark.

This was no way to begin a career as an investigative reporter. Jeez, if she fell for every good-looking guy she interviewed, she'd end up with all sorts of charming memories and not an interview to her name.

She had to pull her feelings into line or she'd be back in the food section writing about melt-in-your-mouth meat loaf and creative Jell-O molds for sensational summer picnics. The thought was enough to drive any ideas of romance right out of her head.

CHAPTER FOUR

THE NEXT AFTERNOON, after a moderately enjoyable couple of hours picking out paint with Liza, Jack sat at the desk in his bedroom and stared in frustration at the document on the screen of his laptop computer. Dave had arrived soon after they came home with the paint and already was at work *refreshing* the walls, as the ladies called it. Liza had taken C.J. out for a walk. And he had come upstairs to get some work done. Except, he'd been up here an hour already and had managed to accomplish absolutely nothing. He forced himself to reread the letter on his screen.

Dear Cordelia,
I'm a thirty-five-year-old female and I always seem to pick the wrong guys. I'm a college graduate, have a good job and people tell me I'm attractive. So why do I always date guys who are losers, are going nowhere or have

some problem like being in major debt, or out of work, or married, or alcoholic? You get the idea. I'm ready for true love. Just tell me how to find it.

Loser Magnet

The words blurred in front of his eyes and he dropped his head into his hands. He could hardly stand it anymore. He'd probably read three thousand variations of this same letter, had probably answered it dozens of times in the column. And no one ever figured it out.

There was no such thing as true love.

After years of reading dozens of books on love, romance and psychology; years of monitoring other advice columns to glean tidbits of insight; years of getting input from his grandmother, all in an effort to be able to answer the questions readers sent to Cordelia, he'd reached the conclusion that true love was a myth. He'd realized that, for all the millions of dollars being spent on love, no one was finding it. Well, almost no one. And he had a sneaking suspicion that those who said they'd found it were lying.

All that the books and columns did was perpetuate the myth that true love existed. Hell, he was as much to blame as they were. Frankly, he was sick of it. Which was all the more reason why Cordelia needed to retire.

Laughter drifted up the stairs and in through his open door. He sighed. Liza must be back from walking the dog. And Davey must be turning on the charm.

Boy meets girl.

And whenever Dave met a new woman... That guy hadn't changed a bit since he was a two-time, all-conference baseball and football star in high school. A ladies' man then and a ladies' man now.

Jack gritted his teeth and began to type.

Dear Magnet,
You like men with baggage so much you should take a trip—to see a psychologist. And if that doesn't work, give it up. True love is an urban myth.

He stared at the screen for a moment, then hit the backspace key, deleting everything he'd just written. Wow, time for a break already; he was letting his cynicism get in the way of work. No matter how sick he was of writing this column, no matter how tired he was of keeping up the deception about Cordelia, he couldn't quit before he got his sports-agenting business on solid ground. Only then could Cordelia retire. Until then, he needed her to maintain his income, his lifestyle…and his freedom.

His cell phone rang and he answered it eagerly, grateful for the interruption.

"Jack, this is Molly. I'm thinking, really thinking, about signing with you." She laughed nervously.

He recognized the voice of Molly Monroe, an up-and-coming beach volleyball player. It wouldn't be long before she was top-ranked. A thrill ran through him. This was more like it. "I'm glad you are," he said smoothly, sitting back in his chair. "Because together, I think we'd be headed for big things."

"I like you," she said. "I like your style. But I can't just base my decision on that. This is *business*. People keep telling me to go with a name, an established place. You know?"

He'd heard this before. It was his number-one stumbling block to breaking into sports agenting. He drew a breath and dived into his pitch. "Molly, all my years in publicity are going to work for you. I know the media. I know how to *work* the media. I took Cordelia to the top. I can take you there, too."

"What do you see for me?"

"Big names. A shoe company, a clothing line. Come on, you'd be perfect for athletic wear. How about a sunscreen manufacturer? Then there's bottled water or a soft-drink company." He raised his voice a notch. "Molly, that's only the beginning—"

"Jack! Hey, Jack, come down here once, will you?" Dave shouted from downstairs. His voice held an urgency.

Jack rolled his eyes and headed into the hall. "I can help make your name synonymous with volleyball. Long after you retire, they'll remember who you are."

"That's all well and good, but long after I retire, I also want to be living off my endorsement earnings."

Jack reached the bottom of the stairs to find Dave giving Liza a lesson in painting. All the dining-room furniture was in the center of the room covered with a big white drop cloth. "You hold the brush like this," Dave was saying as he wrapped his fingers around Liza's to guide her hand.

Oh brother. This was almost as bad as watching Dave give a woman a golf lesson.

"Don't worry about endorsements," Jack said

to Molly. He tried to carry on the conversation and listen to Dave at the same time. "You'll have more than you know what to do with."

"This gives you the best control when you're cutting in around the woodwork." Dave moved Liza's hand along the wood trim that framed the window. Liza looked over her shoulder, spotted Jack and smiled.

He held up one finger in the universal signal for "hold on a minute."

"But my earnings?"

"No problem. Don't even worry about that," he said in a reassuring voice. "When you're ready to retire, you'll be set. I'll make sure of that. You just keep doing what you do best— give people something to take their minds off their day-to-day stresses, help them find happiness—and leave the rest to me."

"Do I do all that?" There was a smile in her voice.

Jack relaxed. "You bet. People love you. You're the best."

Molly gave a self-conscious laugh. "I know I'm probably driving you nuts—"

"Not at all—"

"I'm still not sure. But, like I said, I like you. I just need to talk the idea over with my dad one more time for another perspective. I'll call you in a few days."

"Great. Thanks." Jack shut off the phone and set it on a window ledge. If he could land Molly Monroe—a good-looking, talented beach volleyball player... He'd been working on her for a while and it looked as if all that hard work might finally pay off. It was almost too much to hope for—Molly and a Chicago Bears wide receiver in the same week. If he pulled this off, Cordy might be able to retire sooner than he'd thought.

He gave a self-satisfied grin and looked at Dave and Liza. "So what's wrong? What do you want me for?"

Dave put a hand on Liza's shoulder. "My assistant here thought we should make sure you like the color before we got too far."

"Your assistant?" Jack looked at Dave's hand on Liza and, for some reason, found it irritating.

Liza put the paintbrush in the tray. "I got back from walking C.J. and Dave asked me to help."

Same old Dave. Except the help he'll be looking for is probably different than the help you're offering. Jack gave a wan smile.

Liza shrugged. "I thought I might as well be useful. I was going to hang around and visit with C.J. a while longer anyway."

"Don't worry, Jack. I'm gonna teach her everything I know. She'll be a pro by the time I'm done with her." Dave grinned.

Jack nodded slowly. That's what he was afraid of.

LIZA WATCHED JACK carefully. That phone call had been important. From what she could tell, he'd been in pretty high spirits before he hung up. She thought back to what she could hear of his side of the conversation. Dave had been talking at the same time, so she'd missed a lot. But Jack did say something about being *ready to retire*. And helping people find happiness.

If she didn't know better, it sounded exactly like the kind of stuff you would say to an advice columnist. *Dear Cordelia.* She didn't know who Jack's other clients were, but she was pretty darn certain that Cordelia was nearing retirement row. Her picture sure looked like it. Heck, her name alone made you think of another century. Although it could be a pseudonym… But, add that together with everything she just overheard Jack say and it all pointed toward Cordelia.

The file Mr. Klein had given her back at the newspaper showed that Cordelia was Jack Graham's principal client. As far as she could tell, he didn't have any other clients whom he would be complimenting for bringing happiness to other people's lives.

"So do you like the color?" she asked, racking her brain for how to get at the subject of his phone call. The more she thought of it, the more she became convinced that Jack had just hung up on the woman Liza wanted to interview.

"Looks great."

"That's all we need to know. You can go back to your computer." Dave climbed onto the ladder again and began to apply paint to the wall.

Jack didn't move. In fact, he narrowed his eyes at Dave's back, and then looked at Liza. "You're not really going to paint, are you?" he asked.

"You bet she is. We're a team," Dave said over his shoulder before Liza could reply.

"I guess I am." She smiled.

Jack shook his head.

"I don't have to. If you'd rather I didn't—"

"No, no. Go ahead. I'll throw down some old clothes. So you don't get paint on what you're wearing." He tromped up the stairs and Liza wondered why he suddenly seemed so irritated.

She wandered over to the front windows and looked out at the gray afternoon. Dark, heavy clouds covered the sky like a low ceiling. She didn't need to see a weather report to know that snow was in the forecast. Her gaze landed on Jack's cell phone, still on the window ledge where he'd set it a few minutes ago. Her heart started to pound. Cordelia's telephone number was surely somewhere on that phone. She was too important a client not to be someone he called regularly. Heck, the woman had to be on his speed dial.

Theoretically, all one would need was Cordelia's phone number in order to track down her address. And Cordelia's phone number was sitting in front of her screaming to be had. This could be the break she was looking for; she could be on Dear Cordelia's doorstep before another couple of days passed.

She glanced at Dave. He was still up on the ladder, his back to her. Then she looked at the phone again, wanting to grab it and terrified of getting caught. She reached a hand out.

"Incoming," Jack yelled from upstairs and she snapped her hand back. Spinning round, she hurried to the bottom of the stairs just as an old pair of pants and a long-sleeved shirt landed on the floor. She scooped them into her arms and looked upstairs to thank Jack, but he had disappeared—already back to his computer.

His computer. No doubt there was plenty of Dear Cordelia information on that machine. The only problem was, how did she get at it? When she called Kristin late last night to report she'd had dinner with Jack and his neighbors, Kristin had been beside herself with glee. Then, when she'd learned Liza was going paint shopping this morning, you'd have thought they'd won the lottery. To hear Kristin talk, getting into Jack's computer was just the next simple matter to accomplish.

Arms wrapped around the extra clothes, Liza looked across the room at Jack's cell phone. *Go now.* Heart thudding, she took several steps forward and peeked into the dining room. Dave was still working with his back to the door.

She swallowed hard. Stepping gently across the room to make as little sound as possible, she lifted the phone from the window ledge and shoved it into the center of the clothing.

"I'm going to change," she called casually in Dave's direction, then raced down the hall to the bathroom. Locking the door behind her, she pulled the phone out and set it on the counter as if it were the Holy Grail.

She quickly changed into the clothes Jack had found for her. One look at her reflection and she groaned. She had *never* looked this bad before, even in her own clothes. All of Kristin's admonishments came back to her about making sure she looked stylish every moment she was here. Well, the good news was, she may never have to worry about Jack finding her appealing again. If she got what she needed from the phone, she could get out of Dodge.

Hands shaking in anticipation, she started punching buttons in an effort to figure out how Jack's phone worked. A beep sounded every time she pressed a key. She cringed, hoping the sound couldn't be heard in the hall, and moved to a corner of the bathroom as far from the door as possible. When finally she found his speed-dial list, she scrolled quickly, her optimism turning to frustration as she discovered Jack had a long list of female names and phone numbers—and none of them Cordelia. If only she knew Cordelia's last name. Jack probably had her number under an alias to ensure it stayed safe.

Okay then, onward. She wasn't beaten yet. Punching the keys, she opened the calls history window and exhaled in a whoosh. There it was—the last call taken on his phone. She threw a nervous glance at the door as if expecting Jack to come barging in at any moment, then looked at the phone again. Could this possibly be Cordelia's number?

Or just some other retirement-age client?

There was only one way to find out—call the number. But leave it to her, here she was in the bathroom without a darn thing to write with. She really had to get her investigative-reporter act together.

Cautiously opening the door, she stuck her head out of the bathroom and looked down the hall in either direction. The coast was clear. Her mission, then, was to get into the kitchen, write down the number and get the phone back on the window ledge before Jack came looking for it. Heart thudding from the fear of getting caught, she stepped quickly down the hall, feeling a little like James Bond.

She rounded the corner into the kitchen and spotted a pad of paper stuck on the refrigerator and a pencil hanging from a string tied to the wall phone. She scratched the phone number down, tore the sheet off and shoved it in her pocket. Two steps down, one to go. She mentally congratulated herself on her success thus far. And then the cell phone began to sing and she jerked, juggling the phone, panic ripping through her as she fought to keep from dropping it. Forget James Bond, she was more like Inspector Clouseau. Get the phone to Jack before he comes looking for it! She dashed out of the room and up the stairs.

She rounded the doorway into his room and drew up short, breathing a little hard and grinning inanely as though she was just worried about him missing a call. "Oh! Your phone's ringing," she said on a breath. "You left it downstairs. I found it. Here it is!" *Shut up.*

A sprinkling of sweat broke out across her shoulders. She handed the phone to him and dashed from the room, wanting nothing more than to get downstairs before he saw the guilt on her face or she babbled out her transgression.

TWO HOURS LATER, back in her regular clothes, Liza stood between Jack and Dave as all three surveyed their handiwork.

"It's gorgeous," she said. Both guys nodded.

"Wanna help me do the living room tomorrow?" Dave asked her. "Maybe we could catch dinner afterward."

Jack gave Dave a long look before he said,

"Yeah, come on back tomorrow. C.J. will need a walk."

Liza mentally winced. She didn't want to make any commitments until she found out whether or not she'd gotten Cordelia's phone number. If she was right about this, she wasn't planning to hang around in Coldwater. She felt a twinge of remorse. Jack Graham thought he was about to get a caretaker, and he was going to get burned in a big way. "I don't know. I may have to run over to the culinary institute for a while."

She better talk to Kristin about it tonight. At least Kristin had experience in letting guys down gently. Even though this wasn't a romantic letdown, surely some of the principles had to be the same.

She glanced at her watch and used her fingernail to scrape a couple of paint spatters off its face. "Gosh, look at what time it is. I'd better get going."

"I'll give you a ride back to the inn," Dave said.

"I'll take her," Jack insisted.

Liza glanced up at him in surprise. "Oh. Thanks."

Out in the car, Jack paused to look at her before he put the car into gear. "Liza, I just want to warn you. Be careful with Dave. He gets around."

"You mean, like, he's a player?" Takes one to know one.

"Yeah."

"Why, Jack Graham, are you worried about my reputation?" she teased.

"I just don't want you to get hurt."

She was completely taken aback. Jack Graham, lady-killer, was trying to protect her feelings? For a moment she was speechless, then she said the first thing that popped into her mind. "Don't worry about me, I'm resilient." And then, because she had no idea why she said that, she continued, babbling as only she could, "Look at all this snow. It's like a winter wonderland. Absolutely beautiful. This looks like a good night for staying in."

By the time Jack dropped her off at the inn, she wanted only to race into the building and pretend she hadn't been a nitwit in his car. It better have been Cordelia's phone number that she got, because she had surely just destroyed all chances of having Jack Graham want to spend time with her. Faced with his unexpected concern, she'd gone right back to her usual self—as far from coy and mysterious as you could get.

Once inside the lobby, she shook the snow out of her hair and allowed herself a tiny fantasy about telling Mr. Klein that she, of all people, had gotten the coveted interview with Dear Cordelia.

She hurried to her room, punching Kristin's number into her cell phone as she pushed through the door. "I think I got it," she sang out when her friend answered the phone.

Kristin gasped. "Got what?"

"Cordelia's phone number. I'm not totally sure, but everything points to it."

"Are you kidding? How'd you do this?"

Liza briefly recounted the day's events. "All I have to do is call this number. It's a 312 area code, so she's right in the Chicago area. I can come home."

"Hold on. Let's say you're right and it is her. How are you going to explain where you got her phone number?"

"I'll say Jack gave it to me, that he's out of town and told me to give her a call myself." She did a little two-step in front of the mirror.

"Yeah, and what if she wants to clear it with him first?"

Liza frowned at her reflection. "I'm hoping she won't."

"Bad planning. You can't take that risk. You've got to have a good enough reason to see her that she can't say no."

"And that would be what, oh wise woman?"

"Give me a minute," Kristin said.

"Couldn't I just say—"

"I've got it!" Kristin almost shouted. "I'll make the call. I'll say I'm from Mr. Graham's office, and that he suggests she do this one Valentine's interview to get the press off her back."

"Keep going," Liza said.

"Then I'll tell her he's out of town and I'm supposed to set it up with her. If I handle it right, she'll never know I'm not from his office."

"This could work. Set the date for a day or two from now so she doesn't have much time to get suspicious—or to follow up with Jack. I'll catch the next flight back to Chicago and—"

"Voilà, you're an investigative superstar."

"Oh, Kristin, I hope we're right about this. What if it's not her?"

"Then you haven't lost anything. You just keep going the way you're going. Get into Jack's computer like I said earlier." Kristin paused. "You think I should call right now?"

"The sooner the better. It's only five o'clock there anyway. It's not like you're into the evening," Liza said. "Besides, I need to know to-night if I'm leaving town—the boys want me to come over again tomorrow."

"The boys?"

"Jack and Dave. Dave's the painter."

"My, my, my. How things do change."

Liza grinned. "Will you go make the call, please?"

"Okay, okay. But later I want to hear more about *the boys. And you going back over there again.* I'll call you as soon as I have something to report."

Liza spent the next hour pacing in her room and fighting the urge to call Kristin. She checked with the airlines and discovered she could catch a morning flight back to Chicago for just a seventy-five-dollar change fee. One glance out the window told her that the morning flights might be delayed because of snow, so she got a list of later flights as well.

She had options, she had a destination, and she had an interview—maybe. If only Kristin would hurry up and call back.

Her stomach rumbled. Giving in to her hunger, she drove to the nearest McDonald's drive-thru and got something to eat, her cell phone in her lap the whole time.

Her rental car skidded on the rapidly accumulating wet snow and she twisted the steering wheel to stay on the road. This storm had better end during the night so she could get back to Chicago. She parked her car, raced up to her room and plopped down at the table by the window to wolf down her burger and fries.

As soon as Kristin confirmed that they had Cordelia's number, she would call Jack and tell him she thought it would be too much for her to become C.J.'s caretaker when she was just starting a new job. Guilt tried to make an inroad into her mind and she shoved it away.

Maybe Connie could take the job—she wanted it really bad anyway. Her guilt intensified. It wasn't her fault Jack couldn't find anyone normal to take the job. She pursed her lips. Not her problem—even if he actually was a really nice guy. Even if he had been concerned that Dave might take advantage of her.

Her cell phone rang out in rock and roll and startled her out of her thoughts. When she left Chicago, she'd switched her ring from classical to rock and hadn't yet adjusted to the change.

She glanced at the caller ID. Kristin. *Finally.* "Hi!"

"I called her."

"And?"

"And I said what we decided I should say—"

"Do I have an appointment?" Liza was almost afraid to hear the answer.

Kristen hesitated. "No. The phone number you gave me wasn't Cordelia's."

"It wasn't?" Liza's joy evaporated. Outside, streetlamps illuminated the heavily falling snow, burying the ground just like Kristin was burying her hopes. "Who was it?"

"I have no idea. As soon as I discovered it wasn't Cordelia, I hung up. That was, of course, after I introduced myself as being from Jack's office and asked to speak to Cordelia."

"Oh boy. I'd pretty much talked myself into believing I'd gotten her number. Some investigative reporter I am." She sighed. She was no closer to getting to Cordelia than she had been yesterday. Great. Just great. She hadn't played the player. In fact, she wasn't even in the game.

Then the power went out and the room went black.

CHAPTER FIVE

THE POWER WENT OUT at nine-thirty. Jack swore as he felt his way along the wall into the kitchen and rummaged around in the drawers, crammed with stuff, for a flashlight. This had better be a short power outage because he doubted Billy kept the place well stocked for emergencies.

Unfortunately, based on what it had been like earlier when he let C.J. out, the force of the storm seemed to be growing—not letting up. Heavy, wet snow couldn't be good for power lines. God only knew how many lines were down.

His fingers closed on a flashlight and he triumphantly pulled it out of the overstuffed drawer and switched it on, grimacing at the weak light it projected. The damn thing would be dead in twenty minutes. Aiming the beam into the drawer, he searched for extra batteries—and came up with none. He should have known. Maybe there were some candles in the dining-room buffet, left over from when his grandmother was alive.

Even then, all he'd have was a little light. Once the house cooled down from the furnace being off, the only way to keep warm would be the fireplace. And he had a sneaking suspicion that when he went outside to check the woodpile, he'd discover there wasn't a woodpile anymore. He shrugged into his jacket, stuck his feet into his Sorel boots and pulled on his gloves. C.J. followed him to the back door, wagging her tail as if expecting to go for a walk.

"The snow is probably deeper than your legs, girl. I'll be right back." Jack gave the door a shove; it opened about six inches, then stuck in the snow. He put his shoulder to the door and forced it open enough for him to squeeze out.

Snow whipped cold against his face and he turned his back to the wind for a moment to zip the front of his jacket up through the collar. Unbelievable. The storm had gotten worse. Head down against the wind, he trudged through the snow to the side of the garage where the firewood was always stacked. Just as he'd thought. No woodpile.

Hell.

He didn't have a caretaker for the dog, he

had no batteries for the flashlight, no central heat, no wood for a fire, and he knew the cupboards were only minimally stocked because he'd been eating most meals out. What else could go wrong?

He aimed the weak beam in the direction of Dorothy and Margaret's house, then squinted along the light's faint path as though he would actually be able to see more than a foot in front of him in a blizzard. Those two old ladies were probably in a frenzy with the power out. The least he could do was go over and calm them down.

He set off across the yard for their porch. Wet snow smacked against his face, melting from his warmth and running slowly down his cheeks in icy rivulets. His flashlight did little to illuminate the way, but memory served him well and a few minutes later he was ringing the front bell.

The door swung inward and he was momentarily blinded by the brilliant beam of a huge flashlight. He threw his arm up to shield his eyes. "Dorothy, I'm going blind here!"

"Oh, Jack dear, it's you!" She aimed her flashlight at the ceiling, took hold of his arm and half dragged him through the doorway. "Come in, come in. Can you believe this? When was the last time we had such a storm as this?"

"I think it was the winter I decided it was time to move farther south."

Dorothy tsked. "You didn't get too far."

Jack laughed.

Margaret brushed the snow off his shoulders and arms. "Isn't this exciting? I can't remember the last time we lost power. Well, actually, I do. It was two summers ago—or was it three—no, I do believe it was two—well, it was summer anyway and lightning hit a transformer. You'd never guess how many babies were born nine months lat—"

"Margaret, do stop. I believe Jack wouldn't be coming over in this weather if he didn't have a reason."

"Oh, yes."

Both women looked at him expectantly.

"Actually, I just want to make sure you ladies are okay." He wiped his face with his glove.

"Lord, yes. Margaret is in her glory—that bossy old thing. She's always saying we need to stockpile in case of emergency. Blizzard, ice storm, terrorist attack, tornado, power outage, you know, those sorts of things. We've got enough bottled water for weeks, batteries—"

"You have batteries? Could I borrow a couple?"

"We've got boxes. Come on in."

He followed her into the living room where a cozy fire burned in the hearth, red and gold and blue. *Blue?* "You ladies have wood, too?"

Margaret laughed. "I've got quite a supply of those fireplace logs. I get them at the hardware store. The package says they're made out of sawdust. We like them because they burn so slowly—"

"And in colors too—blue and green," Dorothy said.

"We can be out of power for weeks and not have a problem," Margaret added.

Jack shook his head. These ladies didn't need his help. Quite the opposite, it looked more like he needed theirs. "And to think I was worried about the two of you."

"C or D batteries?" Dorothy went to a box in the corner and held up a package of each.

"C. Thanks." He moved closer to the fire as he unscrewed the top of the flashlight and changed the batteries. "I should have known you two were okay over here."

"Of course we're fine. Two old ladies—what else have we got to do but prepare for emergencies?" Dorothy clucked her tongue.

"Have you got any wood, Jack? I don't remember Billy ever really planning ahead. We can give you some of our logs if you like," Margaret said. "You only need to burn one at a time and they last and last."

"No wood, no batteries, no food."

"Oh, Jack, there's no point in you being home, then. Why don't you just stay with us until the power comes back on. It would be an adventure." Margaret smiled.

"I don't know. Dorothy's allergic to dogs—and I can't leave C.J. alone in that cold house. Maybe I'd better just borrow some of those logs and go back."

A police radio crackled from the coffee table and for a moment they all listened to an exchange about a multicar accident on the nearby highway.

Dorothy shook her head. "I don't know why anyone would be fool enough to go out in this weather."

"Amen," Margaret replied. "Jack, won't you stay a bit anyway? We can all have a glass of beer. C.J. won't get cold right away—she's wearing that fur coat."

"I guess I could stay for a beer." He followed the ladies into the kitchen.

Dorothy took three pilsner glasses from the

top shelf in the cupboard and filled them with Miller High Life from the bottle. "The beer's a little warm," she said as she dropped a couple of ice cubes in each glass.

Jack looked at the ice in his beer and gave the ladies a big grin. *Ice in beer.* It was one thing to get those little crystals in your beer because you were using a frosty mug. But to purposely put ice in beer? He mentally smacked himself. These two ladies were wonderful, and if iced beer was their thing, it would be his thing, too—at least when he was at their house.

Back in the living room, the two ladies took the couch facing the fire and he sat in a chair near the hearth. The scanner cackled out one message after another about cars in the ditch or people needing help.

Dorothy turned the sound down a little. "Just before you came over, the scanner said a truck knocked down one of the poles that brings power into Coldwater—took out the whole southern half of the village. They're using trucks and snowmobiles to move people to the high school where there's a generator keeping the furnace going."

"The whole southern end is out?" Jack asked. "Liza's staying at the Belleview Inn." He wasn't sure why the thought of her stranded in a dark, cold inn bothered him, but it did.

Dorothy nodded. "Your new caretaker is probably sitting in the dark."

"My *maybe* new caretaker. She hasn't decided yet."

"No need to worry about her. I'm sure they'll be taking her to the high school too." Dorothy took a sip of her beer.

"Now, what kind of a how-do-you-do welcome do you suppose that is?" Margaret sat forward on the edge of the couch. "You can't just leave her to fend for herself at the school. The poor girl is new in town, all alone, stuck in the Belleview Inn, with no heat. Why, they don't even serve food in that place, except breakfast—"

"She'll have no reason to want to stay in Coldwater after this storm is over," Dorothy finished.

Margaret looked at Dorothy. Dorothy looked at Margaret. Then they both looked at Jack.

"What?" Jack asked, even though he had a pretty good idea what this pair was about to insist he do. "Look, ladies, I know what you're up to and it's not going to work. Liza Dunnigan is a nice woman. But she and I aren't a match. In fact, here's a news flash—she wants to live in a small town so bad she's moving here. And I get the shakes if I stay in Coldwater too long."

The ladies just stared at him.

"We're only talking about a neighborly gesture," Dorothy said.

"You'd better go get her," Margaret said. "Quick. Before they take her to the school."

"Have you looked out the window lately? We're having a blizzard. I don't have a snowmobile or a plow. So I'd either have to get her on the old toboggan in the garage—or in my rental car. And that little import would never make it in weather like this." He took a swallow of beer. "Besides, didn't Dorothy just say anyone would be a fool to go out in weather like this?"

"Well, yes, but this is different. This is a rescue mission. And what's wrong with the toboggan anyway?" Dorothy said.

Jack rolled his eyes and drank some more beer. He grimaced a little at the watered taste of the beer and thought of Liza in the dark in the inn and wondered how she was holding up. She seemed like a relatively good-natured person, not the type to complain overmuch when things went wrong.

"I've still got Charlie's old pickup in the garage," Margaret said.

Jack tried not to laugh, remembering the Ford Charlie used to tool around town in. That truck had been old for a long time. "What did you keep that thing for?"

"Emergencies," Margaret said with a sniff. "And it looks like it might come in handy."

"I told her to get rid of the truck when she moved in but she refused," Dorothy said.

"Is it still full of all his carpentry tools?"

Dorothy sighed. "No—those are in the basement. We're saving those for an emergency too."

"Yes, well, let's hope we never need them. Now, Jack, that truck will get you there in one piece. You go on and get her before she freezes—"

"Or starves. Or just plain gets scared," Dorothy said.

"We'll take care of C.J.," Margaret began.

"You go get Liza," Dorothy finished.

Jack held up both hands in surrender. "Okay, okay, okay. Where are the keys?"

Once outside, Jack really began to question his sanity. Only a snowplow driver—or an idiot— would go out driving in this weather. And since he had no snowplow, that left the alternative.

After he retrieved C.J. from his grandmother's house and delivered her to the ladies, he headed out on his rescue mission. The wind whipped snow so hard against the windshield of the old truck, he had moments when he didn't know whether he'd end up the rescuer or the rescuee.

The inn was only a mile or so away but it took him twenty minutes to get there. He pulled right up in front. At least there was plenty of parking available. He shut off the engine and sat there a minute, watching as the heavily falling snow covered the windshield like a blanket. He had to admit, he was glad to have this excuse to see Liza again.

BUNDLED AGAINST the cold, Liza waited in the small lobby of the Belleview Inn for a ride to the high-school gym. Several other hotel guests sat nearby, quietly discussing the weather.

She wanted to cry.

Not only did she not get Cordelia's phone number or an interview, but now she was bound for the high school, while the storm raged and the experts tried to get the power going again.

Her plans were falling apart by the minute.

The front-desk clerk had knocked at her door and told her about the evacuation, "for the comfort and safety of our guests." He said each person could bring along one small piece of luggage. So she'd taken the plastic laundry bag she'd found in the closet and filled it with a change of clothes and her toiletries.

The thought of spending the night in a gymnasium of strangers snoring, coughing, crying—and her still without a connection to Cordelia—left her feeling more than a little bereft. She stared morosely at the wall.

The inn's front door swung open and she, along with everyone else in the room, turned toward it expectantly. Jack Graham walked through the door covered in a layer of white. Her heart skipped a beat. He pulled off his stocking cap and shook it, sending sprinkles of snow flying, then brushed off his arms as he looked around the room. When he spotted her, she could have sworn his eyes lit up.

Impossible. Jack Graham's eyes couldn't be lighting up because of her. She looked to either side for the source of his enthusiasm. A middle-aged man sat to her left and an elderly woman to her right. Somehow she didn't think either was Jack's type.

"Liza!"

Trying to contain her surprise, she turned

back just in time to see him heading straight toward her. She stood.

"What are you doing here?" she asked.

He grinned and a blob of wet snow slid from his eyebrow down his cheek. She had to stop herself from reaching up to catch the migrating snow.

"Rescuing you."

"Funny, that's what the guy from city hall said he was doing, too."

"Some rescue—to the high-school gym?" Jack said.

"I'm told what it lacks in atmosphere, it makes up for in warmth."

He laughed. "Come on. I can do better than that. Dorothy and Margaret are set for weeks without power."

"Is this okay with them?"

"Okay? They sent me. Let's get out of here. The snow is probably up to the windows on Margaret's truck already."

Liza made a face. "Margaret doesn't strike me as the truck type."

"It was her late husband's. The truck's a little old, but it gets the job done." He looked around. "Where's your stuff?"

She held up the plastic bag.

He frowned and shook his head. "Better

bring your whole suitcase. Who knows how long the power will be out."

"Really?"

As if to say, *get a clue,* he gestured at the big front window beyond which snow was falling in a steady sheet of white.

"Good point. I just have to pull my stuff all together. I'll be right down."

"I'll come up and get it."

A sudden image of Jack Graham spotting a pair of her white cotton full-cover briefs shot into her mind and she panicked. "No, thanks. I can manage."

A few minutes later she lugged her suitcase down the stairs to the lobby. Jack took it from her and pushed through the door, holding it open so she could step outside. As the door swung shut behind her, the wind gusted and sucked her breath away. She gasped, put her head down and grabbed hold of Jack's arm for support.

Head still down, she lifted her eyes and looked at the old, very faded red pickup truck, now nearly covered in snow. She pulled Jack to a stop and shouted over the wind, "Is that what you came in?"

He laughed and tugged her toward the wreck. "Beggars can't be choosers."

He gave the passenger door a tug and it creaked open. Then he threw her suitcase inside and Liza slid across the cracked vinyl seat after it, grateful for an escape from the weather. Jack hurried around the truck with a long-handled brush, cleaning off the windows, mirrors and headlights before climbing inside to join her. "Not a fit night out for man or beast," he said, starting the engine.

After a harrowing drive, they finally pulled into Dorothy and Margaret's driveway. The ladies greeted her as if she was a long-lost relative. Dorothy gave her a quick hug and drew her into the living room near the fire. "Jack was so worried you'd have to stay overnight at the high school."

He was? Liza turned to look at Jack but he was gone, taking her suitcase into the dining room.

Margaret nodded. "We have plenty enough for all of us to eat and lots of bottled water—"

Liza gasped. "You don't have running water either?"

"Oh, pay no attention to her," Dorothy said. "Margaret's stocked up for emergencies so long, she just wants to use everything. I wouldn't be surprised if she starts putting plastic over the windows in preparation for a chemical attack."

Margaret snorted. "Thank goodness some-one's prepared around here."

Jack rounded the corner and joined them by the fire, effectively ending the discussion. He rubbed his hands together. "This is going to be a little like winter camping—hot by the fire and cold everywhere else." He bent to pat C.J. on the head. "Good old Ceej—thanks for protecting the ladies while I was gone."

Dorothy reached into the cuff of her sweater, pulled out a tissue and wiped her nose.

"Are your allergies kicking up already?" Jack asked.

"It's not a problem." She took an old cribbage board from a side table and held it up. "Anyone for cribbage?"

Margaret clapped her hands together. "Oh yes, it's perfect for tonight."

Jack looked at Liza and she frowned apologetically. "I don't know how to play."

"Two-handed then!" Margaret said. "Partners. Dorothy and me against the two of you."

"You're on." Jack pulled open a drawer in the coffee table and took out a deck of cards. "Still in the same place," he said.

"Jack, can you get the card table out of the first-floor bedroom? And the chairs?"

A few minutes later they were seated around the table in front of the fireplace. Jack bent his head close to Liza's and began to explain the rules of the game. She sucked in a breath at the nearness of him. He smelled of fresh air and gorgeous man and knight in shining armor. It was all she could do to concentrate on his words and not on the man. His forehead touched hers for just a moment and she gritted her teeth to keep from sighing.

"Now, the goal," he said in a loud whisper, "is to keep from losing to these two sharks. I've been trying for upward of twenty years now. *I think they cheat.*"

The ladies giggled. "I do believe we've been insulted, Dorothy," Margaret said.

"Yes, well, we'll let the card playing speak for itself, now, won't we?" Dorothy shuffled the cards and dealt them out.

For the next couple of hours they played cribbage, ate potato chips and drank hot chocolate they had heated in an old pan in the fireplace. Dorothy whipped up some dip from a container of sour cream and dry onion soup mix. And they played and laughed, and much to Liza's chagrin—but not her surprise—she and Jack almost always lost.

When Jack had gone into the bathroom, Liza tried to steer the conversation onto Dear Cordelia. Based on the ladies' last comments about the columnist, she had a gut feeling they knew more than they were letting on. "You know," she said as she shuffled the cards, "I hope this doesn't sound nosey, but I've always been a big fan of Dear Cordelia. And with Jack her publicist and you ladies knowing her, too— well, does she live around here?"

The ladies looked at each other, then back at Liza.

"No," Dorothy said.

Margaret got up and peered out the front window, shaking her head. "I can't remember a storm this bad—it's not letting up at all," she said.

"Desperate times call for chocolate." Dorothy pushed back her chair and hurried from the room.

Liza frowned. *No one* would talk about the woman. Which convinced her all the more that she was on the right path.

Jack slid into the chair next to her and Liza decided it would be better if she waited until everything was back to normal tomorrow before pursuing her story again. Besides, the nearness of him put all sorts of fanciful ideas into her head, few of which were really conducive to investigative reporting.

Dorothy returned a few minutes later holding a bag of assorted bite-size candy bars.

"Are those left from Halloween?" Margaret demanded.

Dorothy nodded, a sheepish look on her face.

"You little oinker. You told me they were gone, and here I find you've been keeping them all for yourself."

"You were on Weight Watchers," Dorothy said.

"So were you."

"But I quit before you did."

Margaret shook her head. "Now I see why. The temptation must have gotten to you."

Jack smiled at Liza, a grin that shot straight to her heart, and she tried not to read anything into what was surely just a gesture of friendship.

"Dig in." Dorothy dumped the candy onto the table. "Liza, have you decided yet about the caretaker position?" she asked.

Liza was glad the only light in the room came from the fire in the hearth so no one could see the lies written all over her face. "Not really. I decided I needed to spend some time getting to know C.J. better. I've never had a dog, so the idea of taking care of one is something I really have to think about."

She looked over at C.J. snoozing near the warm fire. "Although, she does seem like she'd be pretty easy."

Dorothy blew her nose. "Very. We'd take her on but she sets off my allergies. Any dog with dander is a problem for me." She blew her nose again.

"You could get those shots," Margaret offered.

"Allergy shots? At my age?" Dorothy snorted.

"You're only as young as you feel," Jack said.

Dorothy ignored him. "The problem is, Liza, how well can you really get to know what it's like to have a dog if you're only stopping over once in a while."

"Especially now that the weather has gone and done this." Margaret lay her cards facedown on the table as if the conversation was so important she couldn't play and talk at the same time.

"Well, I'm planning to stop over quite a bit. I think that will help make my decision easier." She searched her brain for another subject to bring up.

"Why don't you just stay there?" Dorothy smiled.

"What?" Liza blinked and sat back in her chair. Jack laid his cards facedown and looked calmly at Liza. "What she means is, instead of coming and going all day, why not spend most of the day there."

Dorothy shook her head firmly. "No, Jack, what I'm saying is that she should stay at the house. Overnight. Move in."

Liza lost hold of the cards in her hand, and Jack's eyes widened in surprise. She felt embarrassed for him—and for her. He didn't seem especially taken with the idea. She scrambled to pick up her cards. "Oh, well, I don't think—"

"Use your heads, children," Margaret said, clucking her tongue. "Dorothy's right. Here's Liza, trying to get to know C.J. And then we have a blizzard. Everyone will be housebound for at least a couple of days. How on earth will she *bond* with the dog while she's trapped in a school gymnasium or her hotel room?"

Jack looked from Margaret to Dorothy to Liza. "We only just met," he said.

"No one's asking you to get married—although it's high time you considered the idea. Surely by now Liza can tell you're a decent person, trustworthy enough to move in with." Dorothy looked directly at Liza.

Married? How did they go from caretaker to marriage? "Uh, yes, absolutely. I do think he's a decent person." She looked at Jack and started to laugh at the ridiculousness of the conversation. "I mean, he's really more than decent—he's very nice."

"Oh, thank you." Jack nodded his head.

"Handsome, too, isn't he?" Margaret prompted.

Liza could feel her face flaming. "Oh, yes." She looked at Jack, mortified at this turn in the conversation.

Jack cleared his throat. "Okay, that's probably enough—"

"Margaret and I could tell, from that very first day, that you were a decent person too. It only makes sense that you stay at the house with Jack to get to know the dog." Dorothy smiled in her know-it-all way.

"Ladies, you're putting Liza on the spot—not to mention me."

"For pity sakes, she's already going to spend tonight with you." Margaret picked up her cards and began to rearrange them in her hand.

The fire cracked and popped and no one said a word. Liza mentally replayed the entire conversation. As bizarre as this exchange had been, the ladies had just offered her all-day access to Jack's files, a pathway to Dear Cordelia that she might not otherwise get. It seemed like the perfect opportunity. She cleared her throat. "I think the idea might be worth considering."

Jack's mouth dropped open.

She smiled sweetly at him. "I mean, staying at the house would sure give me a chance to see what having a dog is like day to day."

"It'd save you hotel money, too," Margaret said with relish.

"Jack? What do you think?" Dorothy demanded.

"I...need a caretaker," he said slowly. He met Liza's gaze. "And the best one I've seen to date needs some time to get to know the dog. If she's up for it, I'm up for it."

Margaret yawned. "Well, thank goodness that's settled so I can go to bed. I tried to stay awake as long as I could, but it doesn't look like the power is coming on anytime soon."

"Looks like we'll all be sleeping around the fire. I'll get some blankets," Dorothy said gleefully. She bustled from the room, while Liza helped Jack put away the card table and chairs.

An hour later, long after everyone else had fallen asleep, Liza lay awake, wrapped in a cozy down comforter by the hearth. She looked over at Jack Graham slumbering a mere foot from her. Kristin would die to hear this. Not only was she sleeping next to Jack Graham—well, okay, Jack Graham and his two senior-citizen neighbors and a fat snoring dog—but she was moving into his house tomorrow.

Her stomach hadn't stopped churning since the subject first came up. The whole idea was completely absurd. Single women did not impulsively move in with single men they'd just met. What if the man was a lunatic or a serial killer or…what if the man was Jack Graham, man about town, ladies at his doorstep, in his parlor, in his bed, and, with this move, Liza would probably be next? The thought sent a tremor through her whole body.

Her parents would probably think their properly reared daughter had gone mad. Scratch that, if her parents knew what she was up to right now, they'd have thought she went mad last week.

A month ago, she never would have considered moving into a strange man's house. Now she was not only considering it, she was doing it.

Much as her parents tried to make it so, life just wasn't paint by numbers. You had to roll with the changes. The fact of the matter was, if she wanted to get the investigative-reporter job—if she wanted to change her life—then she had to find Cordelia. And the fastest way to Cordelia was to move in with her publicist.

AT FOUR IN THE MORNING, the lights burst on like an explosion of fireworks. Liza sat up, confused about where she was. She looked around. Oh yeah, she was at the ladies' house, *sleeping beside Jack Graham.*

Jack stretched and blinked several times. "Did you have every light in the house on when the power went out?"

"It's hard to see at night when you get to be our age." Margaret yawned. "You'll find out someday."

Dorothy blew her nose and gave C.J. a long-suffering look. "Well, as long as the heat's coming back on, I think I'll spend the rest of the night in my bed."

Margaret sat up on the couch and rubbed her lower back. "A splendid idea."

Jack looked at C.J. "I suppose I could get you out of here so Dorothy can breathe again."

Liza had a momentary rush of panic. Everyone was going somewhere—was she just supposed to follow Jack? Suddenly, with the lights on, the idea of moving into Jack's house seemed sort of silly. Obviously, now that there was power, the plows would get out, the roads would get cleared, and life would return to normal. She'd be able to stop over and visit C.J. every day if she wanted to.

Jack looked at her as though reading her mind. "Are you still up for moving in?"

Yes. He was practically handing her access to his computer. Say yes. *Throw that damn caution to the wind.* Heart pounding, a sense of exhausted nauseousness roiling her stomach, a sense of unrealness in her brain, she opened her mouth and stepped further away from the well-ordered world to which she was accustomed. "I think it's a great idea, actually."

CHAPTER SIX

THE SNOW STOPPED falling in the afternoon and the temperature began to drop. Jack paused at the end of the driveway, wiped his face and shifted the chute on the snowblower to blow snow in the opposite direction. Thirty inches had fallen since yesterday. Clearing this would be a job of massive proportions. He put the machine into gear and headed up the driveway again.

Looking over at the porch, he saw Liza cleaning off the steps with a shovel. She spotted him watching her, grinned and tossed a shovelful of wet snow in his direction.

He was more optimistic than ever about her taking the caretaker job. It just didn't make sense that she'd move into the house if she wasn't pretty serious about the position.

The sooner he wrapped this up the better. He'd called the airport this morning and learned they already had a couple of runways clear.

Then he'd checked with his airline and switched his flight to one late tomorrow afternoon. As long as Liza was here with the dog, there was no reason for him to stay. By tomorrow night he could be back in Chicago, back to work getting his sports-agenting business off the ground.

From the corner of his eye he saw a motion and looked up. Dorothy was leaning out the front door and waving him over. He shut off the machine and trudged through the snowy side yard until he was close enough to talk. "What's up?"

"Billy always did our walks, too. And with him dying so suddenly, we hadn't gotten anyone else yet," she said. "We've been calling all morning and can't find a soul to do the job. They're all too busy."

"Don't worry—I'll do yours next."

Margaret stuck her head out the door from underneath Dorothy's arm. "Thank goodness. We weren't sure who to call."

"It's the least I can do to thank you for suggesting Liza stay at the house with C.J."

Dorothy smiled knowingly. "A mother always knows best."

Margaret disappeared into the house.

"Not only will Liza get to know the dog, but

it'll really help me out. I've got some work pending back in Chicago and this will be perfect. I can head back for a few days and know C.J. is being taken care of."

"Pardon me?" Dorothy looked confused.

"Well, think about it. Liza said she wanted time to *try out* having a dog."

"Yes, but—"

"If she spends the rest of this week alone with C.J., she'll get a far better idea of what it's really like."

Margaret's head popped out the door again, this time with a bright red scarf wrapped around her neck. "What are you saying?"

Dorothy turned to her. "Jack says he's going back to Chicago."

"He is?" Margaret exchanged a look with Dorothy. "Has Liza accepted the job, then?"

Jack shook his head and explained his plan again.

"But how will she know what to do with the dog if you're not here?" Dorothy asked slowly.

"Come on, how hard can it be? Besides, you two are here. You know what to do. As long as you're willing to help her out, answer questions, give advice—that stuff you two are so good at—she'll be fine."

They stared at him, dumbfounded.

"Is it okay with Liza that you leave?" Margaret sounded almost strangled. She loosened the scarf around her neck.

"Truthfully, I haven't told her yet. But I'm sure she'll understand. She'll probably like the idea—it'll be a lot less awkward for her if she's not sharing a house with a guy she hardly knows. Don't you think?"

The two women continued to stare at him.

"Don't you think?" he repeated. *What the hell was the matter with them? It was a great idea. Brilliant even.*

Dorothy finally nodded. "Is the airport open?"

"A couple of runways are cleared. Besides, I wouldn't go until tomorrow. Plenty of time to get everything in order for Liza's trial week."

"What if she decides not to take the job?" Margaret crossed her arms and shivered.

"I guess I'll have to come back and start looking again." He grimaced. "Or seriously consider Connie…and her brood."

"But what if Liza *takes* the job? Will you just stay in Chicago? And not come back at all?" Dorothy actually sounded alarmed.

"That's my goal. Now, don't panic, you two. Taking care of a dog isn't exactly rocket science."

The ladies exchanged another look.

"Now what's the matter?"

Dorothy pursed her lips and nodded toward where Liza was industriously shoveling snow from the front porch. "That *lovely* young woman—"

"*Adorable, sweet* young woman," Margaret continued.

"Might think you're taking advantage of her," Dorothy finished.

Jack blew out a breath and watched it steam away from him. "No way. I'll put together a list of things to help her out—feeding schedule, walks, all that stuff. It'll be easy. Plus, she'll have the house to herself. She'll love it."

"Is your flight booked?" Dorothy asked.

"Tomorrow afternoon—five twenty-five."

Dorothy looked at Margaret.

"Is there something I'm missing?" Jack asked. "You two seem a little disapproving about this."

"No. Nothing. We're going inside," Margaret said. "It's too cold for old ladies out here. Say hello to Liza for us."

Jack watched the door close behind them. Now, what was that all about? Considering the busybodies they were, he would have expected them to love his idea. With him gone, they'd have plenty of chances to come over and get to know Liza.

Shaking his head, he returned to the snow-blower. There were benefits to living in an apartment in the city. Big benefits—like not having to clear the walks. Getting snowed in there would have meant something entirely different from getting snowed in here. For lack of anything better to do, Kate from down the hall would probably have come down the hall.

He grinned. They would have had an evening by the fire that wouldn't have involved cards at all—unless Kate insisted on a game of strip poker, which she'd been known to do before. And then, instead of getting up early to let out a dog, and shovel, they'd have wiled away the morning doing much the same as they'd done the night before, while waiting for the sidewalks and streets to be cleared.

Not that he didn't have fun last night. The ladies were, well, the ladies. And Liza was really a trouper, she didn't whine about the situation, just made the best of it. Kind of a nice change from some of the high-maintenance women he was used to.

He yanked on the starter again. Nothing. He

turned the engine choke on full, primed it a few times and tried the starter once more. At the silence, he let out a low curse. Oh no. No, no, no. This was not happening. The snow blower couldn't have broken down after a blizzard.

He pulled the starter again. "Shit!" This old blower had to be twenty years old. Why the hell hadn't his grandmother ever gotten a new one? Sighing in exasperation, he pushed the machine down the half-cleared driveway and into the garage.

Thirty inches of snow and he was going to have to *shovel* it all by hand. Yes, this was definitely different than living in an apartment in Chicago.

He lifted a shovel off a hook on the wall and hefted it in both hands for a moment. This was really an old one. No plastic here, just heavy steel...with a corroded blade.

He carried the shovel to the front of the house where Liza was working. "Hey."

She looked up expectantly, a winsome picture. Her nose and cheeks were pink from the cold, and a handful of wavy curls had escaped her hat and were dancing around her face in the wind. *Good thing he wasn't interested in winsome.*

"The snowblower quit working. We have to finish this job the old-fashioned way."

She set her shovel in the snow. "Do I get time-and-a-half for overtime?"

"No. But what I'll do is promote you to vice president."

"I'd rather have the money."

He laughed. "Back to work, then. Break time's over."

He put the rusty blade to the concrete and begin to shovel the snow off to the side. By the time he finished the rest of the driveway, each scoop of wet snow seemed heavier than the last. He'd unzipped his jacket ages ago. Now he pulled it off and threw it in a snowbank.

He leaned on his shovel and stretched his back. Hell, he exercised almost every day, but shoveling this wet snow was like working in a rock quarry—with a pickax.

Liza stopped working and pretended to check her watch. "Another break already? Your contract only allows two a day."

"Easy for you to say—you've got the modern lightweight molded-plastic shovel."

"Yeah. And you've got the muscles. I think we're even." She began shoveling again.

Jack watched her for a moment and admired the determination in her face as she threw each shovelful of snow to the side. "How do you know I have muscles? I could be a ninety-pound weakling under all these clothes."

"Believe me. I know."

She knew? The idea that Liza Dunnigan *knew*—that she'd even noticed—brought a little smile to his face.

LIZA LOOKED UP as Jack trudged down the sidewalk toward her, shoulders drooping. His cheeks were ruddy, his blue eyes sparkled in the brisk air. His old, faded navy Stanford sweatshirt was just tight enough to prove her right—the guy had muscles, nice ones.

She gave her head a shake. This wasn't the kind of information she needed to be gathering. Her mission was to get to Cordelia—not to Jack Graham.

He jammed his shovel into a snowbank and blew out his breath in exaggerated exhaustion. "Wow. Now, *that* was a workout." He held up one hand and she slapped him five.

She had no doubt that by tomorrow every muscle in her body would be aching. She probably wouldn't even be able to walk. "I'm starting to wonder if you came and got me at the inn not to rescue me, but to ensure you had help shoveling the snow."

Jack laughed. "Listen, if you take the caretaker job, I promise to buy a new snowblower."

A plow rumbled down the street and they watched as it filled the base of every driveway on the block with a foot and a half of wet, sloppy, gray snow.

"If I take the caretaker job, I'm hiring someone to clear the snow!"

"Smart woman," Jack said. He looked at the mound of snow and groaned. "There oughta be a law about snowplows and driveways."

"I think maybe I'll look into joining a culinary school in Florida."

"Hell no. You'll *love* Maine. It's hardly ever like this."

Liza threw back her head and laughed.

"Tell you what, you go on inside. I'll clean up after the plows." Jack pulled his shovel from the snowbank and swung into action.

Liza watched him for a moment. He'd be out here until dark clearing these two driveways. Sighing, she picked up her shovel and joined him.

By the time they finished, both were breathing hard. Jack held up a hand again and said, "One more time."

Liza slapped him five with much less enthusiasm than she had forty-five minutes earlier.

They started up the walk just as an older-model Buick pulled in front of Jack's house. The doors popped open and out tumbled Connie's four boys, whooping and hollering as they climbed up onto the mountains of snow on each side of the driveway. Connie got out of the driver's-side door.

"Hey, Jack!" she called, totally ignoring Liza where she stood next to him. "I've brought the boys over to help you shovel. Just tell them what to do."

One of the boys slid down the mountain on his rear end, depositing a pile of snow on the freshly shoveled sidewalk. Two others followed his lead and the pile of snow on the walk grew.

Liza frowned. "I'll tell them what to do," she muttered. "Get lost."

Jack turned to grin at her. "I dare you to say that loud enough for her to hear."

"Darers go first."

Jack widened his eyes. "Okay. Okay." He waved a hand as though this was no big deal at all and stepped toward Connie. "Get…" He glanced back at Liza and made a face. "Get…a shovel and clear off a place in the backyard for C.J. to use."

Liza stepped right up behind him and whispered close to his ear, "Chicken."

He turned slowly to face her. She looked up at him, standing less than a foot away from her. Their eyes met and she could have sworn he could see right into her soul. She gulped.

Somewhere far away, she could hear Connie clap her hands and shout, "Boys! Listen up—clear out a spot for C.J. in the back." She heard the trunk of the car open and the boys screeching as they grabbed shovels and raced up the driveway and through the gate into the backyard.

"Who you calling chicken?" Jack asked, his voice teasing, his eyes twinkling.

She could swear her heart stopped beating as he spoke. Her last resort to gain access to Dear Cordelia was to seduce this guy into giving up the information she needed. Right now, she was thinking there might be definite positives to pursuing that plan of action.

If she only knew how the heck to do it. Where was Kristin when she needed her?

A snowball splatted against the back of Jack's head, saving her from making some stupid comment like *wanna neck?*

His eyes widened and he spun around only to get hit with another snowball in the chest. "Hey!" he shouted.

Connie grinned at him and let fly another

snowball, missing him entirely. Jack bent to grab a handful of snow and form a snowball and Connie took off running, laughing as Jack tossed snowballs her way.

Oh brother. Liza restrained herself from rolling her eyes. Connie had gotten just what she wanted—Jack's attention. Which was just as well. These two could play outside while she sneaked in to nose around Jack's stuff. She started for the side door only to have Connie's four boys jump out of the backyard and begin pummeling her with snowballs, while making kung fu motions and shouting, "Hi-ya!" She threw her arms up in defense and ran back down the driveway with the boys in hot pursuit.

"Incoming!" she shouted.

"Over here!" Jack ran toward her, grabbed her arm and dragged her behind a snowbank. He pounded a fistful of snow into a tight ball and threw it at the boys, reaching immediately for more snow.

"Backup, Liza, backup!"

She swung into action, laughing as the snow began to fly so fast and furious between the two sides it was hard to see. "I'll make a stockpile." She crouched down to make snowballs and pile them up.

Jack grabbed them as fast as she could make them. After a couple of minutes, he dropped down beside her and began to make snowballs, too. "We'll do a blitzkrieg." He laughed wickedly.

Liza stuck her head up over the snow pile to check on the boys and spotted them sneaking along the sidewalk toward where she and Jack were hidden. "They're coming," she whispered. "A frontal assault down the walk."

Jack made a fist with his gloved hand and held it up facing her. Liza grinned and did the same, punching her padded knuckles against his.

A snowball landed on the ground nearby.

"It's showtime," he said.

Grabbing a snowball in each hand, they jumped to their feet and began firing. The boys shot back, diving and rolling down the banks to the sidewalk, throwing snowballs as they fell.

Liza reached for the last snowball, just as Jack did. Their hands met on top of it. "You take it," she said.

He fired it off, then grabbed her hand and started running for the house, all the while yelling, "Truce! Truce!" Snowballs peppered them from both sides as they raced up the steps to the safety of the porch.

They bent over laughing, breath rolling out

of them in white puffy bursts. A snowball landed on the porch and Jack held up his hands in surrender. "Uncle."

Mouth tight, Connie marched up the walk. A snowball smacked into her shoulder. She turned slowly as the boys laughed and pointed at one another, loudly proclaiming each other the guilty party. She shook her head. Two more snowballs landed nearby. She looked up at Jack, smiled and shook her head. "Boys."

Liza couldn't resist murmuring, "Discipline," under her breath.

"Dare you," Jack muttered.

Connie mounted the steps and joined them on the porch. "So, what have you decided about the dog?" she asked.

This was clearly not a woman who beat around the bush.

Jack looked at Liza and raised his eyebrows. She cleared her throat. She wanted to come across strong and in control of the situation. "I, ah, am going to take some time to get to know the dog better before I make a final decision."

Connie's face scrunched in disbelief. "What's to get to know? How are you going to do that?"

"She's moving in here for the next week," Jack said.

Connie's jaw dropped. "With you?"

Liza nodded, taking a full measure of enjoyment from the woman's shock.

Jack shook his head. "Well, not exactly. I've got to get back to Chicago…"

Liza tried not to look incredulous as she turned to stare at him. In the yard, the boys were tackling one another, wiping snow into each other's faces, sliding down the banks to the sidewalk, and shouting and laughing with glee. Connie seemed oblivious to their antics.

"I'm going back to Chicago for a few days," Jack said almost apologetically.

What?

He looked at Liza. "You don't need me here to get to know the dog—"

"Wait—are you saying you're leaving?" Her stomach flopped in horror, and her visions of becoming an investigative reporter began to melt like a snowball in the desert.

He had the good grace to look at least a little guilty. "Yeah—"

"You're leaving Coldwater?" Connie said, shocked.

"When?" both women asked in unison.

"Tomorrow. Five twenty-five flight. Now, Liza, don't worry—I'll write down the instructions about C.J. And you've got the ladies next door if you have questions."

He was leaving? He couldn't leave Coldwater—she was just moving in. Her mind raced for an excuse—any excuse to keep him here. "But—but—I've never taken care of a dog."

"That's why this is so perfect. You can try it out without any interference. Then just let me know at the end of the week."

Let him know at the end of the week? But Cordelia—what about Cordelia? She tried to keep her jaw from hanging slack.

Connie smirked as though she was sure Liza's only motive was a romantic interest in Jack. "The boys and I would be happy to take the job without even a trial period."

"Thanks, Connie, but I made this agreement with Liza first."

"But—"

"I'll let you know if it doesn't work out," Jack said.

Connie set her jaw just as a snowball landed on top of her head. Wet chunks of snow slid down the side of her face. She turned, wiping the snow away, and pointed at the Buick, growling, "Into the car."

The boys tumbled down the sides of the

snowbank into the street. Liza shook her head as Connie and her gang piled into the car and drove away. Poor C.J. would probably pass on to the next world after a week with that brood.

She looked out over the sidewalks and driveways they had just spent hours shoveling. Everything was a mess from the boys and the snowball fight. She closed her eyes briefly.

Jack groaned. "Good thing Connie brought the boys over to help clear the snow." He went down the steps, picked his jacket out of the snowbank where he'd thrown it earlier and slipped it on. Then he put his shovel to the walk and began to scrape it clean.

Liza watched him for a moment before following him. A sense of despair filled her. How could Jack be leaving tomorrow? How could everything be falling apart now, just when it seemed as if everything was falling into place? She couldn't panic; she had to think through her options.

Right, options. *What options?* Insist he stay in Coldwater because she was afraid to be in the house alone with a dog? Oh, that would go over well.

Maybe once he was gone, she could fly back to Chicago, too. Perfect. And leave the dog unattended while she chased Jack around the city for a story. Now, *that* would make him want to spill his guts.

She pulled her shovel from the snowbank where she'd left it and slid it across the concrete, pushing snow off the sidewalk. As far as she could tell, she *had* no options.

AN HOUR LATER, after a hot shower, Liza pulled on jeans and a turtleneck sweater then stood inside her bedroom, ear to the door, listening until she heard Jack go into the bathroom and turn on the shower. She knew the moment he got under the spray because he did one of those half groan, half aahs that people do when they're at a certain nirvana level. She tried not to picture him naked, reaching bliss in a shower. Reaching for her cell phone, she quickly dialed Kristin to distract herself from her own thoughts.

"We have a problem," she whispered into the phone.

"Now what?"

"He's leaving."

"On a midnight train to Georgia?"

"Kristin, this is serious. He's leaving tomorrow, going back to Chicago."

"How can he be leaving? What about the

dog? Weren't you supposed to be getting to know the dog this week?"

"He says I can stay at his place and get acquainted with C.J. while he's back in Chicago." Liza sat on the edge of the bed.

"Oh boy."

"Any brilliant ideas?"

Kristin sighed. "Not offhand. How can you make him stay when you hardly know the guy? The only option left might be to seduce him into staying."

"Excuse me? You mean like promise him favors for the *week?*"

"Something like that," Kristin said.

Liza could feel her face turn red. "I don't think so."

"Oh, come on. What happened to the new Liza?"

"Even the new Liza has her limits."

Kristin laughed. "I'm just kidding. Sort of. Well, if you're not going to do the week-long seduction thing—"

"I'm not."

"Then, I guess you'd better get the information you need tonight." Kristin snorted. "Or tomorrow before he leaves."

"This, I could have figured out myself."

"Where is he right now?"

"Taking a shower," Liza said.

"Oh, the pictures in my mind…"

"Been there, done that. Come on, help me out here, Kristin. I'm desperate."

"Okay, okay. You should be looking around his room right now instead of talking to me," Kristin said.

"Maybe I should just ask him outright—"

"The head-on approach isn't going to work. Look at all the reporters who've called him for an interview. Have any gotten one?" Kristin didn't wait for an answer. "I'm telling you, there's only one way to get answers out of a man who doesn't want to talk."

"I was afraid you were going to come back to that."

"What's to be afraid of? All you have to do is tease—no one says you have to go any further."

Liza's heart began to pound. What had she gotten herself into? It was so easy to talk about beguiling answers out of Jack. But to actually do it? "Kristin, what if he's not interested?"

"He's male. He's interested. Now get out there and go digging around his room while you have the chance."

Liza clicked off the phone and slipped out

into the hall, pausing briefly to make sure the shower was still running. She stepped through the open doorway to Jack's room and spotted his briefcase on the floor by the desk. Adrenaline rushed through her system. She knelt on the floor, popped open the briefcase and tried to keep herself from hyperventilating as she riffled through his papers searching for any reference to Dear Cordelia.

After a few minutes, she gave a sharp exhale and went to the door to listen for the sound of the shower. Silence greeted her. Oh, God, Jack was out of the shower!

She dashed back into the room and closed the briefcase, then ran into the hall and hurried downstairs. She didn't breathe until she was safe in the living room. Dropping onto the couch, she gulped in some air and tried to still the racing of her heart. It wouldn't look good if she was winded when Jack came down.

A fire glowed brightly in the hearth and she laughed at the sight of a pile of packaged pressed logs stacked on the floor. The ladies had obviously stopped over while she was in the shower.

She thought again about the information she needed. Her investigation into Jack's briefcase had been a bust. With him leaving tomorrow, that left her with only two options—ask him outright or tease it out of him. She stared into the fire, thinking. She supposed she could ease into a discussion by asking what it was like to work for someone like Dear Cordelia. Then she could ask if she might ever be able to meet Cordelia. And from there she could go right into a request for the woman's phone number and whether he'd set up an interview for her. That could work.

Yeah, right, and basset hounds could fly.

On the other hand, she could be snuggling on the sofa with the man, his arms around her, his incredible mouth on hers. And when they came up for air, she could, somehow, ask the same questions, in a breathless sort of just-wondering kind of way.

Now, *that* sounded like a plan.

THE DOORBELL CHIMED and Jack bounded down the stairs, pulling a wrinkled twenty-dollar bill from his pocket for the pizza deliveryman as he went to answer the door. "Pizza's here," he called to Liza.

He paid for the pizza, then set it on the coffee table in the living room and popped open the top. Steam wafted up from thin crust with cheese, sausage, mushrooms, black olives and onions. He inhaled deeply and his stomach rumbled.

He looked at Liza seated on the couch, dark hair still damp from the shower, gently curling around her face. There was that winsome look again. Winsome and cute. Not his type.

Although, that didn't mean he couldn't enjoy the moment.

"You want some wine?" he asked.

She smiled. "Sure."

He ducked into the kitchen for a couple of glasses and a bottle of Chardonnay. Back in the living room, he filled both glasses, presenting one to her with a flourish.

"Thanks."

She looked up at him, and he thought that maybe he was wrong about Liza just being cute. There was something really appealing about her. He tried to figure out what it was. Hell, who knew? Who cared? She was staying in Coldwater. She was looking *forward* to living in Coldwater. *Definitely not his type.*

He flipped the CD player on and settled himself on the floor by the coffee table, Japanese-restaurant style. The sounds of Benny Goodman's orchestra slid into the room. "This is about as modern as my grandmother's music collection gets." He reached for a piece of pizza. "At least I got her into the twenty-first century with a CD player. Got her a computer too so she could send e-mail."

Liza took a slice of pizza and scooted down to sit beside him on the floor.

"This shows what hard work will do—I can't remember the last time I was this famished." He ate his pizza slowly, controlling himself from wolfing it down so Liza didn't think he was uncivilized.

"Famished and sore." Liza rolled her shoulders and tilted her head from side to side. "That hot shower was only a temporary fix."

"It didn't help that Connie and her boys showed up. We got to shovel the same stuff twice." Jack shoved a piece of crust into his mouth and chewed thoughtfully, thinking of how hard Liza had worked all afternoon, never once complaining. "I'm sorry you got stuck doing so much shoveling," he said.

She shrugged. "It's the least I can do for my week's room."

Jack drank some more wine and wallowed in the warmth that rolled through him, relaxing his muscles, calming his mind.

Liza closed her eyes, leaned back against the sofa and stretched her legs out in front her on the floor as she ate her pizza. He watched as she chewed slowly and swallowed, as her tongue flicked out to catch some tomato sauce on her lower lip, as she rolled her shoulders in that tight blue sweater. His heart began to beat a little faster.

"This wine is like a muscle relaxant." She opened her eyes and looked at him.

Muscle relaxant? Nah. Aphrodisiac, maybe. A specific set of his muscles weren't feeling exactly relaxed right now.

"Then more is definitely in order." Jack grinned at her and refilled both their glasses.

"Yes, I think so," Liza murmured. "No more one-glass limits. Life is too short to never wear a lampshade. You know—I'm changing my life."

"Right—the culinary school."

She nodded and drank some more wine and he raised his glass in toast. "To success in your new life… And may you find you have a great affection for basset hounds."

Liza clinked her glass against his and took another big swallow of wine. "Do you ever think about changing your life?" she asked.

He shrugged. *All the time.* "Once in a while.

But things have gone pretty well for me—it's hard to complain."

"Owning your own business must be nice. Take time off whenever you want—"

"Yeah, no one makes me use vacation days to come home and look for a caretaker for the dog."

"Unlimited vacation days, right?"

Liza smiled at him, all warm and nice, eyes shining in the firelight. She shook her head. Her dark hair, now almost dry, had softened into waves around her face, waves that he could slip his hands into, comb his fingers through— "What? Oh, yeah, I don't have a limit, you're right. In fact, I really need to plan a vacation— after I find a caretaker—"

He closed his mouth, stunned. He didn't ramble around women. This wasn't him. He prided himself on being smooth and in control. And face it, Liza Dunnigan was no breathtaking beauty. There was no reason for him to be rambling around her.

She put her hands on her lower back, almost on her buttocks, and arched to stretch her muscles. Her sweater tightened across her breasts and his mouth went dry. He reached for his wineglass and took another swallow. She was attractive, yeah, in an ordinary sort of way, but not the kind of woman that men lust after…at least not the kind of woman he lusted after. She was winsome, sweet—not his type.

So what the hell was with him tonight?

Maybe it was the wine. He held his wineglass at eye level. *What the hell?* He finished off his drink and poured himself another. And then refilled Liza's glass too.

It didn't really matter what the reasons were. It didn't matter that she wasn't his type. It didn't matter that he was going back to Chicago tomorrow and she was staying in small-town Coldwater. All he knew was that there was heat in this room tonight and it wasn't all coming from the fireplace.

CHAPTER SEVEN

"HELLO, HELLO!" Dorothy's voice rang out from the back hall.

Jack cringed. So much for the heat in the room. Oh well, he hadn't known where he was going with that anyway. "Out here. In the living room," he called.

He heard boots clunk to the floor and soon after, Dorothy came through the doorway in her stockings, with Margaret hurrying behind her carrying a large box. C.J. rolled to her feet from her spot in front of the fire and wiggled her body in excitement, tail wagging back and forth in greeting.

Dorothy drew up short with a stricken look on her face and Margaret almost banged into her. "Oh, dear, we're not interrupting anything, are we?" she asked.

Jack grinned at Liza. "Not a thing."

"Oh." Dorothy sounded disappointed. "That's

good. Margaret and I are so grateful to you for clearing off our walks."

Margaret bent to pat C.J. on the head. "We could never have done it ourselves."

"And then the snowblower broke. Well, to shovel all that by hand—"

"Even though you're young, we just knew it must have strained your muscles," Margaret said. "No one can lift that much snow and not have their back hurt."

Liza smiled. "We were just talking about the same thing."

Margaret turned to Dorothy. "You see, I told you. I knew this was the right thing to do."

Dorothy rolled her eyes as Margaret held up the box she had carried into the house. "This was Charlie's. Being a carpenter, he often had a sore back."

"'BackMaster,'" Liza read aloud. "'Two-motor back massager helps soothe and relax your back. Powerful massage action. With heat.'" She raised her eyebrows at Jack and it was all he could do to keep from laughing out loud.

"Uh, thanks," he said, for lack of anything better to say.

Margaret opened the box and pulled out a gray rectangular cushion with an attached electrical cord and remote control. "I'll show you how it works." She plugged the cord into an outlet and set the machine against the back cushion of the couch. "Someone sit there, now." She patted her hand against the BackMaster. "Sit, sit. Charlie just loved this thing."

Jack gestured with one hand. "Ladies first."

Liza stood up and repositioned herself on the couch with her back against the cushion. "Can I drink wine while I do this?" She grinned at Jack.

"Just hold your glass tight so it doesn't vibrate out of your hand," he said.

Margaret tsked. "For heaven's sake, the whole room won't be shaking." She picked up the remote control and pushed a button. "Here comes the heat." She giggled.

Liza sipped her wine and sat passively. After a minute, she made a silly face at Jack. "Ooohh. I feel it. I *do* feel it."

Margaret beamed and pushed another button. "Here comes the massage. Slow." She pressed another button. "Or fast."

Liza almost squealed. "My gosh, how could I have not known these things existed?"

She took the remote control from Margaret's outstretched hand and pushed the buttons herself. "Jack, you have to try this—after I'm done with it, of course, which will be in a couple of hours."

Margaret nodded with smug satisfaction. "Well, Dorothy, we've done our good deed. Now we'd better get going. Good-night all." She bent to ruffle the top of C.J.'s head. "Good night C.J."

The dog followed them to the living-room entrance.

"Jack, do you want us to let C.J. out when we go?"

"Yeah, thanks." A minute later, he heard the back door close, then returned his full attention to Liza. "Now, where were we?"

"You were going to try the BackMaster." Liza slid over on the couch and let Jack take her place.

He relaxed into the massaging heat. "Ooh, Margaret is on to something here. This is great."

Liza smiled at him. He stared at her mouth for a moment and the thought came into his mind that he just might enjoy kissing her.

"I've got an idea," she was saying. "If we sit back-to-back we can both use it."

He looked at her and blinked. *I've got a better idea. If we sit front-to-front we can do something else.* He shook his head to clear his thoughts. Don't go getting yourself involved here, he admonished himself. This was the woman who was moving from Chicago and to Coldwater. This was the woman who *wanted* to stay in a small town. He turned up the heat on the cushion and savored the warmth seeping into his muscles.

"Well, do you want to?" Liza's question jarred him back to the moment.

Want to? Hell, don't be asking me questions like that. "I guess we could try it." He shifted on the couch so he was sitting sideways.

Liza plopped herself down with her back to him and reached a hand behind her to position the cushion between them. She started to laugh.

"What's so funny?"

"I was just thinking how my parents would react if I told them what I did tonight. *I shared a vibrating cushion with a guy I hardly know.* They'd probably have a stroke."

"This is something new for you? I do this all the time."

She laughed again. "I bet you do."

"What's that supposed to mean?" He twisted to one side so he could see her face.

"All those women you know in Chicago... surely there's a kinky one or two in the bunch." Her eyes sparkled, teasing.

"Kinky is in the eye of the beholder. You know what they say, one person's kinky is another person's treasure."

"I think it's one person's *trash* is another person's treasure."

He was starting to love the way her mouth moved. This was not productive thinking. He tore his gaze off her lips and brought it to her eyes. *Really unproductive move.*

Her eyes seemed even darker in the firelight. Exotic almost…seductive. Damn.

She leaned back a little. "What? Do I have food in my teeth or something?"

He twisted around abruptly so he was no longer facing temptation. "I think the wine is making me goofy."

"Yeah, me too. Let's have some more. Really, how often in one lifetime can you have a blizzard, power outage and vibrating cushion, all in the same day?"

Liza leaned over to the coffee table and Jack watched her grasp the neck of the bottle and refill their two glasses. He picked up his glass and stared at the wall, his back against Liza's, vibrating, warm, every inch of him knowing she was behind him— Jeez, get a grip. He was leaving tomorrow. And taking advantage of this woman tonight could... Could what? Be fun? There was no reason they couldn't enjoy tonight if she was willing. He didn't want to scare her away from the caretaker job, but if she was willing...

She moved her head a little to the music and he felt her hair against his neck, could smell kiwi, and he thought of burying his hands in that hair as he kissed her.

It would be so easy to do. Except this was the weirdest situation he'd ever found himself in. It wasn't as though he'd just brought her home from a date and they were sitting on her couch saying good night. He leaned sideways, twisting until she was forced to look at him to see what he was doing.

She raised her eyebrows in question. "Yes?"

Oh hell. He was leaving tomorrow anyway. How could he leave town without knowing what it was like to kiss Liza Dunnigan? Screw the discussion.

He raised one hand to touch her hair, ran his fingers along her jaw to gently pull her head toward his. Her eyes widened and he kissed her before she had a chance to protest. Her lips softened and he claimed her mouth. The cushion fell to the floor still vibrating, massaging the coffee-table leg, and he came to the realization, deep in his brain, that kissing Liza was like eating potato chips—you couldn't stop with just one.

From outside he heard C.J. bark, but he ignored her. The dog could wait. He shifted slightly, his aching muscles strained to their limits by the awkward position in which he and Liza were sitting. "Maybe we should get more comfortable," he said.

In the backyard, C.J. barked again.

"Does she need to come in?" Liza straightened and looked anxiously at him.

Her lips were lush and soft and slightly parted and he'd be damned if he'd let C.J. interrupt them now. He pulled Liza up against him, repositioning them both as he nuzzled her hair. "She'll be fine," he murmured, taking her mouth again. He slid down against the armrest, bringing Liza with him, his hands exploring the soft heat of her, trapping her against him.

And then she dragged her mouth from his and drew a shaky breath. He had the distinct impression that he'd moved a little too fast.

"What I'm thinking, actually, is that C.J.—" Liza drew another quick breath. "She's so old— she'll freeze to the sidewalk. Maybe you'd better get her."

"You'll do just fine in the caretaker's job," he said. He pushed himself to his feet and stretched, then grinned at Liza. "Don't go anywhere."

He opened the back door expecting C.J. to amble in, and when she didn't, he squinted into the night hoping to spot her. He whistled and thought of Liza all warm and soft waiting for him in the living room. *Dammit, C.J., where are you?* After another short wait, he shut the door, put on his shoes and grabbed his jacket from a hook by the door.

"Is something wrong?" Liza appeared in the kitchen doorway, her hair mussed, her cheeks flushed pink, her lips looking temptingly kissable. He forced himself to open the door.

"C.J.'s not coming in."

Liza stepped toward him. "Isn't she in the yard?"

Jack shrugged. "I'm kind of hoping she's not frozen to the sidewalk."

"Really?"

"No. I'm sure she's just off in a corner sniffing something." He took the flashlight from the kitchen drawer and went outside.

His optimism faded almost immediately. He shone the light around the fenced-in yard, across the area Connie's boys had shoveled clean so that C.J. had somewhere to move around. Finally he brought the beam to rest on the gate to the backyard. It was swinging open, creaking. His heart fell.

The ladies hadn't closed the gate when they left; C.J. had gotten loose. Damn. That old dog wouldn't have the stamina to last very long outside with the temperature as low as it was.

He pushed through the gate and started down the driveway. Good thing she was old and fat, she couldn't have gotten far. When he reached the sidewalk out front, he shouted, "C.J.," in both directions and waited, hoping to see her waddle out of the shadows toward him.

He looked up at Dorothy's house and discovered the place dark. The ladies sure went to bed early. Last night must have exhausted them more than they'd let on. He'd talk to them in the morning about the gate.

He glanced at his watch. Nine-fifteen. The humane society would be closed. He took the front-porch steps two at a time and went into the house, slapping his hands together for warmth. Liza met him at the door.

"She's gone," he said. "The back gate is open.

The latch is old and rusty—the ladies probably didn't close it tight enough when they were here."

"Ohmigosh, poor C.J. She *will* freeze to the sidewalk."

Jack scowled. "Don't remind me. I'm going to call the police—maybe they found her already."

He flipped open the phone book and dialed, learning moments later that the police hadn't picked up a basset hound but would alert all squads. Alert all squads—for a missing dog? Somehow he didn't think that he'd get the same level of response in Chicago.

When he hung up, Liza was already pulling on her boots. "I'll help you look for her. She couldn't have gotten far—you didn't wait that long to let her in."

"Obviously long enough."

Two hours later, after driving slowly down every block within a mile radius, Liza hanging out the passenger window shouting "C.J." and he out the driver window doing the same, Jack pulled the car into the garage. "I can't believe we lost my grandmother's dog."

"We'll find her."

He exhaled slowly. "I've heard dogs get stolen for medical experiments—"

"I think they want healthy dogs for that—not

the ones already on their last legs." She reached out to pat his arm. "Tomorrow we can put up lost-dog posters."

He nodded. Tomorrow. He was supposed to be flying to Chicago tomorrow. "Maybe she'll come home tonight," he said with more optimism than he felt.

First thing the next morning, Jack called the humane society and the police department to see whether C.J. had been brought in. Liza held her breath, her mind a jumble of mixed emotions. The caring, empathetic old-Liza side of her brain wanted C.J. to be found right away. But the selfish, driven new-Liza side hoped the dog stayed lost until she got the information she needed about Dear Cordelia. It was starting to seem as if she had an entire dysfunctional family living out a full and demented life in her brain. She wondered whether her gray matter could overheat and burn out from all the chaos.

And then, of course, there was the kiss. What was she getting herself into here? Talk about burning up; there was probably smoke coming out of her ears right now.

Jack hung up the phone and shook his head. "No luck, nowhere."

"Then we'll get signs up." She stretched her back, still sore from yesterday's shovelfest. "Good thing it doesn't snow this much very often."

Jack rolled his shoulders. "First dibs on that vibrating cushion when we get back. Listen, I'm gonna go tell the ladies next door about C.J. so they can keep an eye out for her."

Liza couldn't believe her luck. He was leaving her alone in the house. She waited until the door clicked shut behind him, then raced up the stairs and into Jack's bedroom—well, raced as fast as she could considering the muscles in her legs and lower back were painfully protesting. She drew a quick breath inside the door and went to work. This could well be her last opportunity before Jack left town. She opened the laptop computer and turned it on. As soon as the system booted up, she began to scroll through files, scanning their contents as quickly as she could.

Okay, so here were some Dear Cordelia columns. Big deal. She'd expect he'd have those. Come on. There had to be something here. Heart thudding, she jumped up to look out the window and see if Jack was coming back yet. Nope.

She threw herself back into the chair and

began to scroll through the files again. Oh please, let something show up.

JACK WAITED a very long time for the ladies to answer the door. From the corner of his eye, he saw the drape in the front window slide to one side, but by the time he turned to see who was there, the curtain had already swung back into place.

"I hope they don't want me to stay for coffee," he muttered.

The door opened and Margaret stuck her head out. She was wearing pajamas and a shimmery robe. "Oh, it's just you. Good morning, you're up awfully early."

Jack nodded. "I've got bad news. C.J.'s missing—she ran away last night."

Margaret's mouth made an O and her eyes grew wide. She gasped. "No!"

"Yes—"

"Such a shock—our dear C.J. missing."

Dorothy appeared at Margaret's shoulder and sneezed. "C.J.'s missing, you say?"

"She disappeared last night—"

Dorothy sneezed again.

"You sound terrible. Maybe I better come in so you can shut the door." Jack stepped forward.

"Oh, no, it's just a cold." She shook her head.

"Darnedest thing. Came on during the night. You'd better not come in or you might catch it. And that wouldn't be good, would it?"

"No indeed," Margaret answered for him. "C.J. was in the yard when we left. How do you suppose she got out?"

"The latch on the gate didn't hold. It's so rusty." Jack hoped his words didn't sound accusatory.

"Oh. We couldn't have left it open, could we, Dorothy?"

Dorothy shook her head. "I'm sure we closed it. Not to panic you, Jack, but could someone have stolen her?"

"C.J.? Old, fat, shedding, drooling, dandruff, with one-glaucoma-eye C.J.? Stolen?" he asked.

"Well, she does have a lot of love to give," Dorothy pointed out, wiping her nose.

"Love is a many splendored thing." Margaret grinned inanely.

"Love will keep us together." Dorothy's expression mirrored Margaret's.

"What's love got to do with it?" Jack said, getting into the spirit.

"Well, everything, dear. My goodness, it's about time you fell in love, you know." Margaret tsked.

Jack rolled his eyes. "It's a song—'What's Love Got To Do With It'?"

The two women stared at him, not understanding.

"Okay, never mind. Liza and I are going out to put up some lost-dog posters—"

"Are you staying then?" Margaret asked, a definite note of hope in her voice.

"I don't know. I've gotta find C.J. My flight's not until late afternoon—hopefully she'll turn up before then."

He rubbed his hands together to warm them. "Can you keep an eye out in case she wanders back? Or someone stops by who might have found her? You've got my cell number—"

"Absolutely. Yes. Yes. Don't worry, we'll both keep a watch out the window, won't we, Margaret?"

"We always do. And don't forget about canceling your flight," Margaret said.

Jack nodded and headed back to his grandmother's house. He let himself in the back door and looked for Liza in the kitchen. "Hey, Liza?" He walked into the front of the house calling her name again. When she didn't answer, he headed for the stairs. "Liza!" he shouted.

Moments later she skidded around the corner

from the upstairs hall and half limped, half flew down the stairs. "Oh, hi, I was just in the bathroom, you ready to go?" she said breathlessly.

At least she was enthused about doing this. "As soon as we make the signs," he said.

"What did the ladies say about C.J.?"

"It was kind of strange. They seemed out of whack—more than usual, that is. Wouldn't even let me in the house."

"Oh, they probably weren't dressed yet. Maybe they were embarrassed you caught them in their pajamas."

Jack snorted. "There was nothing to be embarrassed about in those pajamas. There were covered from neck to ankle. They couldn't have been less exposed if they had on mechanics' jumpsuits."

Liza laughed. "Better not tell them that."

Two hours later they had visited the humane society, the veterinarian, the pet groomer, the police department, and were back at the humane society a second time, just to make sure someone hadn't overlooked an old basset hound being brought in.

Jack stopped outside a cage holding a golden-retriever mix and reached in to pet the dog. The animal's tail wagged happily. A little Benji-type dog in the next cage pressed itself against the bars and Jack reached his other hand over to pet that animal as well. He moved down the row of cages, giving each dog a minute or two of attention.

After a while, Liza said, "You like dogs."

He looked up. "Yeah, I like dogs. But, even more, I hate seeing them like this. Caged. Dogs are pack animals. When they're part of a family, the family becomes their pack. Here, they're all alone."

He moved to the next few cages and reached through the bars to rub the heads of the dogs inside. "These poor guys just want a home."

Liza watched him, his expression soft and caring as he made his way around the room. This man was becoming dangerous in the worst sort of way. Taking time to pet the dogs in the pound? Oh boy, reporter or not, she wasn't feeling particularly immune to that kind of charm.

"When I was a kid, I used to come down here all the time. Even though it wasn't true, I'd tell the lady at the front desk that I was looking for a dog to adopt." He shook his head. "What I was really doing was making sure all these dogs didn't feel abandoned. I'd stop in and pet them and hope they felt like they were wanted."

"I bet they did feel wanted." Liza reached a hand through the bars and ruffled the hair on top of a little terrier's head.

"I thought I was so sly, saying I was going to adopt a dog. Years later, they told me that they looked for me every Tuesday and Thursday after school. They knew the truth and went along with my ploy anyway."

"Did you ever get a dog?"

"We always had dogs. I just wanted more— to give them a home. My grandmother had a soft heart and lots of love to give. She'd take in strays for the night and end up keeping them for good. She didn't care if they were scraggly mutts. So many people want a purebred with the perfect pedigree."

He stopped in the doorway to the room, looked back at the rows of cages and shook his head. "A mixed breed loves you just as much. Maybe even more," he murmured. "My grandmother knew that. She took in whatever, whoever, needed her love—and made them whole."

Liza watched him and wondered if he was talking about dogs anymore…or someone else. Her heart went out to him and she wasn't sure why.

He headed for the entrance and she followed him outside. The crisp winter air hit her like a slap across the face, and she caught her lower lip in her teeth. She didn't know how long a dog could last in this cold weather, but she was certain it couldn't be days. Especially if the dog was an old one that was used to living indoors.

They drove through town and plastered signs all over telephone poles, announcing a hundred-dollar reward for C.J.'s return. After she hopped out of the car so many times and hurried to keep up with Jack's long stride, Liza's fingers felt as if they were half-frozen in her gloves.

As the morning lengthened, a bitter cold front settled in. *Oh, please, C.J., be somewhere safe and warm.* Inside her gloves, she rubbed her icy fingers against her palms for warmth. She couldn't help it, she began to fantasize about a hot shower, one so long that she drained the entire tank and wrinkled her fingers and toes.

"You look chilled." Jack pulled open the car door for her.

Understatement. "Justalidda." Her jaw was so cold she could hardly speak.

He put his arm around her shoulders and rubbed vigorously. "Get in. I know just what you need."

She looked at his rosy cheeks and the day's growth on his jaw and thought of a really fun way to warm up. Last night he had kissed her as if he meant it. Maybe a little more of the same would do the job.

Gaack! Had her common sense frozen too? Guys like him always kissed as if they meant it—that's how they got all the girls.

Jack slid into the driver's seat and pulled out from the curb, one hand deftly turning the wheel while the other cranked up the heat. "There's a little restaurant downtown. They make strong coffee and hot chili."

Yup. She was thinking of kissing and he was thinking of food. Liza pulled off her gloves and held her hands out in front of the heat vents. Jack reached his right hand over and took hold of her left.

"Does this help?" he asked.

Help? Help what? Help her already racing libido go into overdrive? She nodded, more because she knew he expected an answer and less from an ability to think clearly. "Thanks."

She tried to breathe normally. This whole investigation was taking a decidedly interesting turn. Jack Graham had kissed her last night.

Now he was holding her hand. She was due for a call to Kristin.

Jack pulled into the restaurant parking lot and a few minutes later they were seated inside the Bear Claw Café and Coffee Bar. Liza wrapped her hands around her cup of hot cocoa and sighed as the warmth seeped though her fingers. "With all those signs up, surely someone will call."

"It worries me. This town is so small, everybody knows who C.J. is. If someone found her, they would have called already." Jack almost sounded resigned.

"It's too soon to know," Liza said as brightly as she could, burying her own pessimism. Why did it have to be so cold? "It hasn't even been twenty-four hours. Push comes to shove, we can run an ad in the paper." She picked up a newspaper someone had left behind in their booth and started flipping to the back pages for the want-ad section.

"Hey, look at this, it's your client! Dear Cordelia." She folded the paper and held it up so Jack could see Cordelia's column.

"After ten years, I don't get that excited seeing the column anymore," he said wryly.

"Old hat by now, huh? Do you ever spend any

time with her or is it just an e-mail, phone call sort of business relationship?"

Jack looked at her for a moment. "Well, sure, I see her. She's my client."

Liza couldn't believe he was answering her questions. She forged ahead, afraid to waste a minute in case he clammed up. "So why does she use a drawing of herself with the column instead of a photograph like all the other columnists?"

"Says it's more romantic. Softer edges, or something like that."

"How'd you meet her?"

Jack froze with his coffee cup almost to his mouth. He looked over the rim at her for a moment before finally saying, "Through a friend."

Liza forced herself to slow down. She had dropped into investigative mode and Jack was pulling back. She sipped her cocoa and tried not to blurt out something like, *But where does she live?* Finally she couldn't think of any other way to say it and, with Jack planning to fly out today, she knew asking the question was worth every risk. She opened her mouth.

"Are you Jack Graham?"

They both looked up at the tall, thin man who had stopped at their booth.

Jack nodded.

The man extended a hand. "Terry Schultz. I'm a reporter with the local paper."

Liza could sense a wariness come over Jack. He shook the other man's hand. "Nice to meet you."

"I met your grandmother once," the reporter said.

"Uh-huh."

Liza knew Jack was annoyed, though the reporter didn't have a clue.

"I understand you're the publicist for Dear Cordelia. The advice columnist."

A pained expression cut across Jack's face. "Yes." While his delivery wasn't curt, he didn't elaborate.

The reporter grinned. "I thought so. I'm working on a Valentine's Day story—"

"No kidding," Jack said.

Liza winced at the fake enthusiasm in his voice.

"Yeah. It would really make the issue if I could interview Cordelia—"

"You and every other reporter in the country," Jack muttered under his breath.

"Excuse me?" the man said.

"Cordelia is very private."

"I've heard that. But it would really help my status on the paper if I could get an interview—"

"She doesn't do interviews."

The finality in his voice sent a stab of fear into her. Jack Graham would never set up an interview with Cordelia—not with anyone.

The reporter frowned. "But maybe if—"

"No maybes. No interviews."

The reporter looked taken aback. "Well, you know Cordelia. Everyone has their price—what's hers?"

Jack glanced at the man's worn jacket and his old jeans. "She has no price," he said very politely in spite of the agitation Liza could see etched on his face. "There...are...no...interviews."

"How about if I interview you then?"

"Her publicist? What do people care what I have to say?"

The reporter shrugged. "You could give some insights into what the woman's like."

"No. Thanks for stopping over. Good luck with your Valentine's edition." Jack turned his attention back to Liza, his body language clearly stating the conversation was over.

The reporter stood there for a moment longer as if deciding what to do next. "Okay, thanks. Sorry about your dog," he finally muttered and turned away.

"Damn. Reporters drive me nuts." Jack

looked at her and his expression lightened. "Except food reporters, that is."

Liza's stomach flopped. "Yeah, we don't care about love, only about how good our next meal is."

Jack shook his head. "Investigative reporters are the most persistent SOB's I've ever met. They get something in their heads they believe is true, and no matter how many times you think you've made your point, somehow they never get it."

"I think newspaper editors value tenacity."

"Tenacity? Maybe. All I know is, some reporters aren't above lying to get their story."

A chill raced up Liza's spine.

"You wouldn't believe the lines I've gotten from people trying to get an interview with Cordelia," he said.

"Maybe if Cordelia would give a few interviews, they'd quit being so persistent."

His expression darkened and Liza thought how she'd never want to have Jack Graham angry with her.

He leaned forward. "Like every other person, Cordelia is entitled to privacy. If she doesn't want to give interviews, she shouldn't have to."

"But don't you think some of the pressure

would go away if she'd open up a little? Come on, Jack, half the interest is because she's such a mystery."

"Who cares why? She doesn't want to do interviews and I'll protect her every way I can." There was a fierceness in his voice that Liza both feared and admired. God help her if he ever got wind of her reason for being here.

She didn't want him to think she was one of those reporters who lied to get a story. Because she never had before. This was just an unusual case with unusual circumstances. She had less than two weeks to get the story…and she only wanted this story so she could change her life. This wasn't really what she was like.

A sense of dread settled into her stomach. If Jack found out what she was up to, he would never believe that—not for an instant. She certainly wouldn't. He despised reporters. And he would despise her if he ever learned the truth.

Fear made her heart beat a little faster and she smiled, hoping Jack couldn't sense her nervousness.

He looked at her apologetically. "I don't mistrust all reporters. I'm sure the food-section reporters are ethical."

"Oh, sometimes I'm tempted to stretch the

truth about how many calories are in a recipe. Especially the decadent ones."

Her stomach tightened at telling yet another lie. She didn't want Jack to think she was just like all the other reporters. She didn't want him to think she was a Goody Two-Shoes either. She mentally sighed.

Who the hell *was* she, anyway?

CHAPTER EIGHT

LIZA DECIDED to change the subject. The last thing in the world she wanted to be talking to Jack about was unethical reporters. "So what do we do now? About C.J.?"

"We wait."

The waitress stopped at their table to refill their coffee cups and ask whether they wanted something to eat. "We've got a mean batch of chili simmering in the back," she said. "Just the thing to warm you up on a day like this."

Her words made Liza realize how hungry she really was. "I could go for a bowl—unless you want to get back out and search some more..."

"Hell, it's almost noon—we might as well eat. We can keep searching afterward." He glanced at the waitress. "Make it two bowls."

"You're looking for that dog, aren't you?"

Jack brightened. "Yeah. Have you seen her?"

"Naw. Sorry. But I've heard there's folks that steal dogs, to use in experiments."

Jack threw an I-told-you-so look at Liza.

"Somehow I don't think they'd want C.J.," she said.

"Oh no. They'll take any kind." The waitress nodded knowingly. "That's why so many folks are putting computer chips in their dogs—so they can find them if they're missing. I guess you didn't have a microchip in the dog?"

Jack shook his head. "No microchip. Maybe lots of potato chips, though."

The waitress stared at him and blinked, clearly confused.

Liza smiled. "C.J.—the dog—is somewhat overweight."

"I don't think those experiment places care none about that. They just need dogs."

"Well…C.J. has other issues too. She's got glaucoma, she drools, she has dandruff, you name it," Liza said.

"But who's keeping track?" Jack muttered.

The waitress nodded, looking no more enlightened, and walked away to put their order in with the kitchen.

Several minutes later, she returned with their food. "You know, I've been thinking about your dog," she said. She set two bowls of chili and little paper containers of cheese, onions and sour cream on the table, slowly and deliberately, one at a time. Liza looked at Jack. He crossed his eyes and she stifled a laugh.

The waitress finished arranging everything on their table, then straightened. "Maybe someone took your dog for ransom."

Liza bent her head and focused on dumping the cheese and onions on her chili. She sneaked a glance at Jack.

He cleared his throat and spoke slowly. "I suppose that could be what happened. But who would think an old, glaucomic dog is worth some sort of ransom?"

"Well now, it's hard for me to know, since I don't hardly know you anyway. But, ever since your grandma set up that fund to keep the dog in the house, people have been talking about how much money that old woman really had. Not me, mind you, but other folks. Not mean talk either, just talk."

Jack nodded. "Have you got anyone in mind?"

The waitress shook her head. "Look, I'm sort of like a think tank. I come up with ideas for people. It's up to them to follow through." She ripped their bill off the top of her order pad and set it facedown on the table.

"Tell you what. I'll keep thinking about your situation and if I come up with any ideas, I'll let you know."

"Great. Thanks." Jack stuck a spoonful of scalding chili into his mouth and Liza was certain it was to keep himself from laughing out loud. He reached for the water glass and took a long drink, watching the waitress until she disappeared into the kitchen.

"A think tank?" he said.

Liza grinned. "You don't think there's any credence to her ideas, do you?"

"Give me a break. I don't care that I came up with that ridiculous idea first. No experiment place would want that dog. Hell, *nobody* would want that dog," he said in an offhand way. "That's why her ransom idea is so dumb, too."

"You'd want that dog," Liza said softly.

He jerked his head up to look at her. His eyes met hers and he set down his spoon. "Yeah, I'd want that dog."

"If for no other reason than because nobody else does." She looked into his blue eyes and knew then that he was more than a handsome guy who got all the beautiful girls. Inside him was a strong conscience, a sense of wanting to make the world right for every downtrodden being he came across.

The attraction of that was way beyond what she wanted to deal with. And as much as she tried to shove it into a dark corner of her brain, it kept popping back out at the most inopportune moments. So now she had two problems. Jack would hate her the minute he found out she was just one more lying reporter trying to get a story. And she was more attracted to him than ever.

What a mess.

Maybe she ought to throw in the towel. It seemed infinitely easier than continuing on this path. What did it matter, really? At the rate things were going, he'd be gone by this afternoon anyway, and she'd be back in the food section by next week.

JACK PULLED UP in front of the Belleview Inn and dropped Liza off to pay her bill and get her rental car out of the parking lot. She stepped onto the freshly shoveled sidewalk and waved at him as he drove away. Thank goodness, he was gone. She needed some advice.

Fifteen minutes later she was sitting in her idling car, arguing with Kristin. "I've done my best, but I can't come up with any reason to make him stay here, other than the fact that his grandmother's dog is missing. His flight's out in four hours."

"You can't let him get on that plane." Kristin's voice held a new urgency.

"That could prove harder to do than finding out where Cordelia is," Liza said.

"So? Put some guilt on him about the dog. Forget that he's *Jack Graham* and just think of him as a goal."

"It's easy for you to say all this stuff because you're in Chicago. You're not living it like I am," Liza said testily.

"Right. Which is why I have perspective and you don't."

"The guy is—"

"Which is why you should listen to me."

Liza sighed. "He hates reporters—well, reporters like I'm trying to be."

"Who cares? You didn't go all the way to Maine to get him to like you…"

Liza didn't answer for a long moment. "No, but—"

"Oh Lord! No buts, no buts—"

"But—it's changed."

"No changes allowed. Don't get yourself personally involved." Kristin's voice went up a notch. "You're changing your life, remember? Why would you give it all up because you feel guilty over—"

"I don't feel guilty."

"Oh yes you do. You're the nice girl. You were raised on guilt. You always do what you're told. You don't take advantage of anyone— you're just too nice for your own good. You always let someone else have the empty seat on the bus, you save old bread crusts for the birds, you never tried smoking a cigarette, you never drink too much, or waste money on frivolous clothes that will go out of style, or—"

"Okay, okay, I get it. You don't need to rub it in."

"No, I do need to rub it in. You got fed up with your life and you wanted to change it. You can choose not to change it when you reach the end—but not now, Liza. You can't quit in the middle."

Liza fiddled with the heat button on the console, turning it up higher. "Why not?"

"Because if you do, someday when you're an old woman, you're going to look back and wonder what your life would have been if you had seen this whole thing through. And you're going to wish you could go back, just once, and do it all over again."

"And it'll be too late."

"Uh-huh."

Liza sighed. "I think I *like* him."

"Yeah, you and every other woman, single or otherwise, who meets Jack Graham."

"But he's such a nice guy—"

"He's a guy who needs, I repeat, *needs,* you to take the job to watch that old basset hound. Of course he's going to be nice. He's a charmer, Liza."

"But he really is a genuinely nice guy under all those good looks."

Kristin let out a loud sigh. "These kinds of guys know just how to make women do what they want. In your case, he doesn't want you to fall into his bed—he wants you to take the darn job. I've seen it a hundred times before. Let me guess, he's probably doing stuff to show you what a great guy he is—you know, like helping the poor, or kissing babies…"

Or petting abandoned dogs in the humane society. Liza's heart fell. "You've seen this before?"

"What's he doing?"

"Uh, nothing, really."

"Baloney. Let me have it and I'll tell you what he's up to."

"He stopped to pet all the dogs in the humane society. Said he didn't want them to feel abandoned." Saying it out loud made Liza realize how ridiculous it sounded.

Kristin began to chortle. "Now, *that* is good—"

"We went there looking for C.J. He just wanted to make sure she hadn't been brought in." Liza could hear the defensiveness in her voice. She took a breath to calm herself.

"All he had to do was ask if a basset hound had been brought in."

"He did. But he wanted to make sure they hadn't missed her."

"Ah. He didn't trust the staff to recognize a basset hound? So he went in the back to check for himself?"

Liza fought the disappointment rolling through her. "Yeah."

"Liza, Liza, Liza. This man is playing all the right cards to make you take the job. And that's okay—as long as you realize he's playing you."

How else would he ever have gotten the reputation he had in Chicago? She shook her head at her naiveté. Thank goodness she had Kristin for guidance. "You're right. I've never played in the big leagues before."

"So you get back in there—"

"And win one for the Gipper."

Kristin laughed. "That's right. Have you had any luck finding out anything about Cordelia?"

"No. But I got a really good look at how he treats reporters who approach him on the subject. It wasn't pretty. And let me tell you, every time Dear Cordelia comes up in conversation, it goes nowhere."

"I don't think you have a prayer of getting him to arrange an interview for you. That is, assuming you can keep him from flying out," Kristin said.

Liza exhaled. "I know. I came to the same conclusion after hearing him talk to that reporter this afternoon."

"That's okay. You just have to find the information yourself."

"Yeah, except he never leaves the house. Especially now that we've had a blizzard and the dog's disappeared." She paused. "I know—don't say it. I have to find some way to get him out of the house."

"See? You don't need me."

"Oh yes I do." Liza thought of kissing Jack

and wished it had meant something more to him than just getting her to take the job.

"Listen, Liza, time is short. You keep him from leaving. And you get that information within the next three days. Because even then, you'll have only a week to get an interview lined up."

After saying goodbye to Kristin, Liza shut off the phone and stared out the window at the mounds of snow piled around the small parking lot like walls in a prison. "Oh God, what have I gotten myself into?" She had been so ready to throw aside her plan just because she'd started to like Jack. Boy, old habits were hard to break.

Kristin was right. Strip away her emotions and it was easy to see he was pulling out all the stops to get her to take the job. She just needed to remember to keep her eye on the prize. She had to stop Jack from leaving town, get the information about Cordelia, and then get out of Coldwater before she lost her heart to a guy who probably had a headboard with hearts lined up on it instead of notches.

No problem.

She put her car into gear and began to drive aimlessly, finally stopping at the grocery store to buy the fixings to make spaghetti and meatballs for dinner. As she picked out lettuce and tomatoes for a salad, she prayed Jack had canceled his flight and she wouldn't have to eat alone.

JACK WAS HOME for almost an hour before he couldn't stand being there anymore. The answering machine had no messages about C.J. and the ladies next door reported no sign of her. The only thing left for him to do was wait.

And he didn't do well with waiting. Especially not now, after dredging up all those old memories of his childhood, and the humane society, and his grandmother. He'd lost his grandmother's dog...and it weighed heavy on him.

He felt a need to atone for what he'd done, to be near his grandmother now, to visit her grave. He glanced at his watch; there was plenty of time before his flight left.

Slipping on his jacket, he headed out to the garage, grabbed a dusty red plastic geranium out of a clay pot up on a shelf and drove to the cemetery. The moment he passed through the big iron gates, a sense of peace washed over him. The grounds stretched out in every direction like a sea of white, broken only occasionally by a cross or angel at the top of the taller headstones.

Jack pulled his car to a stop beside a tall pine tree and shut off the engine. He sat there a moment before finally opening the door and stepping out.

Under the gray sky, a chill wind rolled across the open grounds. He flipped up the collar of his jacket and let the hush of the cemetery envelope him. Looking around, he tried to get his bearings so he could find his grandmother's grave. Everything was so different covered with snow—still the same, and yet, the path he would have taken was obscured, the usual landmarks buried.

After a short walk, he stopped to brush off the front of a headstone sticking up through the snow. *Cook.* One of Grandma's cemetery neighbors—he'd known he was close. He went a few feet farther and used his gloved hands to clear away the snow on his grandmother's headstone.

"'Catherine Graham,'" he read aloud. His words almost sounded reverent in the all-encompassing quiet. "'Love never fails.'"

It had been part of one of her favorite quotes. He didn't know the whole thing, just the beginning—*Love is patient, love is kind...* When his grandmother died it had only seemed right to have that quote define her for the rest of time.

"I lost C.J., Grandma." His words were sucked away by the wind. "I'm sorry."

No reply came—not that he was expecting one.

"She was out in the yard and then she was just gone." Now, if that didn't sound like a guilty kid's excuse, he didn't know what did. "You wouldn't be able to get the big guy to help us find her, would you?"

The wind whistled past.

He sighed. He hadn't thought so. A lost dog had to be pretty low on the priority list.

He dug the plastic geranium out of his pocket and stuck it in the snow by the headstone. It looked silly and he grinned. This was just the way his grandmother would have wanted it.

He waited, staring out across the cemetery, expecting something, and not at all certain what. He thought of his flight home—just a few hours away. What should he do? Hell, what choice did he have, really? It would be ridiculous to leave Liza here with C.J. missing. Ridiculous to expect her to fix the whole thing when she hadn't even taken the caretaker job yet. And it would be unfair to C.J. and his grandmother. He exhaled and watched his breath frost in the air.

A golf cart rolled up behind his car and Ernie

Crawford, the cemetery caretaker, stepped out. Jack trudged back through the snow toward him.

"Oh, it's just you, Jack. Didn't know who was wandering out here in the snow, but when I saw you digging, figured I'd better see what was up."

Jack laughed. "Thought I might be robbing graves?"

"You never know these days."

"I suppose not." Jack inhaled and felt the icy air race through his sinuses and down his throat. "Have you heard? My grandmother's dog is missing. An old basset hound—"

"I know C.J. Haven't seen her on the grounds, though. Kinda doubt she could walk all the way here, being as old as she is."

Jack nodded. Where the hell could that dog be?

"Did you ask the ladies next door?"

"They're keeping an eye out," Jack said.

"They're good at that. Margaret tells me you found a new caretaker for C.J." Ernie pointed to another section of the cemetery. "Billy's right over there in case you want to stop by and say hi. Good thing we got him in the ground before this storm hit. Hate to have to move all this snow."

Jack nodded again.

"Margaret tells me Dorothy and him were getting friendly just before he passed on."

Jack turned to stare at the man. "Dorothy? And Billy?" He quashed the visual that leaped into his mind.

"Yeah, except it came to a quick halt because she was allergic to the dog. Margaret says he was wanting Dorothy to stay over there, but all she did was sneeze and blow her nose, which Margaret says Billy said wasn't so sexy."

Sexy? Dorothy? Way too much information. Here he thought his neighbors were two nice old ladies who did volunteer work. And now he learned that Dorothy was getting it on with old Billy... And Margaret—

He cast a sidelong glance at the caretaker. "You talk to Margaret a lot?"

Either the guy blushed or it was getting colder outside. "Oh, well, enough. She's awfully sweet... I mean, she makes a mean corned beef and cabbage."

Jack nodded as though hearing about his neighbors' love lives was just a normal everyday occurrence. Dorothy and Billy. Margaret and Ernie. This was almost as bad as picturing his grandmother with a boyfriend. Parents— and their friends—weren't supposed to do this sort of stuff. He wondered if Margaret got out the vibrating cushion for Ernie.

No! Don't picture it.

A gust of wind blasted across the cemetery, swirling snow up and over them. Jack wiped a hand across his face, the snowy granules melting as he brushed them away. "I think the residents are giving us a sign it's time to go," he said.

His cell phone rang in his pocket.

"There's another sign," Ernie said as he got back in the golf cart. "When you see Margaret, say hi for me."

Jack nodded and answered the phone.

"Jack? It's Liza. I got back to the house just as someone was leaving a message on the machine."

His heart soared. "They found her?"

"It sounds like it, but—"

"What's the address?"

"That's the strange part—they're in Milford. She said she ran into Coldwater on an errand and spotted our posters."

"Milford? How did C.J. get three miles away?" Jack got in the car and headed for the cemetery entrance.

"Maybe some kids found her and took her there as a prank."

"Some prank." He grinned. His grandmother must have more pull in heaven than he thought.

"The woman said they found C.J. wandering

down their street so they took her inside and gave her a hot dog."

"Nice. Are you sure it's C.J.?"

"It sounded like it—same coloring, everything."

Jack pulled up to the curb in front of the house, ran up the steps and burst through the door. "Let's go, Liza! Cross your fingers." He looked at his watch. There was still plenty of time for him to make his flight.

"Oh, I don't need to come along."

"Sure you do."

Liza shook her head. "No, really. I'll just hang out here. I like being alone."

"Keep me company."

When she started to back away, he lifted her jacket off the coat tree and tossed it at her. "Come on—we're in this together. Don't you want to be there when we find her?"

Liza rolled her eyes and gave in. "Okay."

During the short drive to Milford, Jack told Liza about Ernie and Margaret. "You know, I thought the ladies were real strange this morning—maybe Ernie was there and they didn't want us to know. Margaret *was* wearing this silky robe thing."

"That doesn't mean she had a boyfriend

there. If I recall correctly, she was *covered from ankle to neck*."

Jack nodded knowingly. "Yeah but, when men aren't around, women wear cotton and flannel. Enter a man and in comes the silky, slippery stuff."

"You know this for a fact, huh?"

"Remember, I've got an inside line to Dear Cordelia," he said smugly. "She's taught me everything I need to know about women."

Liza blushed slightly.

"I'm not embarrassing you, am I?"

"No, no. But I don't think you can generalize about all women in that regard—even if Dear Cordelia says so."

He looked at her appreciatively, a stirring in his gut reminding him of what it had been like to kiss her. "Why, Liza Dunnigan, are you saying you aren't a cotton-and-flannel kind of girl?"

Her face went from slight blush to hot pink and she pursed her lips, her perfect heart-shaped lips. "I'm not saying anything. A lady doesn't discuss her *unmentionables* with a gentleman...until such point as they are...they are..."

"Being removed by said gentleman?" Jack had to restrain himself from pulling over and checking out what Liza was wearing under her blue jeans and sweater. The idea that this woman, with her matter-of-fact style and kissable lips, might be wearing something not-so-practical underneath was incredibly intriguing. Intriguing, hell. It was an incredible turn-on.

"No! Until such point as they are…in a relationship."

"Oh, same thing."

Liza pushed the button to roll the window down a little and he thought to himself that all the five-degree air in the world wasn't going to cool down the car right now.

She had a certain allure when she was disconcerted.

He pulled himself back. This was not the best time for him to be getting attracted to someone. Unless, of course, they both were in agreement that this was a short-term thing. A *very* short-term thing. He didn't get into long-term things anyway. Especially not with women who were happy living in Coldwater.

They passed the sign announcing they were entering Milford and Jack braked to bring them closer to the lower speed limit. "Here we are. Where do I turn?"

Liza read off the directions and a few minutes

later he pulled to a stop in front of a small white Cape Cod with dirty windows.

"How did C.J. get here?" He hurried up the walk to the house, with Liza right behind him.

A woman stepped out on the porch to greet them. "You looking for the dog?" Her voice had the twang of someone from the Deep South.

"That's us."

She pulled open the door and shouted, "D-wayne, bring that dog out here now. Come on." She looked back at them. "My boy's taken a liking to her already. There's a reward on her, right?"

"A hundred dollars," Jack said.

A boy about ten pushed open the door and out bounced a brown, white and black…beagle. Irritation surged through Jack.

"There she is," the woman said.

The dog raced around the yard sticking its nose into the snow and snorting.

"That's a beagle," Jack said.

"That's what you're missing," the woman replied.

"A basset. We're missing a basset hound."

The woman looked from the dog to Jack and back again. "Are you sure? I coulda sworn the sign said beagle."

Jack glanced sideways at Liza. "I'm sure."

"Since you can't find your basset, do you want this here beagle? Because we found it and we could use that reward money."

"I don't think so. Thanks anyway."

They didn't speak until they were out of Milford.

"I'm sure she'll turn up, Jack. Dogs don't just disappear." Liza tried to sound reassuring.

He glanced at the clock on the dashboard and knew he couldn't go back to Chicago today. He couldn't leave Coldwater without finding C.J....or at least finding out what happened to her. Ever since Billy died, everything that could go wrong had gone wrong. Well, okay, maybe not everything—meeting Liza didn't seem all that wrong.

Although, yes it was, because for some unknown reason, he was finding her attractive and wanting to kiss her and curious as hell about whether she wore silky *unmentionables*. And in the end, she would be in Coldwater and he would be in Chicago and getting involved with her was the last thing he needed to do.

"I'm going to cancel my flight," he finally said. "I can't leave Coldwater until we find C.J."

"Oh, Jack, I'm sorry. If it's any consolation, I bought the fixings for spaghetti and meatballs.

I'll make you a dinner much better than the one you would have gotten on the plane." A smile flashed across her face and it sent a zing right through his breastbone.

A zing? He didn't get zings. The last time he felt a zing he had been a senior in high school and madly in love with Martha Chadwick, who had no idea he even existed, except when she needed help unsticking her locker.

So, that's what this was all about. Martha Chadwick with her short, dark wavy hair and black eyes. He'd almost forgotten about her.

"You know, when I was in high school there was this girl whose locker was two down from mine—Martha Chadwick." He wondered why the hell he was saying this out loud.

"Oh?"

"Her locker would stick. And I had a knack for getting it open. She had hair kind of like yours, and eyes…" He looked at Liza and she looked at him, clearly not understanding at all why he was telling her this story.

He wasn't sure himself. "We never went out…she wasn't my girlfriend or anything." *Why the hell was he telling her this?* He gripped the steering wheel and his knuckles started to turn white.

"And I remind you of her?"

"Yeah." Suddenly he felt again the way he did in high school, awkward around girls, saying all the wrong things, wanting to ask them out and terrified of the rejection. He didn't hit his stride until college. That's when he'd discovered that emotions kept in control meant he could have all the women he'd ever dreamed of. The harder to get he played, the easier the women fell.

Especially women like Martha Chadwick. He'd had dozens of women like her, all self-assured in their high heels and latest-fashion outfits. All confident in their business-meeting behavior. All secure enough to ask him out to dinner and take him home afterward.

And none of them like Liza Dunnigan.

"Actually, you aren't anything like her—except the dark hair and eyes. And that's good."

She grinned and his heart sped up. Liza Dunnigan was a conundrum, a mystery. And he found that incredibly appealing.

He probably should do a short-term thing with her just to get her out of his system. Otherwise no good could possibly come of him getting zinged every time he came back to Coldwater.

CHAPTER NINE

THE NEXT MORNING Liza made an excuse about having to run over to the culinary institute for a meeting, and cut out of the house before Jack could ask too many questions. She still couldn't believe the conversation they'd had yesterday. There she'd been, discussing underwear with him as if such topics were a matter of course for her.

Cotton and flannel? Of course that's what she wore. It was sensible. She'd never given it much thought before. And the worst of it was, even when there was a guy in the picture—she thought of Greg and cringed—she still wore cotton and flannel. Jack was completely wrong as far as she was concerned. She'd never run out and bought new underwear just because a man had entered her life.

Until now, anyway.

For some reason, the thought of Jack finding out she was a total cotton-and-flannel girl bothered her tremendously. She didn't want him to know—and there was no need for him to find out. Because, as of today, she wasn't going to be a cotton-and-flannel girl anymore.

She arrived at the mall in Orono right when it opened and now was deep in a department-store lingerie section, more overwhelmed than she'd ever been in her life. Cotton was so easy—white, off-white, pastels. When she was feeling particularly daring, she might even get something in black.

Silky was a whole other thing. The choices were endless, the styles seemingly unlimited. Colors like lime green and hot pink and neon purple…and brothel red. Oh, for Pete's sake. And then there were the prints—floral and zebra-striped and leopard and polka-dot. And the lace and embroidery and the Brazilian cut and—

A wave of nervousness rolled over her. What kind of girl would Jack think she was if he found out she owned stuff like this?

Maybe the kind of girl he would date.

Oh God, was that what this was about? She already had plenty of doubts about the guy and his motives. Now that he'd decided to stay in Coldwater a little longer, she had to stay focused on getting the information she needed about Dear Cordelia.

Yes, and if the way to that information turned out to be through allure and—she gulped—seduction, well then, she would be prepared.

Upsetting as it was that C.J. was missing, it sure helped her cause when Jack didn't take that flight yesterday. At least he had enough character to stay until they found out if C.J. was alive or dead. With all her heart, she hoped they found the dog—just not too soon. She needed time to capitalize on this opportunity.

She turned a slow circle, letting her gaze roam over the nearby racks, one after another.

She glanced around sheepishly to see if anyone was watching, then turned her attention to the bras. A few minutes later, she was safely hidden in a changing room with armfuls of undergarments that contained not so much as a thread of cotton.

She tried on the silky pink, and baby blue, and pastel floral. And frowned at the sight of each one in the mirror. They seemed a little safe, almost dull, not that much different from plain cotton. Heck, she already had blue and green underwear now. It seemed to her that if she was going to throw caution to the wind, she should really go for it.

Slipping out of the dressing room, she went

back on the floor and quickly gathered a large assortment of bras and underpants the likes of which she had never even considered before. A clerk stopped to ask if she needed any assistance, and Liza looked down at the neon colors and animal prints in her arms and declined, mortified to be caught trying on such things. She raced into the dressing room, firmly shut the door behind her, sat on the bench and drew a breath.

Get a grip, she told herself. *Other women buy this stuff all the time.*

As if to prove it to herself, she rummaged in her purse until she found her cell phone and dialed Kristin at work. "Hi, it's me," she whispered. "Do you have a couple of minutes?"

"You bet. Let me sneak into the conference room so we can talk. What's going on?"

"Jack skipped his flight yesterday," Liza said.

"Great! So now what?"

"I'm out shopping."

"Is that why you're whispering?" Kristin whispered.

"Uh-huh. I'm shopping for—" Liza dropped her voice even lower. "Underwear."

"What happened to yours?"

"Jack likes silky underwear."

"What?" Kristin shrieked. "How do you know that? And how does he know what kind of underwear you have?"

"Calm down. He doesn't know. And he's never going to know if I can help it." She stripped off her jeans and slipped a pair of zebra-striped underpants over her white cotton briefs. Huh. There was nothing brief about them. She made a face at herself in the mirror. These zebra things were probably called panties. *Ewww*—she hated that word.

"What exactly is going on in Coldwater?" Kristin demanded. "Are you and Jack Graham actually hitting it off? This is incredible—"

"No, no, no. It's nothing like that."

"Well, it's something. Because I've known you for seven years now and you're not the type to go buy new underwear just for kicks. Did you buy new underwear for Greg?"

Liza tried to tuck the massive amount of white cotton inside the tiny zebra-striped panties and rolled her eyes at her ridiculous reflection in the mirror. She turned sideways and sucked in her stomach, but the sight didn't get any better. "What?"

"Did you buy new underwear for Greg?"

"No, but—"

"Aha! Liza, be careful. This isn't the kind of guy who falls in love and settles in for the long haul. Hot underwear does not necessarily a lasting relationship make."

"Don't worry. There's nothing going on—" She tugged off the zebra panties.

"Not yet anyway."

"You're the one who said I should seduce him to get the info I needed." Liza pulled on a pair of black underpants with lace panels on the sides.

"*No,* you're the one who said that the very first day. I was the one who said, 'This new Liza is beginning to surprise me.'"

Liza waved a dismissive hand at the mirror. "Who cares who said it? The fact is, I need to get some of this stuff and I need some help picking it out."

She turned sideways again and patted her stomach, grimacing at her little potbelly. "Do they make sexy underwear with a girdle panel in front?"

"Probably. But it would have to be up to your waist. And I can guarantee that no guy—least of all Jack Graham—wants to see you in underwear up to your waist. No matter what fabric it's made of. That's *gramma wear.*"

Liza pulled her sweater down to cover her "gramma wear" and examined the assortment of bras she had hung on the hook. "Leopard or zebra?"

"Huh?"

"What's more...alluring?"

"Oh my gosh, I can't believe I'm hearing this come out of your mouth." Kristin's voice was almost a shout of glee.

"Shh! You're so loud, I swear the lady in the next stall can hear you." Liza took a breath and lowered her voice. "Now, come on, you gotta help me buy this stuff. I'll describe it—"

Kristin's laughter filled her ear.

"Are you quite finished yet?" Liza asked.

"Okay, okay. Describe away."

Liza held up a hanger and looked at the thong hooked to the ends. Heaven help her. "Hot-pink thong." She hung the hanger on another hook and began to list what else she had: "Red Brazilian-cut bottoms. Leopard bikini bottoms. Tiger-striped bra. Black bikinis with lace panels on the sides." She paused. "Do you think that lace will itch?" she asked.

"Liza, Liza! Have I taught you nothing? *Fashion before comfort.*"

The word *cotton* slipped into her mind and she pushed it aside. "Rosebud print—"

"Forget that one right away. Stick with tried-and-true—black, animal prints—"

"I've got a cheetah print too," Liza said.

"Oh yeah, that'll work. How many of these things are you getting?"

"What do you think?" she asked.

"Well, you won't be wearing them every day…"

"Weeelll…"

"You will?" Shock resonated in Kristin's voice.

"At least while I'm here," Liza said.

"Oh boy. In that case, get several. Those hot colors—pink, lime green, whatever—always come in handy."

"I suppose I should get the matching bras?"

"Well, if you're planning to be seen in them, matching is good."

Liza nodded thoughtfully at herself in the mirror. "My mother always said, make sure your underwear is nice because if you get in a car accident you don't want the emergency-room doctors to know you wear ratty underwear."

"My mom told me the same thing!" Kristin said. "She even told me about some lady who got in an accident and made the first guy on the scene pull her old girdle off and throw it in the bushes before the ambulance arrived."

"Yeahhh." Liza pictured herself demanding a passerby pull off her old-lady underwear. "So what happens when the emergency-room doctors cut off my clothes and find leopard underneath?"

"Oh, they'll probably just think you're an exotic dancer."

"A stripper! Coldwater is so small, it would be all over town in minutes."

Kristin laughed again. "You're not going to get in an accident. Now, go out there and buy the underwear and get to work. And keep me posted. This is becoming more fun every day!"

Liza shut off her phone, dropped it in her purse and tried on all the items she had in the dressing room. "More fun every day, my eye," she muttered.

Her stress level was at an all-time high. In the course of a few days, she'd gone from practical and predictable to practically a stripper. And most shocking of all was that she didn't really see a problem with it. Well, not much of a problem—unless, of course, she got in a car accident.

Now that she was about to buy all this stuff, she was more than a little excited about wearing it. The names of these lines really said it all:

Flirty Foundations, the Glamour Collection, Sexy Little Nothings. She had a feeling just wearing a hot-pink thong would make her feel more attractive even if no one else knew she had it on. Comfort? Now, *that* was another question.

On the way to the cash register, she passed the nightgowns and drew to a sudden stop. She'd been so focused on foundations, she forgot about bedtime. Flannel may be nice on bitter winter nights, but she could give it up for the rest of her stay in Coldwater.

She flipped through the racks and selected a nightgown and pair of pajamas, both in slightly sheer, silky fabric that gave her goose bumps just to feel it against her skin.

She set all her purchases on the counter by the register and pulled out a credit card. Who would have guessed when she put this plan into motion last week that throwing caution to the wind would bring this kind of change to her life?

Liza waltzed into the house with her bag of purchases, hoping to sneak everything into her room before Jack spotted her. She was halfway up the stairs when she heard Dave call from the front of the house, "Hey, Liza. I'm painting the living room. Wanna help?"

"I'll be down in a minute," she shouted over her shoulder. She took the stairs two at a time and raced into her room, pushing the door shut behind her.

Heart pounding in excitement, she tore open the bag and began to cut the tags off her purchases with manicure scissors. She lay everything across the bed and looked it all over for a long minute, letting out a nervous laugh before finally choosing the leopard set to wear.

Grinning as though she had a secret, she stripped off her clothes and slid into the new lingerie. She walked from one side of the room to the other, pausing in front of the full-length mirror to stare at herself. Was it her imagination or did her lips look fuller, more kissable, her eyes more sultry? She tossed her hair and gave the mirror a come-hither look.

Wow. Had all those women who always got the best guys figured this out years ago? She spun in front of the mirror, then did a little boogie dance across the room to grab her painting clothes and pull them on.

She looked in the mirror again. Even in these old things, she still felt different, more attractive, alluring. The big question was—would Jack notice the difference?

She stepped into the hall and spotted the half-open door to Jack's room. Tempted, she paused in the hallway and listened. Was he in there or not? When she didn't hear so much as the click of a computer keyboard, she gave the door a little push and stuck her head forward to peer inside.

Jack looked up from his desk. "Hi."

"Oh! Hi!" Shocked, Liza jerked back, slightly off balance, and banged her shoulder against the doorjamb. Well, the bruise would be a nice match for the leopard print. "I'm back." She hoped he just thought she wanted to say hello.

"You get everything done at the institute?"

"All set," she answered evenly. "Any word about C.J.?" She wondered whether he could tell that her brain was screaming, *Leopard! Leopard! I'm wearing silky leopard underwear and I'm the only one who knows it.*

His cell phone rang. "Hold on a second," he said to her as he took the call. He listened for a minute, then said, "Yeah, we can do that. Tell them I'll do whatever they think is best. They know their business better than I do. Just let me know and I'm there. Right, Cordelia will hype it in the column."

He paused, listening. "Yeah. So how many adoptive parents are making this trip? Great. I should be back in a few days at the most. Okay, let me know."

Cordelia? He shut off the phone and looked up at her, offering no explanation for the odd nature of his call. Not that he owed *her* any explanation, but oh boy did she want one.

"So where were we?" he said. "Oh yeah, C.J. Nothing. I've been home all morning and there hasn't been one call about her. I called the humane society and police again, but no one's turned in a basset."

"Let me guess. They said they have your name and number and will call if anything changes."

"Bingo."

She hesitated, the investigative reporter in her not to be denied. Cordelia? Adoptive parents? What was this about? Was Jack Graham about to adopt a child? Or was Cordelia?

"Jack, I just overheard you talking…about adoption. I hope I'm not overstepping…but are you—"

He laughed. "Not me. I'll tell you what it's about, but don't let it get around. It might ruin my reputation as a free-living bachelor."

Liza stepped into the room. This promised to be good.

"It isn't all that exciting," he said. "A few years ago I started an adoption fund to help people pay the costs of going overseas to adopt kids."

Come on. This was a joke. Liza stared at him. Dogs *and* kids? Kristin would have a field day. "You help people adopt kids?"

He nodded.

Why would he care? Bachelor, player, single guy, man about town? "Why? I mean, it's wonderful," she said hastily. "But I don't get it. It doesn't fit your image." Oh, shoot, she wasn't supposed to know what kind of image he had. "I mean, as a single guy," she blurted.

"Yeah, so don't let it get around." He hit a couple of buttons on his computer to save his document and clear the screen, glancing up at her as though weighing whether to say more. "I guess we're all a product of our childhood. I was adopted. Spent my first nine years bouncing around foster homes."

Liza's heart ached for the little boy she didn't even know.

"Catherine Graham and her husband wanted children but they never had any of their own. After he died, she decided to take in a foster child. That was me. I still remember the day I arrived here. She took me in her arms and told me to call her Grandma." His voice cracked. "The last placement I had been at, the woman made me call her Missus. The more she tried to bend me to her will, the harder I fought back. By the time they sent me here, I was a tough little kid."

He sat back in his chair. "Catherine Graham gave me back my childhood. I just want to do the same for other kids."

A lump rose in Liza's throat and she nodded, afraid to speak.

"Eventually, they terminated my birth mother's rights and Catherine adopted me. But I still called her Grandma…'cause she was just like a grandma's supposed to be. Strict in some ways but more lenient in others. She'd lived long enough to know that not everything is of equal importance. *Choose your battles,* so to speak."

"Didn't she take in dogs too?"

Jack grinned at her. "She took in anything that needed love."

"It sounds like she was a wonderful person."

Jack ran a hand through his hair and turned to look at her. "She was. That's why I can't leave until I know what happened to C.J."

Kids and dogs. No wonder the guy made

women fall all over themselves around him. She was coming darn close to it herself. Jack looked so vulnerable Liza wished she could put her arms around him and promise that C.J. would be home by tonight.

In fact, the only thing that saved her from doing that was the ringing of the doorbell. "I'll get it." She hurried downstairs and opened the door to find Connie, Dorothy and Margaret on the front porch. "Oh, hi!" she said.

Connie eyed her disdainfully. "Is Jack here?" She swept past Liza without even a hello.

"How very nice to see you again," Liza muttered. She turned to the ladies with a smile. "Come on in."

Margaret winked at her and stepped into the room. "We've brought you some homemade banana bread for clearing off our walks."

Dorothy held out a loaf of bread solidly wrapped in tin foil.

"You didn't have to do that." Liza took the bread and peeked into the living room where Dave was up on a ladder and Connie was patting his legs in greeting. Then Jack came down the stairs and Connie hurried forward to greet him with a close embrace. Liza exchanged a look with the ladies.

"Oh, Jack, I saw the signs about C.J. all over downtown," Connie said. "Then I ran into Dorothy at the drugstore and she said C.J. disappeared right out of the yard. You don't suppose some medical experiment place stole her, do you?"

Jack glanced at Liza. She could see *I told you so* dancing in his eyes.

"Now who would want to experiment on an old dog with eye trouble?" Margaret asked.

Liza gave her a grateful smile.

Connie looked superior. "Maybe someone who's trying to find a cure for her kind of problems."

Liza exhaled. How could a whole town be obsessed with medical experiments?

Holding on to Jack's arm, Connie looked up at him. "The boys are gong to be devastated when they hear C.J. is gone. What can I do to help? How about if I bring a meal over?"

Dorothy snorted. "This isn't a funeral."

Jack met Liza's eyes. "Yeah. I don't think we need food. Just keep your eyes open for her. Spread the word."

"You can bring a meal over to my house," Dave said. He stopped brushing paint on the wall and grinned over his shoulder.

Connie gave him a wan smile. "In your dreams." She turned her full attention back to Jack. "It's pretty cold out there. You don't think that C.J. might have… I mean when it's cold you can just fall asleep outside and never wake up."

"No." Liza could hardly contain her irritation. What kind of idiot came over and speculated about the death of someone's beloved pet? "She's fat and furry. Both of those things will help her stay warm."

"That's right," Dorothy said. "I wouldn't doubt if she's safe and sound in someone's house right now—"

"You think someone stole her just to have her?" Connie asked, incredulous. "Who would want her?"

Margaret tsked.

Jack disengaged his arm from Connie and took a step back. "What Dorothy means is maybe she ran away and someone found her. They just haven't gotten around to calling the police or humane society yet."

"Well, if someone does have her, it won't take long for them to notice that eye and her drooling and shedding. You'll probably have her back in no time," Connie said.

Liza decided she'd had enough of this conversation. She handed Jack the loaf of bread. "The ladies brought this over—for shoveling their walks."

Jack unwrapped a corner. "Is this—"

"Your favorite. Banana bread," Margaret said.

"Our famous recipe." Dorothy beamed.

"I'd say you shouldn't have, but I'd be lying. Thanks." Jack broke off a small chunk of bread and popped it in his mouth.

"Now don't be rude," Margaret said. "We'll cut some slices so everyone can have a piece." The two ladies disappeared into the kitchen.

Liza picked up a paint roller and poured some paint into a tray. "Dave, I'll start on this wall over here."

She glanced up just as Connie stepped closer to Jack and lowered her voice. "A bunch of us are gong out to the Mosquito Inn tonight. It's Wally Dixon's birthday—you remember Wally, don't you? We'having a party. He'd be really surprised to see you."

Oh, brother. Liza zigzagged the paint roller on the wall. What an obvious ploy—Connie was certainly not a master of subtlety.

Not like Liza and her new leopard *unmentionables.*

Dave turned around and sat on the top rung

of the ladder. "Jack, you should come out. It'll be like old times."

Liza looked at Jack. He was grinning down at Connie, clearly considering going. Well, and why not? What guy would turn down the obvious?

She dipped her roller in the paint tray, then pressed it to the wall and began to roll with ferocity. *Fine, go out with her.* It didn't matter anyway. Jack was just the guy she was staying with for a few days, the guy who had the information she needed.

She turned her head slightly to look at Connie again—the woman had the look of a vulture going in for the kill. Connie wasn't giving up until she got a definite *yes.* "Lots of people from the old days will be there. Will you come?" she asked in a cajoling voice.

"Well…" Jack glanced at Liza and she quickly turned away. She wasn't getting into this discussion.

"Please say yes," Connie said in a throaty voice that she probably thought was sexy.

Please say yes, Liza repeated snottily in her head.

"Did I mention it's South Seas night at the bar? I'll be in a floral sarong."

"In that case I may have to come," Jack said.

Liza smirked at the wall. All guys were the same. And Jack Graham was probably worse than most. He was so used to women throwing themselves at him. Ha! Well, no way was she ever going to do that. If she and Jack Graham ever got together he would have to do a lot of romancing before she—

What was she thinking? If *they* ever got together, it would be for one reason and one reason only—because it was a means for her to get information on Dear Cordelia.

"Come to what?" Dorothy asked.

Liza looked up just as Margaret held out a plate of banana bread toward her. She took a slice.

"A party at the Mosquito Inn," Jack said.

"Party? That would be perfect for Liza," Margaret said with glee.

"Oh—no—that's okay—" Liza shook her head. "I wouldn't even know anyone—

"You'll know me." Dave winked at her.

"And me and Connie." Jack smiled and Connie glared.

"No, really. This sounds kind of like a reunion." Besides, if Jack was out, she'd have several hours to search his computer. Yesterday she'd failed in her quest to stay home instead of going to Milford with him. Her adrenaline kicked in a little. Tonight, however, would be a whole other story.

"It *is* a group of old friends," Connie said.

"Now that's just silly, don't you think, Margaret?" Dorothy asked. "If it's at a tavern, anyone can come."

"Besides, this is going to be Liza's hometown now. She might as well make some friends," Margaret added.

"I couldn't have said it better myself," Dave said from atop his ladder.

Oh, no, not again. "I'd feel like the third wheel, or odd man out, or something. Really, no. I'll stay home."

"Nah, come on out," Jack said. "The ladies are right. You should meet some people who live here."

Liza sighed. Once again, she didn't have a good reason to keep fighting this.

"Well?" Jack was grinning that killer smile at her and she felt her determination begin to crumble.

"What if someone calls about C.J.?"

"They'll leave a message," Jack said.

"You tell her, Connie. Tell her to come along," Dorothy said with a sly grin.

"It's really up to her," Connie said.

"Oh…all right," Liza said weakly. This was okay, she rationalized. She would stay for one drink, meet a few people, plead exhaustion and cut out, leaving Jack behind. He'd be at the bar partying and she would have plenty of time to get into his files.

CHAPTER TEN

JACK PULLED OPEN the door to the Mosquito Inn and the mingled sounds of music and voices shattered the frosty night. He looked at Liza. "Sounds like the party is well under way. Hope we didn't miss too much."

They stepped into the barroom, illuminated by neon beer signs on the walls, colored Christmas lights still up from the holidays and turn-of-the-century modified gaslights hanging from poles on the ceiling. Plastic blow-up palm trees adorned the entire room. Jack looked around for familiar faces, spotting Connie, Dave and other old friends gathered at some tall tables near the bar. Moments later he was shaking Wally's hand and wishing him a happy birthday and introducing Liza around.

"So you're the new caretaker," Mary Ellen Wilson, an old high-school friend said chirpily. She was wearing some sort of coconut bra and a grass skirt, both of which revealed way more of Mary Ellen than anyone probably ever wanted to see. She hung a lei around each of their necks. "Welcome to Coldwater. Connie tells us you'll be on the staff at the culinary institute."

"That's right," Liza said, nodding.

Jack bent close to Liza's ear and spoke loudly in order to be heard over the din. "What do you want to drink?"

"Just a glass of Chardon—" She frowned and bit her lower lip, thinking, as though this were an important decision. "I always have Chardonnay. How about a...a..."

"Beer?" Jack offered, gesturing at a pitcher on the bar.

She wrinkled her nose. "Too mundane. I'm changing my life, remember?"

Mary Ellen leaned into the conversation and held up a large, curved glass topped with a paper umbrella. "It's two-for-one specials on exotic drinks. Mai tai means *the best* in Tahitian," she said happily.

"Wanna go native?" Jack quipped. "With *the best?*"

Liza tilted her head back and looked up at him. Her mouth opened as if she was about to say something. His heart started to hammer. He shoved his hands in his pockets to keep his fingers from tracing the beguiling shape of those lips. And then following his fingers with his mouth. And then letting his fingers slide down the V-neck of her close-fitting sweater.

"O-kay."

Dave leaned over from his bar stool and smiled at Liza. He held out his glass. "Try this. It's a zombie. Fruity. You'll like it."

Jack frowned. "Aloha," he said, looking at Dave's wild Hawaiian-print shirt.

Liza's mouth shifted up at the corners, slowly breaking into a brilliant smile. She looked flattered. "I will?"

Dave's eyes stayed locked to Liza's and Jack felt a twinge of annoyance.

"I guarantee it. Or your money back." Dave leaned in closer and Jack could swear the jerk was trying to look down Liza's sweater.

Jack looked from Dave to Liza and back again. Behind them the blinking Christmas lights seemed to be dancing on the wall. "Mai tai?" He suddenly felt displaced and he didn't like it one bit.

Liza dragged her attention back to him. She shook her head. "No, I'll have what he's having."

"The lady has taste," Dave said smugly.

Jack headed for the bar feeling out of sorts. "Hey, Jack, what'll you have?" he muttered to himself. "A beer would be great, thanks for asking."

He flagged down the bartender and ordered their drinks. A few minutes later, he returned with a beer for him in one hand and a zombie for Liza in the other. As he neared the table, he noticed Liza had taken the bar stool next to Dave and they were chatting up a storm.

"How soon before you decide?" Dave asked.

"This week. Of course, we have to find C.J. or it's a moot point."

"Cocktail time." Jack handed Liza a tall glass spilling over with slices of pineapple and orange, a cherry on a stick and an umbrella.

"Oh, it's like a salad," Liza said brightly.

Dave laughed too hard and Liza smiled at him in a way Jack had never seen her smile before.

"Had a few of these already tonight, buddy?" Jack said under his breath.

Liza pushed her dark hair behind one ear and put her lips around the straw to take a drink. Jack took a swallow of his beer and watched Dave's eyes fixate on Liza's mouth.

Mine, his brain whispered. I claimed that mouth last night—it's mine.

Dave reached up to wipe a drip of zombie from Liza's lower lip, and irrational anger surged through Jack. He watched as Dave plucked the umbrella from Liza's drink and tucked it slowly into the hair over her left ear. "You can wear this like a flower," he said, grinning.

Jack clenched his teeth and resisted the caveman instinct to lay claim to this woman. He felt an arm slip through his and he turned to find Connie cozying up.

"Hey there," she said.

Connie's eyes lit on Liza and Dave at the bar. She smiled loosely, as if she'd had a zombie or two herself. "Looks like your caretaker has found herself a boyfriend."

"They're just talking." He heard the defensiveness in his voice. *A boyfriend?* Liza couldn't have found a boyfriend in Coldwater. It seemed to him she had other more important things to concentrate on than meeting a guy. She needed to put her energy toward getting ready to start her new job, moving in, maybe even on finding C.J.

But not on getting a boyfriend.

Connie squeezed his arm and he dragged his attention back to her. "Do you want to dance?" she asked.

"Jack!" Liza called. "Did you know Dave played for the New England Patriots for two seasons?"

His irritation intensified. Those two years on the practice squad were going to carry this guy for the rest of his life. Jack turned to Connie. "Yeah, let's dance."

Out on the dance floor he took Connie loosely into his arms. Somehow, what she had to offer just didn't seem very appealing anymore.

"Jack, you're so preoccupied—can I help?"

"Just worried about C.J.," he said.

"Have you ever thought that she might have run away?"

No valedictorian, this girl. He pulled back to look at her. "Uh, yeah. That's pretty much what we thought."

"I mean, ran away to…escape someone."

"What? Like the dog *reasoned* this out first?"

Connie smiled a little. "Well, yeah. I guess."

"No. I've never thought of that." He wondered how much longer this song would be.

"I bet C.J. would come home if you got rid of that Liza."

Jack pushed back from her then. "Connie, give me a break. The dog isn't out there hiding, waiting for a change in caretakers."

"How do you know? Think outside the box."

"We're talking about a dog. C.J. doesn't even know Liza's the caretaker—"

"The *maybe* caretaker. And how do you know? She never ran away when my dad was caretaker. What does that tell you?"

It told him she was missing a screw or two. The song ended and Jack took another step back. "Thanks for the dance."

He left Connie on the dance floor and stopped at the bar for another beer. Across the room, Liza and Dave were looking cozy at their corner table. Dave reached up to brush Liza's hair back from her face and she laughed up at him. A stab of envy swept through him so deep it took him aback. Jealous? Him?

Highly unlikely.

He had no reason to get jealous—there were plenty of women in the sea—or was that fish? Besides that, he would be a fool to get involved with a woman whose dream life included settling down in a small town. Let Dave have her.

Out on the dance floor, Mary Ellen Wilson was doing some sort of bizarre dance, a combination of the swim and hip-hop, arms and legs whipping out in every direction. She spotted him watching her and began to dance toward him, hair flying, breasts heaving in her coconut bra, hips shaking, grass skirt swaying. She never could dance. He grinned, remembering many good times with Mary Ellen during their high-school and college years.

Gyrating wildly from the dance floor to the bar, she made her way to him, laughing when he rolled his eyes at her. "Jackie, Jackie, wanna dance? I can see it in your eyes. We could win the dance contest—just like junior year."

The memory made Jack laugh out loud. How they won was still a mystery to him. At one point he and Mary Ellen had actually gotten down on the floor and done *the worm*.

"I just got off the dance floor," he said. "How about Dave?"

Mary Ellen looked at Dave and gave Jack a big mai tai grin. "Okay. Hey, Davey, let's dance!" she shouted. She grabbed him by the arm and, despite his protests, forced him out of his seat. The guy threw an apologetic look Liza's way.

Jack tried not to take a turn at feeling smug. *Too bad, Dave. He who dances with Mary Ellen loses his bar stool.*

He took the seat next to Liza. "How's your zombie?"

"Sweet." She grinned. "How's your beer?"

"Hoppy." He paused. "Hey, Liza. Remember, Dave's...not someone you can trust."

"He seems like a nice enough guy."

"Well, not that he isn't. It's just that he...he..."

She drank some more of her zombie and he tried not to pay attention to her mouth. "Has his way with women and then discards them?" she asked innocently.

"That's a nice way of putting it."

Liza waved a hand. "Well, don't worry about me. No one is going to take advantage of me."

She pursed her mouth and Jack wished that kissing Liza hadn't been so good last night because then he might not be so tempted to do it again right now.

"Not even me?" he asked in a low voice, every rational brain cell warning him to back away, and every instinct pushing him forward.

Liza slowly swirled her drink with her palm-tree stir stick and looked up at him. "Especially not you."

His heart dropped.

"I have a sneaking suspicion, Jack Graham, that you and Dave Butler are two peas in a pod."

He looked at her, taken aback. He wasn't as bad as Dave. *Was he?*

"I think you're confusing me with someone else." He took her hand. "Will you dance?" he asked, pulling her up until she was standing.

Liza set her glass on the bar and looked up at him. Her expression made him want to put his arms around her and dance right here as if they were alone in the room. He turned and led her through the crowd. They popped out onto the dance floor right beside Mary Ellen and Dave, and Connie and some guy he used to sit next to in high-school geometry, but whose name was escaping him right now.

The music played, fast and loud. The dance floor was a writhing mass of Hawaiian shirts, bright colors and leis wrapped around wrists, ankles and necks. When the song ended and a slow one began, Jack pulled Liza into his arms without even asking for the dance.

"So tell me. How are you different from Dave?" she asked.

He thought he would say he wouldn't ever hurt her. But he realized that probably wasn't true. Then he thought he would say he would always be honest with her. But that probably wasn't true either. How *was* he different from Dave, then? He bent close to her ear, his cheek brushing against hers, and said, "Because I see the person you are and Dave sees only another conquest." He hoped that didn't sound like a line, because for once, it didn't feel like one.

He caressed the nape of her neck. She was affecting him and he couldn't let her. He had to keep this carefree. They could have some fun together while he was here—that would be okay. But there could be no more.

A moment later, he felt a tap on his shoulder and turned to find Dave standing at his side. The guy was cutting in? Who the hell cut in during this day and age?

Scowling, Jack graciously moved aside and let Dave take his place. Mary Ellen intercepted him on his way back to the bar. "I did my best to keep him busy," she said.

"What for?"

"So you had time with her." She gave him a loopy grin.

Jack looked at her sharply. "I don't want time with her—she's the caretaker."

"Oh, come on, Jack. You're still the same as you were in high school. I can tell when you like someone."

"I don't like her."

Mary Ellen snorted, then let out a laugh.

"Okay, I lust her. But that's it—no like."

"Maybe. And maybe not. I don't see you enough anymore. But I did know you pretty well at one time. I've seen Jack Graham lust and this isn't it. Not to say that isn't there, too, but…"

Jack glanced at the crowded dance floor. "Pheromones," he said. "I'm attracted to hers. It's a physical thing."

"Okay, just keep repeating that to yourself." Mary Ellen sipped her mai tai.

They stood on the edge of the dance floor watching for another minute or so until the song ended. Then the deejay grabbed a portable microphone and boogied out onto the floor holding a long pole and shouting, "How low can you go?"

It was definitely time for him to return to the bar. Liza brushed past him and said, "Quick, let's get away before they make us limbo."

"You too?"

"Please. I have no athletic ability."

"How much athletic ability does one need for limbo?"

"More than I have. No flexibility. I lose right away." She hurried to her chair, plucked her glass off the table and took a long drink through the straw, emptying the glass. Then she waved at the barmaid, who went off to make her another zombie.

"Do you need another beer?" she asked him. Her dark eyes met his and his chest tightened. He wondered whether she had the same effect on everyone—or was it just him?

He slid into the seat next to her and hoped Dave was stuck on the limbo floor all night. The scent of kiwi wafted off her hair and he thought about slipping his fingers in those waves again and kissing her until she was senseless. It would be so easy, really. Here they both were just inches apart—

In a bar.

He hadn't done the making-out-in-a-bar thing since college, but for some reason, it seemed like a really good idea right now. "You know, Liza. If C.J. is gone for good—"

"Don't say that. We'll find her."

"But if she is and you don't become the caretaker, and even when I go back to Chicago—" What was he doing? He was about to tell this woman he wanted to see her again—in direct contradiction to what he'd decided just minutes ago.

"Yeah?" She looked at him quizzically.

He shrugged. What could it hurt? He would only see her while he was in Coldwater anyway. "I'm trying to say, I'd like to see you—" *Naked.*

Oh hell. That thought just proved Mary Ellen wrong—it *was* lust, pure and simple.

He actually felt disappointed.

"THAT'S THE MAI TAI talking," Liza said when her brain finally registered what Jack was saying.

"No, it's not. I'm drinking beer."

Oh brother. "Jack, that's a line straight out of Dear Cordelia's book. *I'd like to see you?* You've got to be able to do better than that."

"I can." He leaned toward her. "You're bright and funny and—" His mouth hovered inches from hers. "And you have a mouth that makes me crazy."

"I do?" She couldn't remember ever reading anything like this in the Dear Cordelia book. "Why?"

"Say that again."

"What?"

"No. *Why.*"

She stared at him in confusion.

"Come on. Say it."

She formed the word with her lips.

"Stop!" he said before any sound came out. He brushed a thumb across her pursed lips and she sucked in a breath. "God, but you're made for kissing." He swept his lips across hers, kissed her hard, and then pulled back to grin at her.

Shock filled her—shock and confusion and irrational attraction. Jack Graham had just kissed her in the bar in front of all these people? And his line—*I'd like to see you...*? What was that all about?

Just then, Dave sauntered up, oblivious to what had just occurred. "Liza, can I get you another drink?" he asked.

Jack eyed him antagonistically and Liza jumped in before he could say a word. "No thanks, I've got a full one." She held up her glass.

Dave dragged another bar stool over and hoisted himself up on it.

Jack scowled. "Hey, Dave, Liza and I are sort of in the middle of something right now."

Dave wasn't buying it. "Yeah? Like what?"

A dispute? Over her? Never in all her life had two guys ever had a disagreement over her. Especially not guys who looked like these two. Guys like them never looked at girls like her. *This was insanity.* Kind of a nice insanity, but insanity nonetheless.

She leaned forward. "Jack, I think it's okay if—"

"We're working on vowels," Jack said.

Vowels?

"Vowels?" Dave asked in disbelief. "Like A, E, I, O, U?"

Jack nodded. "And sometimes *why*." His gaze dropped to Liza's mouth and her heart started to pound. Nervously she whetted her lips with her tongue.

Dave looked at her for confirmation.

She swallowed hard. "Well, that is what we were doing. We just did Y, and—it's all about proper form and pronunciation."

"If you need help with vowels, I can help just as much as Jack can. A, E, I, O, U, and sometimes Y," Dave said, slurring slightly.

"What're you guys talking about?" Connie pulled a bar stool over from another table and plopped down.

"Vowels," Dave said.

"Like A, E, I, O, U?"

They all nodded. Jack winked at Liza.

"Why?" Connie asked.

"That's right," Jack said. "And sometimes Y."

Connie stared at him as if he was crazy.

"We're helping Liza with her pronunciation," Dave said.

"*I'm* helping her," Jack said.

Liza sighed and tried to figure out a way to

settle the boys down. The only problem was, the zombies had disconnected the part of her brain that might have helped her. The drink may taste like punch, but obviously it packed a wallop.

What she didn't need was a brawl in here. In fact, if she really forced herself to focus, what she needed was to remember that both these guys were *players*. She had to quit being so flattered that the men liked her—they liked all women—and get back to her original plan to cut out early and sneak into Jack's computer. She glanced at her watch. Jeez, she'd been here over two hours already. At the rate she was going, she'd lose this opportunity—and who knew if she'd ever get as good a chance again?

She dragged her zombie-sodden brain back into investigative-reporting mode. "You know what? Between all the snow shoveling and the painting, I'm really beat. So, I'm gonna take off. Why don't you guys work on vowels with Connie." She stood.

"I'll drive you home," Dave offered.

"No, I'll take her home," Jack said.

Absolutely amazing. Two guys fighting over her. She should have bought silky underwear years ago. "No, no. I'd rather walk. Those zombies have my head spinning—the fresh air will do me good. Besides, Jack, these are all old friends of yours—I don't want you to cut your night short because of me."

Connie pressed up against Jack's side. "Stay out a while—we never get to see you."

"Yeah, but—"

"No buts." Liza snatched her jacket up from the chair and slid it on. "You never get to see these people. I'll be fine. Good exercise. Besides, I already ordered you another beer." She kept prattling on so he couldn't disagree with her. "It was great meeting everyone." She waved at Connie and squeezed her way to the door, hoping Jack didn't wait too long for his beer to arrive, since she'd never actually ordered one.

The outside air tingled in her nostrils and she sucked in a deep breath, hoping to cleanse the zombie from her system. She started down the block, quickening her pace, intent on getting to Jack's grandmother's house as soon as possible. If she was going to track down Cordelia, she would need every minute she could get before Jack decided to call it a night.

She moved into race-walker speed and then began to jog. After half a block, she began to breathe hard. Too bad she didn't do this sort of thing regularly so she could keep the pace up longer. She pushed herself to keep going. Her left foot hit the ground and skidded outward on a patch of ice, ankle twisting as she fell. She hit the sidewalk, landing on her left hand and hip. Moaning, she lay there, eyes closed. Her ankle throbbed, her hand throbbed, her hip throbbed.

At least her brain was intact. Or as intact as it could be full of zombie juice.

Exhaling from between gritted teeth, she pushed herself to sitting and pulled off her glove to look at her hand. No abrasions—the pain must just be from the impact. She forced herself to her feet, brushed the snow off her jeans and limped forward, jaw clenched tight. Only another couple of blocks to go.

What had ever made her think investigative reporting would be fun? What had ever possessed her to go after this job?

She tried to limp faster. *She'd wanted to change her life.* And boy oh boy, had she succeeded. This was exactly what she'd gone searching for. The thrill of investigation, the fear of discovery, the pain of…falling?

Okay, so maybe she hadn't gone searching for pain. But she'd gotten it. Someday down the road, long after she had flushed out Dear

Cordelia, when she was sitting back at her desk in the newsroom regaling her colleagues with details of her latest exposé, she could tie it all together with some trite comment like, *no pain, no gain.*

Wincing against the ache in her ankle, she hopped up the back steps and went into the house. She tossed her jacket on the kitchen table and headed upstairs, stopping outside the closed door to Jack's room for a moment to catch her breath. Then she turned the knob and opened the door, stepping carefully across the room in the dark to turn on the desk lamp.

The clothes Jack had been wearing earlier lay in a heap on the bed. The faintest smell of his aftershave lingered in the air and she spotted the open bottle on the dresser. She reached up and screwed on the cap—no need to have the stuff evaporating. Yeah, and no need to have a subtle reminder of him tantalizing her in his bedroom.

She slid into the chair at the desk, opened the computer and turned it on. "Come on baby, time to give up everything you know," she said aloud.

She started a methodical search of the files on the hard drive, opening each and reading a bit before moving on to the next. The first time she glanced at her watch a half hour had already passed. She exhaled sharply. She had to work faster—Jack could come back at any time.

She scanned the names of the remaining folders, hoping one or another would jump out as a possible clue, but nothing sounded promising. Fine, she'd go through them individually.

Time and again she opened files that contained old columns from Cordelia. If what she wanted was advice on her love life, then she'd be all set. But this was no help at all in her quest to find Dear Cordelia's location.

Somewhere on this computer there had to be some real information about Cordelia. Another half hour passed. She clicked over to Jack's internet connection. Maybe Cordelia's personal e-mail address would be listed in his address book. Though she was hopeful, she wasn't optimistic. If he didn't have her phone number on his cell phone, she doubted Jack would have her e-mail address openly listed. Moments later her fears were confirmed—no listing for Cordelia.

She slumped back into her chair and stared, dejected, at the screen.

Unless… Unless Jack used more than one e-mail address on this computer. Each one would have its own address book. She sat up straight, clicked on Switch Identity and gasped as three addresses appeared:

JackGraham1@il.drf.com

JackGrahamPublicity@il.drf.com

DearCordelia@il.drf.com

"Jackpot," she whispered out loud. She grinned at the screen. DearCordelia@il.drf.com. She highlighted the address and waited for a second while the screen switched identities.

"This has to be it. Please, please, please let it have something that will help me," she said.

One look at the address book and she was disappointed again. "How can you work for Cordelia and not have an e-mail address for her? What kind of a publicist are you, Jack?"

The machine dinged as several new messages entered the in-box. Liza glanced at their subject lines— "Help!" "Is this love?" "How do I find my dream man?"

"How do you find your dream man?" Liza said aloud as though she'd been asked the question herself. "Well, first you find the best-looking guy you've ever seen. Then you follow him halfway across the country and move into his house, ostensibly to watch his dog." She sighed. "The question, dear reader, isn't how you find him. It's how do you make him fall for you? Or in my case, how do you make him tell you what you want to know and then make him fall for you?"

She put her elbows on the desk and rested her chin in her hands. Here she was in her dream man's bedroom and a fat lot of good it was doing her.

She was tempted to take a look at the messages that just came in, but didn't dare open them or Jack would be able to tell someone had been in his computer. She could, however, safely look at his Sent Items folder. So she clicked on it.

It opened a long listing of documents, all with a different date as the subject line. She furrowed her forehead at the screen and opened one file and then another. And then another.

These were Dear Cordelia columns. The original letters and Cordelia's reply.

Why was Jack getting all the letters people sent to Dear Cordelia? Her heart started to pound. And why was Jack sending out the column?

Maybe he just forwarded everything on for Cordelia. *Maybe.* She narrowed her eyes at the screen, then slowly turned her head to look at the painting on the wall, as though a change of scenery would make everything clear. Without turning her head, she let her eyes slide back to the computer screen.

No way.

No way was Jack Graham answering Dear Cordelia letters.

Was he?

Her heart thudded harder. Holy cow. What had she just found? *Nothing*—it couldn't be anything important. All he was doing was forwarding the columns once Cordelia had written them. That was it—nothing more.

Fingers flying now, she clicked back into the files she had looked at earlier. The dates at the top sent a shiver through her—these were columns that hadn't even run yet.

There was a logical explanation for this—there had to be. Maybe Cordelia was sick, or on vacation, or behind in her work…or nonexistent.

Ohmigosh.

"I need to verify this. I need proof." She stared at the computer screen, in awe of what she might have just discovered. The clock on Jack's nightstand showed she'd been at this over two hours now. It was well past midnight. Hopefully Jack was having a rip-roaring good time and would stay out until the bar closed.

Now, where to find the truth? She opened the

Deleted Items folder and frantically clicked through the messages.

Could it be possible? Had she been living with Dear Cordelia these past few days? If she was right, this would be a major scoop. At least in entertainment circles.

"Investigative reporting, here I come." She grinned. "Just get me the proof—"

A sound in the hall made her jerk her head up. Her mouth dropped open and she stared at the closed door, eyes widening in horror. Someone was coming down the hall and it could only be Jack.

She exited out of the open screen, then closed the laptop, cringing because she hadn't properly shut it down first. Well, as Dorothy said, desperate times call for desperate measures. She flicked off the lamp and held her breath, praying Jack would go into the bathroom so she could get out of here without getting caught. She held her breath and stared at the door, at the knob, and watched as it turned.

CHAPTER ELEVEN

FIGURE SOMETHING OUT, her brain screamed at her—and so she did. She sat on the edge of the bed and smiled at Jack when he came through the door.

He stopped, obviously taken aback. "Hi."

She kept smiling, though her stomach was a mass of jumping grasshoppers and her brain was like a puppy chasing its tail. She smiled as if being found in a man's room wasn't an out-of-the-ordinary experience for her.

He looked a little confused, and his gaze slid around the room before coming to rest on her again. "What, ah, are you doing here?"

Liza swallowed and her smile faded. There was one way out of this.

"Waiting for you." She smiled again, hopefully in that mysterious way Kristin had tried to teach her.

Head cocked slightly as though not sure he

believed her, Jack slowly crossed the room to the bed. She stood before he got there. His eyes were narrowed and dark and hot, and what had seemed like a reasonable idea when it popped into her head a moment ago now was feeling like one of the worst ideas she'd ever had. She was Liza Dunnigan, for goodness' sakes. She went on many, many, *many* dates before she even got remotely close to situations like this.

And, need she add, she never got in situations like this with men who oozed sex out of every pore on their body. Not that she hadn't wanted to get into situations like this with men like this, but...

"But I can go," she blurted. She took a step to one side and he countered, blocking her path.

"No. Don't."

Her heart pounded so hard she'd swear he could hear it. She should have said she was looking for an Ace bandage to wrap her ankle, not waiting for him. Why hadn't she thought of that before? What was she supposed to do now? Where was Kristin when she needed her? What did Dear Cordelia have to say about situations like this?

Cordelia? Her advice was to avoid situations like this. Don't get caught in the wrong place.

Jack's head dipped toward hers—and her brain felt as if it were about to explode. Cordelia? If she was right about Jack, she could just ask him—her—

And then his mouth covered hers and all coherent thought fled. He tasted of beer and rum and strawberries and exotic beaches in the summer—if she'd ever tasted an exotic beach, that was. He pulled her up against him, took her mouth fully, one hand in her hair. She let herself sink into the heat of him and thought, ohmigod this guy could kiss. Which was not really a good thing because she should probably put a stop to it and mention that Ace-bandage thing.

In a minute, she should.

The hand that had been holding her head slid down her shoulder, along the side of her breast, and she shuddered as every goose bump on her body bumped to attention.

And then he slid that hand up under her sweater, along the soft curve of her waist to caress her breast. His mouth was on her throat and her head was back and her skin was tight and aching for more. She really thought that maybe this was going too far and not the sort of thing she typically found herself doing but— Oh! When his lips found that spot right at the base of her neck and his hands were finding those other spots—all of them, every one—she thought maybe she would put off interrupting this for another minute or so.

Jack pushed her sweater up and pulled it over her head. His hands skimmed over her *leopard bra.*

"Liza Dunnigan, I would have pegged you for white cotton," he murmured.

Leaning into her, he pressed her tight against him and she gasped, "I graduated from cotton a long time ago."

His body pushed her against the wall and his hands held her head as he kissed her so long and hard and deep she thought her knees might give out.

She should have bought leopard underwear years ago.

Hips still pressed to hers, Jack began to unbutton his shirt with one hand. She cleared her throat and watched his fingers undo one button after the next until his shirt fell open. She gulped as he undid his cuffs. She was far too straight for something like this. They needed to date and all that. Have awkward phone conversations. Fall in love. Make a commitment. This was just not how she did things.

"I was looking for an Ace bandage…" she said.

He tossed his shirt to the floor and she looked at his broad, bare chest, and the definition of the muscles in his arms. Her heart hammered. Every nerve in her body was on high alert. "Because…"

He took a step back from her and opened the fly of his jeans. She tried to make her mind work so she could finish her sentence.

He slid his pants to the floor and stepped out of them to stand in front of her in black silk boxers. "Ace bandage," he murmured as he pulled her into his arms again. "That's a new one. What do we do with it?" But then his mouth was on hers, and she forgot about the bandage as he steered her down onto the bed. And somehow, there she was on her back in only her new leopard underwear—was her stomach sticking out?—and Jack Graham, man of a thousand conquests, was lying on the bed beside her, his hands moving over and under her animal-print unmentionables until she couldn't bear it any longer and moaned out loud.

Moaned. Out loud. Liza Dunnigan. Get in control, she admonished herself just before she sank under the erotic assault of his mouth and hands.

He shifted on top of her, their bodies separated only by the silky layer of her underwear and his boxers, and those did precious little. He was good at this, she had to grant him that.

But she didn't need to become his thousand and first conquest.

She lifted her head and tried to push up on her elbows. "The Ace bandage was for—" She gasped as he pushed her bra up, and the sensations rolling through her forced her back onto the pillow. Okay, so another minute or so and then she'd put a stop to this thing. No reason she couldn't take advantage of his expertise for a few minutes longer. After all, it wasn't often she was able to apprentice with a master.

"We can try kinky the next time," he whispered in her ear.

Kinky? What the heck did he mean by that? Oh no, he didn't think she wanted to do something with an Ace bandage, did he?

What could one possibly do with an Ace bandage?

She opened her eyes, ready to clear the whole thing up, but just then his fingers began working magic on parts of her that she swore had never before been touched. And his mouth was on her throat and it had been forever—okay, her entire life—since she'd had an experience like this. Besides, she could hardly breathe, let alone speak. It crossed her very pleasure-saturated mind that investigative reporting could be a very fulfilling field and that it was probably good she keep investigating this particular process.

Suddenly he rolled off her and a wave of cool air moved in to take the place where she had once been heated to a delicious degree.

"Hang on a minute." He disappeared into the bathroom and reappeared holding something behind his back.

She shivered and knew it was now or never. This guy thought she was going to make love with him and she really couldn't. They hardly knew each other after all... This was totally wrong for her. "I really think—"

"Shh. I know, I know." He punched a button on the CD player beside the bed and the soft sounds of classical music filled the room. Then he handed something to her as he settled full length beside her on the bed. She took it in the darkness. Oh brother, an Ace bandage.

He ran a hand up her leg, from calf to thigh to breast, and every inch of her waited for more, wanted more.

"Well?" he whispered as he nibbled at her ear, his breath warm, his voice low and seductive.

His hand moved to her breasts, his touch more urgent. "What do we do with it?"

"Nothing," she murmured. "Next time."

"Ah, a woman after my own heart." On the CD player the symphony played and she sighed and gave in to what she knew she would later admit was what she'd wanted all along.

JACK WOKE the next morning with his head pounding and his mouth dryer than the Sahara Desert during a drought. Eyes shut, he rolled over and caught the scent, the sweet floral scent Liza had been wearing last evening.

Liza.

The memory of last night flooded back to him and he reached out to pull her into his arms—and came up empty. He opened his eyes hesitantly, squinting against the sun beaming in around the edges of the window shade.

No Liza.

He drew a long, slow breath and focused on the nightstand clock. Eleven in the morning. No wonder Liza wasn't in bed any longer. He groaned and thought about getting up and decided instead to procrastinate longer.

Any minute, surely Liza would be up to check on him. Women had a certain predictability to them. She'd have a hot cup of coffee for him, would open the shades and offer to whip up some scrambled eggs. Then she'd come over to the bed and commiserate with him over his headache, and before long they'd be making love again. He thought of her leopard *unmentionables,* as she called them, and how she must have been wearing them all day yesterday and he hadn't had a clue. Liza had a wild side.

The very thought almost cleared up his headache by itself. He rolled onto his back and put his hands behind his head in anticipation. Considering the time, Liza would have to be coming up soon.

He waited a little longer and began to get antsy. His stomach growled. Well, hell. Where were the scrambled eggs?

He rolled out of bed and padded down the hall to take a shower. The powerful spray was like a massage on his shoulders and neck, cleansing away the poisons he'd ingested last night.

On second thought, it would be better if Liza came upstairs now. She could sneak into the shower with him. Nothing like a slippery, sudsy start to the day. He waited, the hot water rolling over him, and still she didn't arrive.

As he climbed out of the shower and toweled

off, a twinge of regret flashed through him that he didn't have much time left to share with Liza before he went back to Chicago. What little time they had, they should put to good use.

So where was she?

He pulled on jeans and a sweatshirt and went downstairs, stopping to glance in every room, growing more perplexed by the minute. She didn't get scared off by last night, did she? What if she'd decided to move out?

The thought sent another stab of regret through him. He didn't want her to leave—he liked her.

He opened the front door and went out barefoot onto the porch to look for her car. It had snowed sometime during the night and the light dusting of fresh clean white sparkled in the morning sun. He squinted against the brightness.

He heard the sound of a shovel scraping along concrete and leaned over the porch rail to look down the driveway. Liza was clearing away last night's snowfall. He watched her shovel in steady rhythm. A warmth went through him and he smiled. This had to be a first; he'd never had a woman leave his bed to shovel.

"Good morning," he called.

She jerked her head up in surprise. "Oh! You startled me." She walked toward him, smiling tentatively. "Good morning. How do you feel?"

"My feet are cold." He stuck a bare foot through the porch-rail slats.

"My gosh! You'll get frostbite! What are you doing out here barefoot?"

"Looking for you."

She frowned slightly. "Why?"

He almost said, *because he was afraid she'd left and he didn't want her to,* but decided it sounded too needy. "Do you want to go out for breakfast?"

She grinned. "Sure."

"I need some thick black coffee and greasy fried eggs. How about you?"

"I don't need them but they sound great. Just let me finish shoveling and I'll be ready."

"You're kinda nice to have around—keep this up and I might give you a raise."

Liza tossed a shovelful of snow in his direction and the wind blew it back in her face. She let out a screech.

"Didn't you ever learn about not pissing into the wind?" He started to dance from foot to foot because his feet really were getting cold.

She sputtered and wiped her face with a mittened hand. "Yeah, and haven't you ever heard that a wise man wears shoes in the winter?"

He laughed. She could give as good as she got. He was half tempted to march down to the driveway and kiss her until she was breathless. "Touché. Let me get some shoes on and I'll help you finish up."

LIZA WATCHED JACK go into the house, a sick feeling in her stomach. What did he think about last night? Did he have regrets? She'd awakened early, still in his embrace, warm and safe, and had lain there thinking, her emotions tangled and confused. Slipping gently out from under his arm, she'd rolled onto her side and watched him sleep, his chest rising and falling, his breath coming soft and easy. She had almost reached out a hand to touch him, to slide her fingers down his arm and over his chest. She almost had.

But early-morning sunlight had begun to stream in around the edges of the shades and the room had gotten brighter and suddenly she had felt a little like Cinderella the morning after the ball. Like her clothes were in tatters and her hair was a mess and one of her shoes was missing.

This was Jack Graham after all. And she was Liza Dunnigan, most recently a very practical woman. So, as much as she'd wanted to awaken him with a kiss, she'd been terrified he would open his eyes and look with horror upon her as something the mai tai's brought home. Of course, then he'd be nice—and give her one of those lines that both of them knew wasn't true. Like, *I'll call you.*

After what they'd shared last night, she couldn't deal with that kind of rejection. So she'd slipped from his bed and gathered up her clothes and escaped.

Which was just as well, because once she was out of his room, it had hit her just what kind of game she was playing. She had moved into his house on a lie, had broken into his computer, and then slept with the guy—all in the name of investigative reporting. What kind of a person did stuff like that? Not her.

Not the old her anyway. Her stomach started to churn.

"Sleep well?" Jack's voice jerked her out of her preoccupation.

She nodded.

"So did I. Best night's sleep I've had in a long time."

His eyes locked with hers for a long moment, almost too long. "Thanks."

Liza felt faint. He was thanking her? Had she just provided a service? "Glad I could help." *Glad you could help?* What kind of idiocy was that?

"So am I." Jack grinned and began shoveling.

An hour later, the sidewalks clear, they headed into the coffee shop. Margaret and Dorothy waved from a booth along the far wall.

"Join us, why don't you." Margaret scooted over in her seat. "Dorothy, you come over by me so they can sit together."

"Oh, that's not necessary," Liza said.

"No, no trouble at all." Dorothy climbed out of the booth and over to the other side, sliding her plate of scrambled eggs and hash browns with her.

Sit, sit," Margaret said, fluttering one hand. "Do you want some bacon?" She held a piece up as Liza scooted into the booth and Jack followed.

"No thanks," Liza said.

"I'll eat it," Jack said. "I'm starving."

"Did you two have fun last night?" Dorothy asked.

Clearly they were to have no secrets from the ladies next door.

Jack nodded as he crunched on the bacon. "Too much fun," he said wincing.

As Jack spoke, Dorothy narrowed her eyes at

Liza. "How was Connie?" she whispered across the table.

"About what you'd expect," Liza said.

"Oh, that woman, she's always wanted him. You'd better watch her—"

"Watch who?" Jack asked.

"We're talking about a television program to watch—girl stuff," Dorothy lied. She began to dig through the little packages of jelly stacked in the plastic holder at the end of the table. "All orange marmalade and mixed fruit. Don't they ever check these things? Jack, would you be a dear and find me some strawberry?"

"Sure." He slid out of the booth.

Margaret snickered. "There isn't any strawberry anywhere—we already looked."

"Shh," Dorothy said. "Now, back to Connie. She's got those four wild boys—"

"And she wants Jack," Margaret added.

"But nothing would be a worse match. We know Jack—"

"And we know Connie—"

"And so does every man in town, if you get what I mean," Dorothy said in a low voice.

Liza's head bobbed from left to right as the two women shot out their statements like machine-gun fire.

"She just isn't right for Jack." Margaret stabbed some scrambled eggs with her fork and stuck them in her mouth.

"Why are you telling me this?" Liza looked from one to the other.

Dorothy reached across the table and patted Liza's hand. "He seems a little taken with you."

Her jaw dropped. "Me?" Jack Graham was taken with her? Ha-ha.

"Yes, you. We know him well enough to tell. He might not realize it himself yet, but give him time. You just need to watch out for Connie— she'll give you a run for your money. Whenever Jack is back in town, she comes hanging around." Dorothy looked at Margaret for confirmation and Margaret nodded emphatically.

Liza had no doubt what Connie came around for. The same thing Jack went to see Connie for. Her heart slowed as she thought of last night. She hoped she hadn't just taken Connie's place—same service, new girl.

"We have to be careful about what we say, though. Jack thinks we're being—" Margaret's voice dropped lower "—busybodies. But we think you and he—"

"There isn't any strawberry jam in the whole place," Jack said as he slipped back onto the seat.

"Was it fun for you too, dear?" Margaret asked, not missing a beat.

"Whaaat?" Liza tried to hold down her panic. How much did these old women know?

"At the party. Did you have fun too?"

Oh. "Everyone was really nice."

"That's Coldwater for you. It's what you'll have to look forward to once you settle into the house for good," Margaret said.

"That is, if we find C.J.," Liza said.

"I'm sure you'll find her. You have to stay upbeat about this. Dogs are funny—they come back just when you least expect it." Dorothy forked some hash browns into her mouth.

The waitress arrived and cast a sympathetic look Jack's way. "Any luck finding your dog? You two want coffee? How about breakfast?"

"No, yes, and yes." Jack grinned.

As soon as they'd placed their orders and the waitress stepped away, Dorothy was right back on track.

"You haven't given up on finding C.J., have you?" she pressed.

Jack shook his head. "No. I don't know. We have to be realistic—how long could an old dog like that survive in this kind of weather?"

"She has that fur coat, you know," Margaret said. "And an extra layer of fat."

"Or two. Plus, dogs lived outside when they were wolves," Dorothy added.

"She's pretty far removed from the wolf bloodlines." Jack shrugged. "I'm more worried because she's so old."

Margaret frowned. "Old is just a frame of mind."

Dorothy nodded. "You're only as old as you feel."

"Old is as old does," Liza chimed in.

Jack snorted. "She's a dog."

Dorothy waved a finger. "You'll find her, I just know it."

"Well, it better be soon, because I've got clients I keep putting on hold."

"When you didn't go back a couple of days ago, all your clients were fine. The sky didn't fall or anything," Dorothy said.

"Right, but—"

"You certainly can't leave until you know for sure about C.J.," Margaret said.

"Maybe she's not out in the cold. Maybe someone found her and has taken her in their house." Dorothy absently toyed with a little bag of sugar.

"Well, if that happened, why haven't they called the humane society or the police yet?" Jack asked.

The two old women shrugged in unison and looked at one another as though each expected the other to have an answer.

Dorothy finally spoke. "Maybe they're busy—"

"Or maybe they like C.J.," Margaret said.

Jack shook his head. "I'm afraid we're grasping at straws. She's already been gone almost forty-eight hours. Much as I hate to say it, I'm not holding out a lot of hope." He looked at Dorothy's plate. "If you're done, can I have the rest of your toast?"

Dorothy handed it over. "Liza, what do you think?"

She scrunched up her face. "The longer this drags on, I think—it just doesn't look good."

Jack exhaled. "Which brings me back to work I keep putting off."

Dorothy looked alarmed. "You can't be talking about going back to Chicago—not with C.J. out there somewhere."

"Not just like that!" Margaret added.

"It isn't just like that. I haven't made any firm plans yet—but I've gotta think ahead. I've got a really important appointment that I've already put off once. Look, Liza could stay at the house for a while, C.J. or not. If C.J. is found, Liza can be the caretaker." He looked at her. "If that's what you decide to do."

She turned to look at him, a sense of unreal-ness rolling over her. He was talking about leav-ing *again?* She had to wrap this up, had to confirm whether he was Cordelia or not. And if she discovered she had misinterpreted what she saw on the computer, if Jack Graham *wasn't* Cordelia, then she had to find out where Cor-delia was. She fought down the panic rising in-side her.

But what if he really was Cordelia? She thought of last night and her stomach wrenched. Even if he didn't *like her* in the way the ladies seemed to think he did, she liked him as a human being. How could she reveal his secret? This would be the ultimate betrayal of a friend.

She shoved away her fear and guilt. A week ago, Kristin had said something to her—a good investigative reporter doesn't get emotionally involved. Well, now she could see why.

The waitress arrived with their food. She set it in front of them and tucked their bill under the saltshaker.

Dorothy dabbed at her mouth with her napkin. "We really should get going. We have some errands to run. Right, Margaret?"

Margaret nodded. "Several."

The two women slid out of the booth and walked to the register to pay. Margaret turned back to say, "Now, don't gulp your food or you'll get indigestion."

"They sure seemed to be in a hurry to get out of here suddenly," Liza said.

"They're kind of like that. If you ever talk to Dorothy on the phone, as soon as she says what she called for, she hangs up. No chitchat for her."

From across the restaurant, an ethereal-looking red-haired woman waved at them. Liza smiled back. This must be more small-town friendliness.

A moment later, the woman was sliding into the bench seat vacated by Dorothy and Margaret. "Oh, Mr. Graham, I wanted to give you a call," she said.

Jack's expression looked strained.

"I've seen the posters about your missing dog. How tragic. Have you heard anything yet?"

Jack shook his head.

The woman leaned forward and her long red hair fell around her face, obscuring all her features except her nose. "My sisters get around the city quite a bit, you know," she whispered. "They tell me your dog has been taken in— she's not being mistreated."

Jack gave a weak smile. "That's good to know."

Liza smiled, feeling hopeful. "Your sisters have seen C.J.? Where?"

Jack kicked her under the table. She gave him a look that said, *Watch your manners, buddy.*

"I don't know exactly—"

"Jack, maybe we should talk to her sisters," Liza said.

The woman nodded. "I can talk to them for you."

Jack sighed. "Do that. Give me a call if they come up with any other information."

The woman went back to her booth and Liza reached down to rub her shin. "What did you kick me for? And why don't you want to talk to her sisters?"

Jack shook his head. "She's nuts. She applied for the caretaker's job—"

"So what? Her sisters—"

"Her sisters are cats."

"What?"

"And her brothers are birds." Jack laughed.

"You're kidding, right?"

"That's what she thinks anyway. So her sisters must have been out on the prowl one night and spotted C.J."

"Oh. Never mind." She turned her attention back to her breakfast.

Half an hour later, they had finished eating. Liza pushed through the door and blinked at the brightness of the day, the sun reflecting off the newly fallen snow.

Jack shaded his eyes. "Finally my eyes have opened all the way and now I need sunglasses."

Liza looked up at him, into his ice-blue eyes. Heaven help her, but she really shouldn't be looking into this man's eyes after last night. Especially knowing that there was a reasonable chance he was Cordelia.

Jack pulled open the passenger door of the car for her. "Last night really took me back... seeing all those old friends."

Liza got into the car. "Do you ever miss living in Coldwater?"

"No. Not a bit. There may be a sense of belonging in a small town. But as you've probably noticed, there's also an almost total loss of anonymity."

"You do a lot of things you want to hide, do you?" Liza grinned and raised her eyebrows.

"I've got nothing to hide." He paused. "Well, okay, *almost* nothing."

Did he answer too quickly, too decisively? Liza watched his expression carefully for any sort of clue. Was he thinking about Dear Cordelia? Or was she reading something into nothing?

They reached home a few minutes later and Liza discovered an envelope lying on the floor in the foyer that had been dropped through the mail slot. She handed it to Jack. "You've got mail," she said playfully.

"This better not be a communique from the cat lady." He tore it open and pulled out a single sheet of paper. The expression on his face changed from mild interest to confusion to anger. "What the hell is this?" he asked. "A ransom note for the dog?"

CHAPTER TWELVE

LIZA TOOK THE PAPER from him. The words "We have C.J. We'll be in touch" were scrawled in large sloppy printing across the unlined sheet.

"Someone kidnapped C.J.? Why?" Her mind went into overdrive. Maybe someone else had discovered Jack was Cordelia and was going to use the information to blackmail him. She wasn't sure why they needed the dog to blackmail Jack, but then, who could figure out the criminal mind?

Calm down. This was paranoia, pure and simple. After all these years, there was no way two people would have figured out at exactly the same time that Jack Graham was Cordelia.

Except there was that thing she'd read once about something called "simultaneous creation." It had to do with the fact that everyone watches the same TV programs, and reads the same newspapers and magazines... So because everyone's exposed to the same stimuli, many people develop similar ideas.

Yeah, but she had one stimulus no one else had. *She'd moved in with Jack Graham.*

Okay. She was overreacting. No one else was on to her story. Nonetheless, the sooner she verified that Jack was Cordelia—or not—the better off she'd be.

Jack threw his keys on the dining-room table and his jacket over the back of a chair. "This is bizarre. Who would hold C.J. for ransom? I'm calling the police."

Five minutes later, he hung up the phone, discouraged. "He said if we get another note with an actual ransom amount, let them know. Otherwise, it's probably a prank—someone who saw all the lost-dog posters thought they'd have some fun."

"That's it?"

"Well, first he laughed out loud. A lot."

"Nice. Remind me not to call the police next time I need help."

"Actually, it was an old high-school friend of mine, so he was yukking it up more than I think someone else might have."

"Do *you* think it's a prank?" Liza wandered into the living room.

Jack shrugged. "Who knows? Prank or not, if someone has C.J., we need to get her back."

"Can you think of anyone who might have a motive for taking her? I mean, really, who would want a fat, old basset hound with a bulging eye?"

"Who slobbers," Jack said.

"And sheds," Liza said.

"At least our suspect list will be short."

Liza snorted. "That's an understatement."

"Seriously, what motive would someone have to take C.J.?" Jack asked.

Liza stood up straighter. "Remember that waitress yesterday? The *think tank* one? She said someone might have taken C.J. for ransom."

"She also said people think my grandmother had a lot of money. And, the fact is, she didn't."

"Yeah, but does anyone really know that? Maybe the think-tank waitress has C.J.," Liza said.

They looked at each other for a long moment before Liza shook her head and said "no" at the same time Jack did.

"But, Jack, how about you? Maybe it's your money they're after. Are you secretly rich?" Liza held her breath, hoping he'd say something, anything, to help her out with her quest.

"Not rich enough to pay a big ransom for a dog."

Unless he really was Cordelia. Then he probably had a lot more money than he was letting on. Liza crossed the room and dropped onto the couch. "Suspects. We need a list of suspects. Did your grandmother have any enemies?"

Jack rolled his eyes. "Even if she did, why would they wait three years to kidnap the dog? C.J. could have kicked off before now and the opportunity would be lost."

"We should talk to the neighbors again. See if anyone noticed a stranger skulking around out here."

"This is nuts. Why would someone deliberately take C.J.?" Jack stared out the window, then turned slowly to face Liza. "Unless one of the candidates for the caretaker's job took her."

"And they stole her because they got really attached to her in the space of an interview?" Liza tried not to sound incredulous.

"No, Watson. Because they want the job."

"Jack," Liza said as calmly as possible, as though he were a small child. "Why would anyone think stealing the dog would get them the job? That's sort of like stealing the ice-cream machine to make Dairy Queen hire you. It's not logical."

"Bingo. I wouldn't exactly say I had logical candidates apply to be the caretaker."

"Oh really?" She raised her eyebrows. "And what am I? Dry dog food?"

He held up a hand and smiled at her. "Except you, sweetheart, except you."

Her heart skipped a beat at his words. He sat beside her on the couch and put an arm around her shoulders, and she felt her self-control waver. His fingers played with her hair and a shiver coursed right up the middle of her.

"Let's think about those candidates, shall we? Which ones seem the most likely to have a criminal bent?" she asked brightly. She shifted to break body-to-body contact with Jack and looked up at him.

Big mistake. His eyes didn't look at all as though he was thinking about dognappers—they were thinking about last night. Well, she wasn't going to—she couldn't. She had a job to do, information to find. She was changing her life, and just because last night was…the most incredible experience she'd ever had and just another step toward the new Liza— His arm tightened around her, bringing her back in contact with him, and her brain faltered. Just because last night—

And then his lips touched hers and her brain shut down.

She leaned into him, kissed him back long and hard, took hold of his shirt and pulled him closer. And when finally they broke apart, breathless, all she could think was, oh good God, what if he really was Dear Cordelia? What would she do then?

No more kissing, no more nothing until she knew for sure either way. Otherwise, she would be a basket case. She drew a hand across her lips. "So, ah, really then, which of the candidates might be suspects?"

Jack threw his head back and laughed. "Okay. We'll stay on track. There was that woman you just met at the coffee shop—the one with the cat sisters. You have to admit she's a little off."

"Just a little. Maybe she's looking for a long-lost cousin and thinks C.J. is it."

"And then there was this chain-smoker…and the teenager you met when you arrived for your interview, and some woman who decided the whole place needed redecorating," Jack said.

"Did it seem like they all wanted the job—I mean, *really* wanted it?"

He nodded.

"Okay. Did anyone get mad that they didn't get the job? What about Connie? She seemed pretty upset you didn't hire her."

"Aw, Connie just gets— She would never—" Jack stood abruptly and walked across the room, shoving his hands in his jean pockets.

"What *about* Connie?" Liza repeated.

"What about her?" he said. He turned back slowly. "I should have thought of this before."

"You think Connie might have C.J.?"

"Maybe. Hell, more than maybe. Look at how adamant she's been about wanting the job. And last night she told me— She said she thought C.J. would come home if you were gone." He grimaced.

"What? Like C.J. didn't like me?" Liza almost laughed.

"More like, she ran away from home because she didn't like her new stepmother."

Liza snorted. "Now, *that* sounds sane. The dog hasn't known me that long—why would she run away so soon?"

Jack raised his eyebrows. "Oh, and *that* sounds even more sane."

"Well, think about it. That was so unfair of her to say. I hardly know the dog and she hardly knows me—"

"All right already. We've established that C.J. had no reason to dislike you yet."

"Yes, but Jack, you're missing the point. C.J. hated Connie and the boys. You could tell the minute they arrived—she was always trying to get away from them. Especially that little one."

"So your point is that C.J. ran away because she thought Connie was going to be the caretaker?"

Liza grinned. "Works for me."

"I think we won't share that theory with the police. Let's go see the ladies."

Five minutes later they were talking to Dorothy on her front porch, telling her about the ransom note for C.J.

Dorothy gasped and shoved open the door to shout inside, "Margaret! Come quick. C.J.'s been dognapped!"

Margaret hurried out onto the porch and closed the door behind her. "Dognapped? How do you know?"

Jack handed her the note and she read it aloud, clucking her tongue and shaking her head. A blustery wind raced across the yard and swirled the top layer of snow in the air. Dorothy sneezed and dug in her apron pocket for a tissue.

Jack motioned toward the door. "Should we go inside?"

Both women looked startled by the suggestion.

Dorothy wiped her nose again. "You know I've got this dandy cold. And I'd hate for you to catch it. Better that you stay out here."

"That way you won't be exposed to all the germs in the house." Margaret shivered and held her cardigan closed at the chest.

Jack slanted a look of amusement at Liza as if to say, *See what I told you? These women get more eccentric every day.* She swallowed a smile.

"By any chance, did you notice anyone at the house earlier?" Jack asked.

"Well, there was the meter reader from the power company."

"Anyone *suspicious?*" Liza couldn't keep the urgency from her voice.

The two women looked at one another and shook their heads. "But then, we only just got home ourselves. We've been running errands," Dorothy said. She wiped her nose again.

"Nothing at all? No unusual cars? People?"

The ladies shook their heads. "We'll keep an eye out in case another letter shows up," Dorothy said.

"Yes. And I'm freezing." Margaret opened the door and went inside.

"I'll never get well if I stay out here." Dorothy followed Margaret.

"Well, thanks," Jack said as the door shut. He gave Liza a quizzical look. "That was bizarre. Maybe they're getting senile in tandem."

"They're probably just worried about Dorothy's cold."

Jack frowned. "She didn't seem sick at breakfast."

"Whatever. Let's go check with the other neighbors."

Two hours later they'd learned nothing to help them with their investigation, but knew plenty of the neighborhood gossip, including every illness currently being experienced by every senior citizen on the block.

"I'm gonna go have a talk with Connie," Jack said when they reached his grandmother's home. "I've got a sneaking suspicion she knows what's going on." He pushed open the front door but didn't step across the threshold. "I'll be back in a while. Wish me luck."

"Good luck." Liza waited on the porch until he drove away, then went inside and closed the door behind her. One part of her really hoped Jack learned Connie had taken the dog so she could quit worrying. But another part of her knew that C.J. and Jack couldn't be her concern right now.

She turned the lock. She had a job to do. And she was terrified of what she would learn. This was eating her up. She took the stairs one step at a time, and knew, deep in her heart, that she hoped she was wrong about Jack Graham.

Lifting her cell phone off her dresser, she punched in the speed dial for Kristin at work, then slipped into Jack's room and opened the laptop computer. After five rings, just when she thought voice mail would kick in, Kristin answered.

"Oh thank goodness you're there!" Liza said on a breath. Her stomach fluttered with nervous excitement.

"Liza? What's the matter?"

"Nothing. Well, everything. I got into Jack's computer—"

"Fantastic! Did you get an address for Cordelia?"

"No—"

"Phone number?"

"No—"

"E-mail?"

"No, will you let me—"

"Liza, you're running out of time!"

"You don't have to remind me of that. I'm

aware every day of how little time I have." She thought of Jack and last night.

"So? Have you got *anything?*"

"I think so." She watched the computer screen flash its self-promoting messages as the CPU booted up. What if she was wrong? *Please God, let her be wrong.*

"Well? Don't keep me in suspense. What is it?"

"I don't know for certain. I mean, I could be all wrong. This could be a false lead and all that—"

"What is it?" Kristin almost shouted.

"Do you think it's possible that Jack Graham could be Dear Cordelia?"

Laughter filled the earpiece. "Not on your life."

Unbelievable relief slid through Liza. She knew it was a good idea to call Kristin with this. "Why not?"

"Why not? You've read Dear Cordelia's book. He doesn't do anything the book says to do. He lives his life completely different from the way Cordelia advises people. There's no way he'd be able to write that column."

She'd never quite thought of it like that.

"What made you think he was Cordelia?"

Liza suddenly felt stupid. "Oh, well, he's got all these files, questions people sent to the column—and answers to the questions."

"That doesn't mean he's writing the answers. Maybe she e-mails them to him to proofread or something like that."

Liza calmed a little more and punched in the keystrokes that took her back into his e-mail folders. "There's one more thing. An e-mail address—a separate one. It's DearCordelia—"

"Yeah?"

"All the messages people send to Cordelia come into that mailbox."

"And?" Kristin sounded intrigued.

"And there are completed columns that haven't even run yet."

"Really. Huh." Kristin blew out her breath. "I don't know. If this is the story, you'll need more proof than that."

"I know. I better get at this—I don't know how long Jack will be gone. Call you later."

She set the phone on the desk and began to search his computer files again, this time more methodically, checking the Properties file and noting that several documents had been created just yesterday and the author was Jack Graham. She popped open one after another. Upcoming advice columns. For Dear Cordelia. She clicked on one that had been created yesterday and began to read.

Dear Cordelia,

I'm thirty-two and have fallen hard for a guy that I'm not sure feels the same way about me. We have a lot of fun, he's very attentive when we're together, charming even. But he has quite a reputation as a man about town and I can't shake the feeling that I may be one in a long line of many. Do guys like him ever settle down? Or am I wasting my time?
Dating a Playboy

Liza sat back in the chair. Change the age, make the person be lying about their identity, and it could be her and Jack. She scrolled down and discovered an incomplete answer.

Dear Dating,
There are a myriad of reasons why men don't settle down. Some get bored easly, or are perfectionists, or are protecting themselves from a broken heart, or even hiding something. As to whether you're wasting If you think you're wasting You're not wasting time if you Try to look at this from his point Maybethe best thing for you to do is Maybe he really does like you

Huh. This column wasn't even finished. Very suspicious. But it didn't necessarily mean Jack wrote it—Cordelia could have e-mailed it to him because she couldn't figure out how to respond. After all, it did seem like a topic he could relate to.

She exited that document and continued searching, scanning files as quickly as she could, finally opening a message received from his grandmother more than three years ago. As she read, she got an ache in the pit of her stomach. She felt as if she had opened Jack's diary and was peering into the most private secrets of his life.

Dear Jack,
It's late and I can't stop thinking about our phone call tonight. I took Cordelia Jane out for a walk and her sad basset face made me remember a sad little boy named Jack who blossomed when he finally came to a place where he was loved. Don't be so hard on yourself. These have not been wasted years.

You help people find love. A finer thing you couldn't do. When you are very old, you will look back and know that your life had purpose. If you have helped even one relationship grow stronger, or one couple find the love they seek, then your time has been well spent. Love never fails.

I know you never meant the column to be forever. I'm glad you're finally going after the career you always wanted. Be content. Keep the faith.

All my love,
Grandma

Liza stared at the screen and then blinked hard to clear away the tears blurring her eyes. She drew a slow shuddering breath and hated herself. She'd gone looking for proof and she'd found it. Cordelia was a basset hound. Dear Cordelia was Jack.

She shut down the computer and slowly closed it. The click as it locked shut seemed overly loud in the room.

She slipped into the hall and hurried downstairs. What was she going to do? She had just sneaked onto someone's computer, invaded their privacy, and was about to turn their life upside down by telling the world all their secrets.

This wasn't what she'd planned. All she'd wanted was to change her life. *All she'd wanted was an interview with Dear Cordelia,* a chance to prove to the newspaper that she was good enough to be an investigative reporter.

She began to pace from the living room to the kitchen and back again. What did she do now? Jack Graham may not be perfect but he was a pretty nice guy. Did he deserve what she was going to do to him?

She had to think. And she couldn't think here—not with reminders of Jack everywhere she turned.

JACK LOOKED at Connie and tried to figure out how to ask if she'd taken C.J. without sounding as if he was accusing her of dognapping. A couple of little white lies might help things along he finally decided.

"I'm so glad you stopped over." Connie dropped onto the couch next to him, shoulder to shoulder, thigh to thigh. "We've hardly seen each other while you've been back this time."

Jack smiled his gee-I'm-glad-to-be-here smile and looked into her eyes. "I feel the same way," he said. "That's why I'm here."

It took all his inner strength to hold himself back from throttling her and shouting, "Where's the dog?"

"I really should be mad at you, the way

you've been ignoring me. In fact, I *was* mad at you. But then I decided you had a lot on your mind with all this C.J. stuff." She smiled. "And I forgave you."

"Thanks." He resisted the urge to roll his eyes. "I wanted to tell you in person that, since we haven't found C.J., I'm going back to Chicago."

Connie straightened. "Already? But what if C.J. shows up?"

"Liza will be staying a few extra days." He hoped this led them down the right path.

"Hmmph. Well, there's the problem. C.J. will never come back if she's there. I already told you—the poor dog probably ran away just to avoid her."

"Connie, the dog can't open her own gate."

She blinked. "All I know is if I were a dog and that was the caretaker you hired for me, I would be hightailing it out of town as fast as I could."

He figured he'd let that "if I were a dog" remark slide. "This isn't just sour grapes about your not getting hired as the caretaker, is it?"

Connie jumped to her feet. "How can you say something like that?"

Jack started to lose his patience. He stood.

"Listen, Connie, why did you say you thought C.J. would come home if Liza was gone?"

"To help you get C.J. back. I was looking at it from the dog's point of view. Why?"

"Well, you sound like someone who knows where the dog is. Like you might have her."

Connie's mouth dropped open. "Why would I have the dog?"

"Because you wanted to be the caretaker—bad."

"Are you accusing me of stealing your dog? I might want the job, but I wouldn't steal C.J. to get it," she said with a sniff. "Anyway, if the dog is gone, there is no job. My stealing the dog wouldn't help me at all," she said in a high, excited voice.

"It would if Liza left."

Connie's eyes flashed. "I can't believe this. After all these years, after how close we've been, I'd think you'd know me better than that."

Jack eyed her for a moment, trying to gauge whether she was telling the truth or not. "You're sure? Because I'm going to trust you on this."

Connie walked toward him and stopped a foot away. "You want to know what I think? I think that Liza woman took her."

"Right."

"She was afraid you would go back to Chicago, so she took the dog to make you stay."

"Why would she care if I went back to Chicago?"

"Men are so stupid." Connie flipped her hair. "She—wants—you."

Jack shook his head. "I don't think so."

"Oh, I know so. Women can see through other women. She actually thinks she might be able to land you."

"No—"

"Oh Jack, get real. You offered her the job, then you say you're going back to Chicago, and, suddenly! oh! shock! the dog is missing. She knew you were leaving, right?"

He thought for a minute. "Uh, yeah, actually, she did."

"And then the dog disappeared—right?"

He nodded.

"Mark my words. There's your thief."

"That's pushing it. The dog disappeared at night—I'm the one who discovered her missing." He thought back to what he and Liza had been doing on the couch that night... "Liza didn't have any opportunity to steal C.J. I was with her during the time C.J. got loose."

"Then she's got a partner."

"Connie, this is so far-fetched, it's bordering on absurd."

"Truth is always stranger than fiction, you know. Where did she come from anyway?" Connie pointed a finger at him.

"Chicago."

"Uh-huh. What a coincidence. Someone from Chicago just happens to come to Coldwater and apply for a job working for you?"

Someone who worked for a newspaper in Chicago.

Oh God no, this couldn't be about Cordelia. A pain started in his chest and began to spread outward. Not Liza. She didn't have ulterior motives. She couldn't.

"I gotta go." He pulled on his jacket and headed for the door.

"Mark my words—she wants you. And my bet is she's got someone helping her *set you up.*"

Jack stepped outside and inhaled deeply, hoping the crisp air would clear his mind. Connie was seeing conspiracy theories everywhere she turned.

Liza was nothing more than a nice woman— an incredible woman—who used to work in the food section of the *Chicago Sentinel,* who just happened to stop at his house and ask if it was for sale. And who was considering the caretaker job but kept putting off accepting it.

He got into his car and started the engine. Could Connie be right? The dog disappeared one day after he'd told Liza he was going home. Then, this morning, after mentioning he wanted to get back to Chicago for a meeting, the kidnapper's note appeared in the mail slot—and Liza was the one who'd found it.

The night Liza had come to dinner with the ladies next door, she'd spoken as if she still worked at the newspaper—and then corrected herself. He'd chalked it up to the fact she'd only recently quit.

If she had really quit at all.

An inkling of fear slid cold through his veins. Suddenly, everything about Liza and her reason for being here seemed suspect. Too many coincidences. Was she up to something? Had she really been waiting for him in his room last night—or had he caught her there searching for the truth about Cordelia?

Not Liza.

He exhaled sharply. He hadn't realized how hard he'd fallen until this moment.

This was nuts. With only the accusations of a jealous woman for proof, he was finding Liza guilty of the worst possible motives. All he had to do was ask her, just come out and say, "Liza, tell me straight. Did you steal C.J.?"

Right. And if he was wrong, that would be the end of whatever it was that was going on between them.

She couldn't be faking everything—quitting her job, joining the culinary institute. She'd been at the institute just yesterday morning. *Hadn't she?*

It would all be easy enough to check. Two calls. That's all he'd have to make. One to the newspaper to see if she was still an employee. And the other to the Maine Culinary Institute.

Heck no. He trusted Liza. He wasn't going to go checking up on her.

And if Connie was right? What if Liza was up to something? What if it wasn't about getting him at all, but getting to the truth about Dear Cordelia?

He drew in a long, slow breath. Everything about him, his livelihood, his reputation, his budding sports-agent business could be on the line right now. For his own protection, he had to make sure Liza was everything she said she was.

He arrived home and spotted a note from Liza on the kitchen table saying she'd gone out for a walk. This was perfect. He could check out the culinary school and the newspaper and put his fears to rest. Liza would never need to know.

He flipped open the phone book and dialed the Human Resources Department at the Maine Culinary Institute. Using his ultraprofessional voice, he explained that he was a landlord in the area and wanted to check the information on a rental application. Could they confirm for him that Liza Dunnigan had taken a position on staff?

After what seemed like an inordinate wait, the woman returned to the phone. "We have no one by that name who has been hired recently," she said, clearly confused. "Are you sure you called the right school? Perhaps she's going to be on staff at the university in Orono."

Stunned, he nodded. Liza wasn't going to work at the culinary institute?

"Sir?"

"Uh, yeah, maybe I have it wrong. I'll double-check."

He hung up and stared at the phone. "Liza, what the heck are you up to?" Fear nipped at the edges of his mind, tried a full-frontal assault on his consciousness, but he shoved it away.

Not his Liza.

He dropped onto the couch. Of all the women

who had been in his life, all the casual relation-ships he'd had with gorgeous, fun women, he'd always been able to keep himself free of entan-glements. Until now.

It served him right—poetic justice, as it were. Here he was, falling for a woman who proba-bly not only didn't want him, but was up to no good besides.

He sprang off the couch. The newspaper. The paper could clear this whole thing up. Liza's phone number should be on the *Sentinel* Web site. If she was still working there, her voice-mail message would tell him everything he needed to know.

He ran upstairs to his computer and, minutes later, had her *Sentinel* phone number and e-mail address on the screen. He flipped open his cell phone and dialed.

The call connected and he listened to Liza Dunnigan's voice message tell him she would be out of the office for two weeks on vacation, and to press zero to talk to someone else. He snapped his phone shut, slumped down into his chair, and thought he might be sick.

Liza Dunnigan wasn't moving to Coldwater. She wasn't looking to buy a house. She wasn't going to go to work at the culinary institute.

Deep inside, he knew what Liza Dunnigan wanted, what every reporter wanted.

Cordelia.

And then he spotted the cell phone lying on the desk. *Liza's* phone.

She'd been in here again. And she'd called someone.

He picked up the phone, anger filling every inch of his body and soul. He clenched his teeth, the feeling of betrayal so strong he could hardly stand it. Holding the phone in his hand, he hit the redial button and held his breath. Moments later, an excited female voice answered, "Liza! I've been dying to hear! Is he Cordelia or not?"

Jack's heart dropped into his gut and he ended the call.

CHAPTER THIRTEEN

JACK STARED at the phone in his hand as if it could give him the plague. He'd been set up. My God, all the years he'd been so diligent about keeping this secret, and here he'd been found out by a reporter from the food section.

He walked slowly out into the hall and down the stairs, gripping the phone tightly in his hand. It took all his willpower not to throw it against the wall, to take some sort of adolescent satisfaction from destroying Liza's phone.

What was this about anyway? Since when did food section reporters do investigative reporting? Was she planning to create a new dish and name it after him? Like Cordelia Casserole? Or Transgender Tacos?

He groaned. Not even funny. She was probably working in cahoots with that guy from the *Sentinel* who had been calling him for weeks. No doubt the two had put together a plan. That guy would go after the interview with Cordelia so Jack wouldn't get suspicious when another reporter showed up at his door, ostensibly to buy his grandmother's house.

"What a gullible fool," he muttered. That story about wanting to buy the house—why didn't she just say she was applying for the caretaker job? Damn, but she was brilliant. By not initially applying for the job, she could stall about accepting it. That forced him to stay in Coldwater and gave her more time, and opportunity, to get into his computer and find out exactly what she needed to know.

He shook his head. He'd looked into her dark eyes and swallowed every bit of her story—hook, line and sinker. Hell, he'd even invited her to live in his house so she could get to know C.J. better. She and her partner must have had a real laugh over that one. How many times had she gotten into his computer before he finally caught her?

And what about C.J.? Connie was probably right. Liza had to have arranged for someone to take the dog. He should have hired Connie in the first place—at least with her, what you saw was what you got.

A numbing ache started in his chest and he squeezed his hands into fists at his sides, as if the action could stop the pain. *Liza.* She'd been so commonsensical, so matter-of-fact…and so damn appealing. Never in a million years would he have expected her to wait for him in his room.

He blew out a sharp breath. Except, as it turns out, she hadn't been waiting for him in his room. Obviously, he'd caught her snooping and she had been forced to improvise. That incredible night they'd had together *had been an act.*

"I should have known," he said aloud to the empty house. "After all these years writing that column, I should have been able to tell something wasn't right with her."

He set Liza's phone on the mantel, then walked up to the front windows and stared outside, not really seeing. She'd fooled him completely—and he never got fooled. She was good; he had to grant her that. But to be that good, she had to be completely without scruples—hell, probably even a psychopath. She was in Maine for one reason and one reason only—to find out who Cordelia really was.

The question was, did she?

The wall phone jangled and he went to answer it. Ernie Crawford's voice rolled over the line. "Jack? This is Ernie. You know, from the cemetery." He paused a beat. "I got a little problem and I'm wondering if you can help."

Jack blew out a quick irritated breath. He wasn't feeling particularly helpful right now. "Sure, Ernie. What is it?"

"Well, I know you know that Dear Cordelia woman…"

Oh hell.

"I've got a question."

"Why don't you just write to the column?" Jack asked as pleasantly as possible.

"I suppose I could. But I kinda need an answer fast. And since you know the woman, I thought maybe you could just ask her for me. As a favor, you know. I'd owe you for this one, Jack." Ernie sounded desperate.

Jack sighed. "Okay, fine. I'll ask her. And you don't owe me anything. What's your question?"

Ernie cleared his throat. "It's Margaret…"

He should have known.

"We've gotten kind of close."

"I gathered that."

"The thing is, all of a sudden she's acting sort of strange."

Jack rolled his eyes. He'd heard this problem a million times before.

"She won't let me in the house."

"She won't let me in, either. Dorothy has a cold."

Ernie snorted. "She told me that, too. Only I know her pretty well and I think she's lying."

"Maybe she's not, you know, interested anymore." Jack pictured Margaret in the house with another man and Ernie at the front door. If he wasn't feeling so shitty right now he would have laughed.

"I know it's not *that*. She'll come to my house—she just won't let me in hers. So, what I want to know… Can you ask Cordelia what I can do about this?"

"Sure. No problem." Jack shook his head. "It might be a day or so before I hear back from her."

"That's okay. Thanks, Jack, thanks. I really appreciate it."

Jack hung up the phone and wandered back to the window. He wished his problem was as simple as Ernie's. Right now, all he could think of was Liza and what she'd done. Every cell in his body wanted to throw her out of his house the minute she got back. And every inch of his heart wanted to take her into his arms. But he could do neither. Not until he learned whether she'd found what she'd come for. He shoved his hands deep into his pockets and let his shoulders slump.

He'd disabled the password on his computer while he was here, never thinking he'd have to worry about security. He shook his head. In essence, he'd helped Liza Dunnigan discover his secret.

Staring out the window, he formulated a plan. When Liza got back, he'd have to handle her with kid gloves. If he pushed too hard too fast, she'd probably walk out. And he needed to know exactly what she knew before he sent her packing.

Half an hour later, the front door opened and Liza stepped into the room, cheeks rosy, eyes sparkling from the cold. "Hey," she said, grinning. She slipped out of her jacket and hung it on the coat tree.

The warmth on her face made him sick. Looking at her made him sick. "So where'd you go?" he asked.

"Just walking, wanted to get some fresh air, clear my head. Sometimes I get a little stir-crazy in the winter."

Just plain crazy might be more like it. He looked at her a moment, just looked, and wished he could lay it on the line but knew he couldn't.

"I've decided to head back to Chicago," he

said. "I just don't think we're going to find C.J.—not after this many days."

"Oh Jack, I can't believe she won't show up somewhere."

He wanted to shout at her, *You lying witch.* Of course the dog was going to show up…just as soon as Liza went back to Chicago and filed her story.

He shrugged. "If she does, the ladies will let me know. I'm, ah, going to close up the house and put it on the market. You'll have to find somewhere else to live. That is, unless you're still interested in buying?"

"Oh, I might, maybe…" She looked a little stricken. Yeah, well, she wasn't the only one feeling a little stricken right now.

"Last week, you said you wanted to buy the house," he said, taking a perverse pleasure in making her uncomfortable.

"I did. But you're catching me a little off guard here. I'd pretty much put the home-buying idea to rest when I began to seriously consider taking this job with C.J."

"No C.J., no job," he said. "I suppose you could stay here until you find another place. Be pretty hard to start a new job and be homeless at the same time."

Liza nodded.

Screw the kid gloves. "You're starting in a week or so, right?"

She nodded again, her smile fading.

"Because the oddest thing happened today." He strolled across the room and turned to face her. "I called the culinary institute. They said you weren't on staff at all. And I was wondering what exactly that might be all about."

Liza's eyes widened for the briefest moment and then she smiled sheepishly. "Well, I'm actually not on staff yet. I'll be working on developing recipes for a cookbook with them and they'll be putting me on the payroll by spring."

He marveled at how easily the lies came out of her. Bitter disappointment coursed through him. This was so opposite from what he thought Liza Dunnigan was all about.

He walked to the hearth and lifted her cell phone off the mantel, holding it up like a trophy. "Here's your phone." He tossed it to her. "You left it on my desk—by the computer."

Liza paled and a small gasp escaped her. "Oh, I was in there…looking for that Ace bandage—"

Jack snorted in disgust. "Oh hell, Liza, not that again. What for? Were you hoping to seduce me as I came in the door? Try wrapping yourself in plastic wrap—it's a little sexier than a brown elastic bandage."

Liza flushed. "I fell coming home from the bar last night and twisted my ankle."

"Looks like you're walking okay today."

"Why are you acting like this?" Her forehead creased.

"Acting? This isn't acting. Maybe you should tell me about acting."

"Fine. Behaving. Why are you behaving like this?" Her lips quivered and she pressed them together. He remembered what it was like to kiss those lips, to feel Liza's soft body beneath his own, her breath mingling with his— He rammed the memory into the darkest recesses of his brain and covered it with hatred. It had all been a lie anyway.

"Anything else you were looking for in my room?" He willed her to tell the truth, to come clean, to apologize and ask his forgiveness, to tell him she loved him—

Where did that come from? To tell him she loved him? *As much as he loved her.* He had fallen in love with the woman who was to betray him. This was bordering on melodramatic. If it wasn't his own life, he might laugh out loud at the ridiculousness of it all.

"What else were you looking for in my room?" He kept his voice steady and cool.

Liza shook her head.

"Because I talked to your friend on the phone—and she wanted to know. Did you find what you were looking for about Cordelia?"

Liza gasped. "Oh Jack—"

"Oh Jack what? You're sorry? Sorry for pulling a fast one? Or sorry for getting caught? It's kinda late for sorries, you know."

He leaned toward her, mentally crushing all feelings for her beneath bitter contempt, his words coming out one by one, curt and demanding. "What did you learn about Cordelia, Liza? I have a right to know."

She stared at him, her big, dark eyes welling with tears. She bit her lip.

"Tell me what you learned."

She raised her chin, looked him straight in the eye, and he had to hold himself back from reaching up to brush the tears off her cheeks. And then she said, "You're Cordelia," as though daring him to deny it.

For a flicker of a moment he was filled with

a grudging admiration for her and what she'd accomplished. He walked toward the window and looked out, his back to her as he spoke. "I'm Cordelia. Ten years and no one ever figured it out. I gotta hand it to you. You're good."

Outside, the day was already beginning to darken as dusk shot gray through the winter-afternoon sky. He turned to face her and narrowed his eyes. "What do you get out of it? A big raise? Recognition? A promotion?"

She flinched a little at the last one.

"A promotion? You're getting a promotion for this story?" he said, resentment in his voice.

She shook her head. "I'll leave." She started toward the stairway and he stepped into her path.

"You *are* writing a news story, correct?"

She stared at him a long time before nodding.

"I thought so. Make sure you put something in your article about what it's like to—screw—Cordelia." He knew he was being crude and he didn't care. "In every sense of the word."

Anger flashed in her eyes for an instant. "Maybe I'll recommend that Cordelia read her own book. She might especially benefit from the chapter about honesty."

"Oh, the pot calling the kettle black, is it?"

Liza tried to step past him and he reached out

and took hold of her arm. "Who the hell are you anyway?" he demanded.

She pulled away from him to race up the stairs and Jack watched her go. Then he went into the kitchen, popped open a beer and chugged half of it down.

A few minutes later he heard Liza's footsteps on the stairs. He leaned against the doorjamb in the entry to the kitchen and watched her hurry across the room for the front door.

"Just one more thing, Liza," he said in an over-nice voice.

She turned, her expression wary, all her body language telegraphing flight. "Yes?"

"Where's my grandmother's dog?"

"How should I know?"

"Oh, come on. You had someone grab her to make me stay in Coldwater."

She let out a sharp laugh. "I most certainly did not."

Jack straightened and walked toward her. "Look, I've figured everything out—you might as well fess up because otherwise I'll have to get the police involved."

"You really think I took C.J.?"

"You or an accomplice. Maybe that woman who answered your phone when I hit redial."

Liza's mouth dropped open and she quickly recovered. "I don't know where C.J. is. You may think I'm the lowest possible human being on the planet right now—and who knows? Maybe I am. But I didn't take the dog. No one associated with me took the dog. *I don't know where C.J. is.*"

She reached for the door handle and tugged at the door, but it stuck. She tugged several more times before setting her suitcase down.

Jack sighed and stepped forward. "Here. Let me." He pulled open the door.

Liza picked up her suitcase and marched outside. He stood in the doorway, watched her open the trunk to her rental car and hoist her suitcase inside. The wind swept a chill through him and he welcomed the cold, some other sensation he could feel besides disgust.

LIZA SLUMPED into the seat on the airplane and closed her eyes so the woman in the window seat next to her wouldn't try to start up a conversation. She let her breathing go soft and slow. She had accomplished the impossible. She'd gotten the story that reporters all over the country had tried to get and failed. So why didn't she feel victorious?

Her mind replayed the conversation she'd had with Jack, the look on his face—disgust, revulsion—when he'd confronted her just a few hours ago. The memory brought an ache deep within her chest.

She'd gotten the story and lost the guy.

Oh, brother, she had to get over that delusion. He'd never been hers to lose. She'd known from the beginning that all he wanted was a caretaker for the dog and a short-term fling.

Just as all she'd wanted was the information to give her a new job. Oh, all right, and to live happily ever after with the man of her dreams. Too bad the man of her dreams turned out to be the same guy whose pockets she had to pick. Kind of destroyed any chance at happily-ever-after.

Oh, this was just swell. Her first real assignment as an investigative reporter and she fell in love with the subject. It would be a long and painful career if she made a habit of this.

She thought of never kissing Jack again and a knot formed in her throat. If she had taken the job as caretaker, at least she would have had contact with him on a somewhat regular basis. Maybe they would have had a chance—

Good heavens, she was a raving lunatic. This

is what she'd come to—confusing a made-up story with reality.

And all because of Jack Graham.

She tried to work up some self-righteous indignation. If he hadn't always been so darn protective of his client—okay, himself—this never would have happened. At some point, with some reporter, he could have had *Cordelia* give written responses to questions or something like that. At least it would have removed some of the aura of mystery that surrounded the woman.

Besides that, he was a man. People didn't want advice about love from a man, they wanted it from a woman. How many advice columnists for the lovelorn were men anyway? She couldn't think of even one.

That settled it. So how come she wasn't celebrating? How come she felt like a schmuck? She sighed. Self-righteous wasn't working. He wasn't at fault here. She was. She could complain all she wanted that he'd been putting one over on his readers for years. But the bottom line was, she had purposely gone into his life and lied about herself and her motives. Not a very ethical person.

"Would you like something to drink?"

She opened her eyes and looked up at the flight

attendant in her smart navy blue uniform offering beverages and a minuscule bag of pretzels.

How about a double martini?

Liza straightened. "Uh, a Diet Coke, please." She took the pretzels and set them on her tray table.

The woman next to her ordered the same and promptly wolfed down the pretzels. After a few moments, she quit staring out the window and began staring at Liza's untouched pretzels.

"This is my first time all alone on an airplane," she said.

Oh great. She should have kept her eyes shut. Liza gave the woman a wan smile, the kind that was supposed to deliver the message she wasn't in the mood to talk.

The woman smiled sheepishly and didn't get the message. "I have a phobia about flying—so I'm in therapy. My therapist came with me on two flights before this one. But now, it was time for me to fly on my own."

"Good for you." Liza nodded and pulled the in-flight magazine from the pocket in front of her. Selfish as it sounded, she wasn't in the mood to hear all about this woman's life and her problems.

"I was pretty nervous before we took off, but

once you're up here, it's about the same as being on a bus. Except when you look down." The woman laughed a little at her joke. "I had to change my life. You know, I couldn't take vacations unless I drove, I couldn't take a job that involved travel. Do you know what it feels like to want your life to be one way and be trapped with it another way—just out of fear?"

Liza stared at her. "Actually, I do."

The woman glanced out the window. "I'm glad I went through everything I did to get here. I'm a different person than I was before—stronger, braver." She looked over at Liza's bag of pretzels again.

"I was so nervous, I didn't have lunch." She swallowed. "Are you going to eat your pretzels?"

The unexpectedness of her question caught Liza by surprise and she laughed. For some reason, the whole conversation struck her as absolutely ridiculous. "No—" A laugh bubbled up from inside her and she fought to hold it in. She handed the bag to the woman as a chortle burst out of her. "Have them." One laugh rolled out upon another until she was near hysteria. Tears spilled over her cheeks, and still she couldn't stop laughing. She gasped for breath and forced herself to calm, only to be overcome again. And the tears kept rolling from her eyes, until she was no longer laughing, but crying.

The woman in the seat next to her held the open bag of pretzels and stared at her as if she was insane.

Liza drew the back of her hand across her eyes and sucked in several breaths to calm herself. She wiped her eyes roughly with her hands, saw the mascara on her fingertips and sighed. She must look like a wreck. "I'm so sorry," she said. "I'm not laughing at you—not at all."

The woman set the pretzels on her tray table. "Did he end it? Or did you?"

Liza gaped at her a moment before recovering her composure. "No, it's not that—I mean, we weren't really even dating—not really. Although…I don't know what we were doing." She sighed. "Oh, he ended it. Because of what I did."

The woman nodded sympathetically. "Are you sure it's really over?"

Liza considered what she had done to Jack. He had used the word *betrayal*. No, she didn't expect to be hearing from him anytime soon unless it was to bring some sort of lawsuit against her for breach of trust or some such lawyerly thing.

"I'm sure. It's over. Done. Finished. Complete."

"Sounds pretty serious."

"Well, I did a pretty serious thing." Tears welled in her eyes again.

The woman just looked at her. Finally she said, "If you could take back what you did, would you?"

"It's too late."

"If you could change it, would you?"

Liza tilted her head back against the seat and contemplated the question. Would she? She sighed. Would she give up the certain chance for promotion into her dream job in exchange for the uncertain possibility of having Jack Graham permanently in her life?

Certainty versus uncertainty. A bird in the hand versus two in the bush, and all that stuff. "I don't know," she finally said. "I don't know that I ever meant anything to him anyway."

A long silence settled over them, which was fine with Liza. She didn't really want to talk this whole thing out with someone she'd just met and would probably never see again in her life. She closed her eyes.

"Have you thought about apologizing?"

Liza opened her eyes and shook her head. "I

don't think there's any way to apologize out of this one."

"But you haven't tried."

"Right. I haven't tried. But—" What did she think she was going to say? *But, I want to apologize and still file the story? But, I want him to love me even if I expose his secrets? But, I want everything on my own terms just for once in my life?* Yeah, right. It was too late for this anyway. By her actions, she'd guaranteed that she had lost any chance of ever having a relationship with Jack.

Dwelling on all this didn't even make sense. She'd known from the beginning that she would write this story if she got the information she needed. She'd known all along that what she was doing with Jack was strictly to get a story. She'd known in her head this was a job.

So how come her heart hadn't gotten the message?

"Will you be okay?"

Liza jerked her attention back to the woman. "Oh sure, I'll be fine. Don't worry about me. I'm very resilient."

CHAPTER FOURTEEN

"WHAT DO YOU MEAN Liza went back to Chicago?" Dorothy's face was a perfect picture of shock and Margaret's face was the same. The two women exchanged a quick look of dismay. "We thought she was going to be the caretaker."

Jack shook his head. "She left yesterday. Can I come in?"

The women exchanged another look. Dorothy held up her index finger. "Just one minute—"

Margaret nodded vigorously. "We just need to pick up a bit."

The door slammed before he could assure them it didn't matter to him what the house looked like. He made a face at the lion's-head door knocker. "Okay, then. Don't mind me. I'll just wait out here until things are in order."

He turned and walked across the porch to the steps. The ladies never cared before if their house was spic and span. He hoped they weren't planning to vacuum before they let him in—it was a little cold out here. For lack of anything else to do, he looked up the street one way and then the other. He felt surprisingly calm considering that Liza Dunnigan's story was about to explode his life.

He heard the door open behind him and turned to find both women in the doorway, breathing as though they had just finished a stint of hard work.

"Oh!" Dorothy said on a gasp. "Oh, well, everything is just—"

"Spiffy," Margaret said. "Tip-top. Neat as a pin."

Dorothy nodded. "Shipshape."

They stood there grinning. Jack looked from one to the other. Guilty. They were guilty of something. Hiding a lascivious hobby they'd taken up? Hiding men? He thought of Ernie's concerns and wasn't sure he wanted to know.

He shrugged his shoulders against the cold. "Great. Can I come in?"

"Oh! Yes!" Dorothy said, stumbling backward into Margaret.

Jack stepped into the house and glanced over his shoulder, puzzled, at the ladies' behavior. On second thought, who cared what they were up to, he had enough problems of his own.

"We were just having our morning coffee—

would you like a cup, Jack? It's fresh." Margaret didn't wait for an answer before disappearing through the swinging door into the kitchen.

"Okay," he said to the door. He sat on the brocade sofa while Dorothy perched on a chair by the hearth. She sneezed and blew her nose. Her eyes watered until he thought tears were going to flow down her plump cheeks.

"Maybe you have a sinus infection," he said.

She waved a hand dismissively. "Oh, I'll be fine soon. These things never last long."

Margaret came back into the room and handed a steaming mug of coffee to Jack, then settled into the chair on the other side of the hearth. He glanced from one to the other. They looked like folk art bookends, up to no good.

"Now, what happened with Liza, dear? Will she be coming back?" Margaret asked in a worried voice.

"I don't expect we'll ever see Liza Dunnigan again—except on the evening news."

Dorothy gasped. "What did she do?"

"Is she in jail?"

No, but that might be a good place for her. He shook his head. "Nothing like that. She…" How did he tell them? Even *they* didn't know he was Cordelia. "She wasn't actually moving here to take a new job."

"She wasn't?" they asked together.

"No. It was all a lie. She wasn't moving here at all. She was working on a story for the *Chicago Sentinel* and lied about moving here so she had a reason to get close to me."

Dorothy chuckled. "That seems to be a common problem for you, doesn't it? Women doing all sorts of silly things just to get close to you."

He gave a wry smile. "She didn't want to get close to me because she liked me. She wanted information…wanted to find out something I've kept secret for a long time. And she succeeded. I expect, within the next couple of days, we'll see a big story break about… me…and Dear Cordelia."

Dorothy looked at Margaret, and Margaret looked at Dorothy, and then both looked at him.

"You mean that you're Cordelia?" Dorothy finally asked.

"You know?"

The two women nodded in unison like those little dog bobbleheads people put in the back windows of their cars.

"For how long?"

The women looked at each other again.

Margaret shrugged. "Oh gosh, almost ten years now."

"Ten years?" The words burst out of Jack. "Since the beginning?"

"Just about," Margaret said.

"My grandmother told you."

Dorothy smiled. "Not exactly. Do you remember when you used to call home asking for help answering some of the questions? Sometimes your grandmother would ask our advice because she didn't know how to answer either."

"It didn't take long for us to put two and two together." Margaret leaned forward. "Especially when we saw some of our advice show up in Cordelia's column."

"Your grandmother swore us to secrecy." Dorothy sipped her coffee.

"You two were Dear Cordelia, too?" Jack sat back into the cushions and shook his head. He'd been giving romantic advice to America based on the input of three old women in Coldwater, Maine. "You've known all these years and never said a word."

Margaret nodded. "We figured at some point you'd take your own advice and settle down."

"Find yourself someone to love and who loved you—"

"And start a family and tie the knot—not in that order, of course. We thought with all those girls in Chicago, surely one would be *the one*." Margaret sighed. "They were all so…pretty and fashionable and—"

"Young—"

"Yes, but lovely—"

"And flighty." Dorothy frowned and shook her head in disapproval.

"And sophisticated and worldly." Margaret frowned back at Dorothy.

"And young and gold-diggerish. Admit it."

Margaret sighed. "Yes, I suppose so."

"Suppose so? We've had this discussion a million times." Dorothy clucked her tongue. "Looks aren't everything and Jack knows it. Why do you suppose he never married any of them. Right, Jack?"

"Enough, enough." He held both hands up in surrender. "Why I'm not married isn't going to be our discussion today."

Dorothy ignored him. "When Liza came into the picture, she seemed like just the right sort of girl. Perfect for you."

Dorothy's words lay open his heart and he

drew in a long breath to ease the pain. Liza *had* been different from any woman he'd ever met. Or so he'd thought. Why the hell did she have to be the same as the rest after all?

"Who cares if she found out you're Cordelia?" Dorothy said. "You couldn't keep it a secret forever. It had to come out sometime anyway."

"She lied about everything."

"Oh, that's just what reporters do." Dorothy flipped one hand up as though to say *so what?*

Not *his* reporter. He shook his head. "Besides, I think—do you think—she could have had something to do with C.J.'s disappearance?"

"Liza?" Margaret's eyes grew wide.

"Connie actually thought of it. When she first said it, I thought she was crazy—"

"Jealous, more like it," Dorothy muttered.

"But with everything else she's done, I think she might be guilty."

"Did you ask Liza about it?" Margaret squeaked out.

Jack nodded. "She denied it—had the audacity to act hurt. I guess I'll have to get the police involved."

"I wouldn't." Dorothy blew her nose. "You see, I have allergies."

Jack looked at her. "The cops won't care about your allergies, Dorothy."

She didn't say anything and suddenly he thought of Ernie and how Margaret wouldn't let him in the house anymore. How the ladies wouldn't let Liza and him in the house either. How Dorothy's cold seemed to be nonexistent at the restaurant, and yet was back in full force here in the house.

How could he be so blind? Or stupid? *Or maybe just falling in love.* He stood and walked to the room's entrance then turned to face them, absolutely certain they had his grandmother's dog. "Where's C.J.?"

Dorothy leaped up, a look of dismay on her face. "Don't be upset, Jack. We didn't mean anything bad by it."

"You dognapped C.J.?"

"Dognapping sounds so harsh," Margaret said in a soothing voice. "We just gave her a little time away from home…"

Dorothy took his arm and pulled him down to sit on the couch. She sat beside him. Margaret moved to his other side and patted his knee as if he were a child. "We only did it to help you," she said.

"Help me? Help me what? Lose my mind?"

Dorothy bent to straighten the magazines on the coffee table. "We were helping you and Liza…get to know one another."

Margaret nodded. "You said you were going back to Chicago. We had to do something to make you stay—"

"She seemed like such a nice girl." Dorothy said.

"And pretty, too, in her own way. Maybe not as quite as sophisticated—"

"But certainly not a bit flighty—"

"And not too young either," Dorothy added.

Jack closed his eyes. Liza may be pretty, and not flighty, and not too young, and fun to be with, and approachable, and incredibly appealing, and— "Ladies, I think you've forgotten something. She's a fake and a liar and about to expose me to the world."

Dorothy sniffed. "Well, we didn't know all that then."

"I still think she's perfect for you," Margaret said. "People do things for their jobs. Look at you, Jack. You pretend to be an old woman."

"I don't pretend to be her, I just use her name."

"That's pretending," Margaret said.

"Someone else might call it lying," Dorothy said.

"Why is it I suddenly feel like the bad guy around here?" Jack frowned. "You're supposed to be on my side."

"Well, we are. But Jack, maybe if you'd have put forth some effort, you know, romanced her a little, she would have stayed here."

"And you two could have gotten married—"

Married? "Ladies, time for a reality check. If she had agreed to stay, I would already be back in Chicago. And she would be in Coldwater. No romance, no love, no marriage."

"Not with C.J. missing." Margaret smiled.

Jack snorted. "The ransom note was a nice touch."

"Margaret remembered it from a TV show— an old movie from the 1940s," Dorothy said. "It just seemed like the perfect solution."

"Oh yeah, it was perfect," Jack said.

"Who would have guessed Liza was a reporter?" Margaret sighed. "She did seem so right for you."

The ache Jack had carefully buried surfaced for a moment and he stomped it back into place. There were millions of women in the world, millions of women who could replace Liza Dunnigan—if he felt like looking.

"So where is C.J.?" He pushed himself off the

couch. "I might as well take her home. Ease Dorothy's allergies."

"Upstairs. We had to carry her up there when you came to the door," Margaret said.

"She's so fat and her legs are so short. She's got the same body as a pig." Dorothy frowned.

Jack let out a bitter laugh at the image of the two of them lugging C.J. around. He started upstairs. He'd found the dog, Liza was an undercover reporter, he didn't have a caretaker, Dear Cordelia was about to be exposed, he'd probably lose his chance to succeed as a sports agent, and there was a gaping hole in his chest where his heart once was.

Things were looking up.

TWO DAYS AFTER leaving Coldwater, Liza sat at her kitchen table, reading the food section of the *Chicago Sentinel* as she had every Sunday for the past seven years. Mmm, one of the features was beurre blanc, a wine sauce with shallots, bound with butter, and served over black sea bass. Her mouth watered. It sounded like something romantic she could make for Jack.

Except she'd never be making dinner for Jack again. The thought hurt like a stab and she pressed her lips together against the pain.

She quickly flipped the page and spotted a story about Super Bowl menus *guaranteed to score big*. That was supposed to have been her story—someone else had obviously written it while Liza was out. She sighed and dropped back into her chair.

They would replace her so easily in the food section—so many reporters hungry for a by-line. Why did she care? She was on the verge of filing a story exposing Dear Cordelia's identity. She should be overjoyed; she would never have to work in the food section again.

This was her new life. She was the new Liza. She'd succeeded. She'd changed herself into someone exciting and mysterious and different.

She just wasn't sure she liked herself anymore.

Standing, she walked over to her computer and picked up the stack of neatly printed pages from the printer tray. Plopping down sideways into a chair, she reread the article she had just finished writing.

She held the pages in her flat hand as if weighing them on a scale. These typed sheets were like gold—they held her future as an investigative reporter.

The fact that she'd uncovered what so many others had failed to learn would probably do wonders for her career. Respect like she'd never seen before would likely come her way from all sorts of important people in the industry. Who knew what lay ahead for her? Maybe job offers. Maybe the *New York Times*. Maybe network news. Well, maybe not that. Regardless, she was about to get a chance at the future she'd always dreamed of.

At Jack Graham's expense.

She stared at the pages and relived what it had been like to kiss him, to hold his hand, to talk with him and laugh…. She inhaled and closed her eyes, remembering his smile, the one that made her feel as if she was the most important person in the world. The smile that she'd first seen when he opened the front door the day she arrived at his house with a cockamamie scheme that had actually worked. The smile she'd fallen in love with.

It was about time she admitted it to herself. She'd fallen in love with Jack Graham that day. He opened the door and smiled at her, and after that, she'd never been quite the same. As much as she tried to deny it these past few days, as much as she tried to bury it beneath rational thoughts and logical evaluations of what she had done, she knew it was true. She loved Jack Graham. She would probably love him forever.

And he hated her. With good reason.

Tears bit at the back of her eyes. There would never be any chance for them. Not that a guy like him ever really picked someone like her anyway. She was always the girl who did the homecoming decorations—not one of the chosen few on the Court.

She wondered whether C.J. had been found and hoped Jack didn't still believe she'd had something to do with the dog's disappearance. But even if C.J. was back, she had no right to hope Jack thought any better of her—she'd probably lived up to his worst expectations.

She set the pages on the coffee table and reached for her cell phone. Kristin answered after a few rings.

Liza smiled just hearing her friend's voice. No matter what happened, Kristin would always be there for her. "Hi, it's me," she said.

"Omigosh, what happened to you?" Kristin's voice was all excitement. "What did you find out—I've been on pins and needles for two days. I almost called you a couple of times and then decided I couldn't risk it. I feel like I'm waiting for the next episode of a serial mystery program."

Liza squeezed her eyes shut to force away the

tears. Then she laughed. She could always count on Kristin to raise her spirits.

"Well? Spill it. Is he or isn't he?"

She looked at the story, neatly typed on clean, white sheets of twenty-pound paper. Boring white paper. Very practical. But then, the paper was only the backdrop. The words were what mattered. And what a set of words this was. All she had to do was turn this story in and she would never be called boring again.

"Or practical." She didn't realize at first she'd said the words aloud.

"Practical? What does that have to do with Cordelia?"

"Nothing." She picked up the top sheet of her article and examined it. "Kristin, isn't it amazing how plain white paper can become something valuable just because of what's printed on it?"

"Yeaahh."

"It's kind of like life, don't you think? We all start out as blank sheets of paper. But what makes us valuable is what gets written on our souls and in our conscience." A chill ran through her. The words on the pages of her life didn't always have to be predictable. But they had to be true to her values.

"Liza?" Kristin said. "What are you talking about? You're scaring me a little."

Liza set the page back on the rest of the stack. From one perspective, turning in that story was the right thing to do. The smart thing to do. After all the work she'd done, after all the lies she'd told, after falling in love with a guy she could never have, it was only logical that she turn the story in.

Yep.

But then, this wasn't just Cordelia's story—it was her story, too. She could write whatever she wanted to on the blank pages of her life. She'd already decided she wanted to change her life; just because people expected certain behavior from her didn't mean she had to oblige them.

"Hello? Liza, are you there?" Kristin sounded frantic.

"Uh-huh."

"What's going on? I need to know. He's Cordelia, isn't he?"

Liza picked up the stack of white typed pages and walked into the kitchen. When he'd confronted her, Jack had asked, *Who are you?* At the time, she hadn't known how to answer. Now she knew.

She was the woman who would never betray him.

"Jack Graham? No. I was wrong. He's not Cordelia."

"What?" Kristin was incredulous. "You seemed all but certain two days ago. What happened?"

"That's why I didn't call you back right away. It took me that long to ferret out all the information. He works so closely with Cordelia... And I was rushing looking at his files that first day—I was in such a hurry and so anxious to be right that I leaped to the wrong conclusions."

Kristin groaned. "I can't believe this. Did you at least find out where she is so you can get an interview?"

Liza opened a cupboard drawer and pulled out a book of matches. "Nope. I didn't find anything." She set the pages in the sink, then lit a match and touched it to the corner of the stack.

"Liza, I'm devastated. I had headlines written—Love Lady Is a Man. Dear Cordelia Is Actually Dear Cornelius. And my favorite was, Love Is a MANy Splendored Thing."

Liza snorted. "Based on those headlines, it's probably good I didn't get the story. You'd better stick to writing about cooking."

"That's it then? You're done?"

Liza watched the paper curl and burst into flame, the letters dissolving as the paper changed from white to black and then into ash. "Actually, I think my dreams just went up in smoke," she said, amused that she was even joking about it.

"You sound way too cavalier about this whole thing. What happened?" Kristin asked, bewildered. "You wanted out. You wanted to change your life. And you were on the verge of succeeding. Something's out of whack here. What happened?"

"I like the food section."

"You hate the food section."

"Correction. I used to hate the food section. Now I look forward to working there with my friends." Liza smiled.

"You fell in love."

She hesitated. "No, I didn't."

"Oh man, I've got this all figured out. You can't tell me the truth about Cordelia because you fell in love with the guy. Are you two getting married? Lalalalalala! Oh I can't believe this, *you fell in love with Jack Graham, the player!*" She chortled gleefully.

Liza laughed, a pain in her heart from the truth of Kristin's words. "Absolutely not.

There's no love going on here. In fact, I doubt if Jack Graham and I will ever speak again."

"Lovers' spat?"

"No. He has his life, I have mine. Maybe you haven't noticed, but Jack Graham and I don't move in the same social circles here in Chicago."

"You're kidding. Why, this is absolutely the first I've heard of that." Kristin let out a laugh. "Ha-ha."

"So tell it to me straight. I want you to say the words—I'm not in love with him."

Liza squeezed her eyes shut and pressed her fingers to the bridge of her nose to keep the tears burning in her eyes from spilling out onto her cheeks. "I'm definitely not in love with him."

"And you didn't get the story."

"No. I didn't get the story."

Kristin heaved a long-suffering sigh. "Okay, whatever you say. I'm sure the boss will be happy to hear you're sticking around."

"Feel free to let him know. I've got to give Mr. Klein a call and tell him I failed—just like everyone else. He can reassign the story to that guy who was on it before."

She hung up the phone and rinsed the ash in the sink down the drain. A small piece of paper remained unburned and she picked it up and

read the few words that were there: *of integrity.*
She'd written that Jack Graham was a man of
integrity. For a fleeting moment, she wondered
whether he would ever say the same about her.
Instantly, she knew the answer was no.

Determined to remove all vestiges of this assignment from her life, she deleted the Cordelia
file from her computer—and emptied the computer's garbage can so no one short of a computer geek on a mission could ever retrieve the
exposé she'd written. A weight lifted off her.
Then, even though it was Sunday, she called
Mr. Klein and left him a voice-mail message
telling him she'd failed, and thanking him for
giving her the opportunity to try.

She rested her elbows on her desk, dropped
her head into her hands and thought of Jack
Graham. She wished he was there to hold her
and tell her everything would be okay.

A lump formed in her throat and she tried to
swallow it down. Of all the dreams she'd ever
had, this one with Jack was the one she knew
would never come true.

CHAPTER FIFTEEN

"IT'S GOOD TO HAVE you back, Jack."

He looked up from his computer and smiled at the young woman who had stepped into his office to set the mail and the newspaper on his desk.

"It's way too lonely around here when you're gone," she said.

"Things got a little more complicated in Coldwater than I expected," he replied. He picked up the newspaper and a knot formed in his gut. It had been over a week since Liza left Coldwater. Every day since then he'd expected her Dear Cordelia story to appear in the paper. Today was no different. It bothered him that the paper hadn't called him for comment, hadn't called to verify that Liza's story was true, but if they were going to do a half-assed job of reporting, there was nothing he could do about it.

"But it's all fixed now?"

Everything but his heart. "Yeah. Got a caretaker all settled in. Turns out the ladies next door knew someone from their church and it all fell into place." After he'd confronted them about the dognapping, those sweet ladies couldn't do enough to help him find someone to take the job.

His secretary smiled and made eye contact with him. "Well…if you need me, I'll be at my desk."

"Okay." He glanced at the newspaper.

She waited another beat before stepping out of the room, long honey-blond hair swinging across the back of her formfitting sweater that was tucked into her equally formfitting slacks. Nice to look at. But young. Way too young.

The ladies were right. He needed someone like Liza. Hell, he needed Liza. The joke had truly been on him. What bugged him the most was that she had awakened something in him that he never knew existed. He wanted a future with one woman, wanted to share his life with one woman, wanted to love one woman. And the one that he wanted he couldn't ever have.

He used to believe true love didn't exist. Now he just believed it didn't exist for him.

He shoved the mail to the side and opened the main section of the newspaper, flipping through the pages and scanning each for a story on Dear

Cordelia. When he reached the editorial pages at the end, he sat back in his chair. Huh. He would have thought he warranted Section A at least. A quick check of the rest of the paper didn't turn up a story either.

What the hell? When was this story going to break? He was beginning to think the waiting was worse than the actual disclosure would be. Calmer now, he flipped to the front page of the newspaper and began to read.

The intercom screeched. "Jack, there's a guy on the phone from the *Chicago Sentinel*. Same guy who was calling about Cordelia before you went to Coldwater. Do you want to talk to him?"

This was it. They were calling for his comments. Who knew why it took so long for them to get to this point. Who cared? The fact was, they were on the phone now. Maybe they'd gone out and gathered all sorts of other information about his past, what he'd been doing in the years before he started the column.

"Yeah, I'll talk to him." For about three seconds Jack thought about lying, considered telling the guy that Liza had come up with the story just to make a name for herself, that none of it was true at all. But he couldn't do it. It was time for the truth—no more running away from Cordelia.

Muscles tense in anticipation, he picked up the phone. "Jack Graham."

"Mr. Graham, this is Tom Calloway from the *Chicago Sentinel*. Thanks for taking my call. I'm calling—"

"I know why you're calling."

"Right. I guess you would know by now. It's about Cordelia."

Jack felt a stab of irritation. So, Liza got the story and now she was too afraid to face him to get his comments on it? Baloney. She had no qualms sleeping with him just to get the scoop, but she sent in some other guy for the kill? No way. Let her finish the story. If they wanted his comments about Dear Cordelia, they would have to get Liza to call him.

"Why isn't Liza Dunnigan calling on this story?" he asked abruptly.

"Oh." The reporter sounded taken aback. "Well, it was originally assigned to me. She just took it over for a couple of weeks while I was on vacation."

Jack frowned. "You mean, they took her off the story once you were back?"

"Yeah. It was my assignment."

"So she isn't even getting any credit for it?" Jack couldn't keep the surprise out of his voice.

Liza did all the work and this guy was going to get the accolades? What kind of newspaper was this?

"She did what she could while I was gone, but the story was assigned to me—"

"Will her name even be on the byline as a contributor?"

Several seconds of silence greeted him. "Uh, would you like her name on the byline?" the reporter asked slowly.

"I think she deserves it," Jack said.

"Okay. Sure. I can talk to my editor. I'm sure he'll agree that if you grant us an interview with Cordelia, we can put Ms. Dunnigan's name on the byline with mine."

"You want an interview?"

"R-right. That's what I've been calling for all along." He sounded confused.

Jack sat back in his chair in stunned silence.

"Mr. Graham?" Calloway said. "If you like, Ms. Dunnigan can accompany me on the interview."

"With Cordelia?" he managed to choke out. "The columnist Cordelia?" He knew he sounded really stupid, but he had to buy some time to figure this out.

"Right. I'm sorry, I didn't realize you and

Ms. Dunnigan had connected on this story. I thought she had no luck at all reaching you." His words started to come faster. "Like I said, I'm sure my editor would bring her right back on for the interview. We'd love to have it in time for Valentine's Day. How does this Thursday sound?"

Liza didn't turn him in.

She didn't tell the newspaper. She didn't file a story.

Calm slid over him followed by regret so deep it hurt.

"Mr. Graham? Would you like Ms. Dunnigan to be present at the interview?"

Jack snapped back to attention. "Cordelia doesn't do interviews."

"But I thought—"

"No interviews—"

"But Ms. Dunnigan can be there, I guarantee it."

"I'm sorry, Mr. Calloway, Cordelia doesn't do interviews. She likes her privacy. Have a nice day." Jack set the phone back in its cradle and stared at it for a long moment.

Liza hadn't done it.

He spun his chair so he could look out the window. Though the day was gray and blustery, not unlike the one when he'd gotten the call that the caretaker had died, it felt suddenly as if the sun was shining.

Liza had dug up the information that every newspaper in America had been trying to get for years. And she hadn't used it. She'd earned herself a promotion—and she'd given it up for him.

He wanted to call her to ask why, to thank her, to look at her face again, to touch her hair, to kiss her…to love her.

Oh, God, did he love her.

He almost felt giddy. Almost. What was it he always said? There was no such thing as true love. Since when was he an expert anyway? Suddenly it felt great to be so wrong.

Dorothy was probably right—who cared if the world knew Cordelia was a man? If he lost out on the opportunity to represent certain macho sports figures because of it, well, their loss. With the right PR, he could probably turn this to his advantage. He'd have to think it through, but there were probably benefits to having a sports agent who had a good understanding of the human psyche.

He steepled his fingers and tapped them against his lower lip. Liza's only means to a promotion had been to get an interview with Cordelia.

No problem. It just so happened he had an *in* with Cordelia.

Five minutes later he was on the phone with Bill Klein, the editor at the *Sentinel.* The man sounded stunned.

"*The* Dear Cordelia? The advice columnist *Cordelia* wants to give an interview to the *Sentinel?*" Klein asked.

"Yes, but there are some stipulations."

"Absolutely. Whatever she wants."

"The interview will be with Liza Dunnigan."

"Liza?" There was definite bewilderment in the man's voice.

"Don't you know who she is?"

"Oh sure, yeah, I know. It's just she's in the—"

"Food section. I know. Nevertheless, that's who Cordelia wants to meet with." Jack was enjoying this immensely.

"Works for us. Is there any chance Cordelia would be open to doing this before Valentine's Day?"

"That's her goal."

Jack heard Bill Klein exhale. "Great. Is there a specific location where she'd like the interview to take place? Here in the office? A restaurant?"

"As you know, Cordelia's very private. She asked that the interview take place in my apartment where she knows the privacy is guaranteed. I hope that's all right."

"Fine. Absolutely fine. Can I send a photographer?"

Jack smiled. "She's agreed to do the interview. But no pictures."

"No problem. Just had to ask. How about questions—is anything off limits? Can Ms. Dunnigan ask about her childhood, education, family…"

"She can ask. I'll leave it up to Cordelia what she'll answer." Jack looked at the calendar on his desk.

"Great. And a date. Does she have a date in mind?"

"How about Friday night, seven-thirty." He gave the man his address. "Cordelia asked that Ms. Dunnigan have dinner with her that night. She finds it less stressful with strangers when there's something to do. Oh, and tell Ms. Dunnigan there's no need to dress up—casual, jeans would be fine." *Leopard underwear would be a nice touch.*

"Fantastic. I'll set it up. Mr. Graham, thank you. Tell Cordelia we'll do a great job. We'll do a story that makes her proud." He sounded like a man who'd just won the lottery.

"There's just one more thing. Would you tell

Ms. Dunnigan that Cordelia asked that she bring along an Ace bandage?" He grinned at the silence that followed.

"An Ace bandage?"

"Right. You know, those brown elastic bandages you use to wrap injured knees and twisted ankles?"

"Yeah, I know what they are. I'm just curious... What does she want it for?"

Jack held in a laugh. "Who knows? She's got quite an eccentric streak. It's always good to humor her, though. Especially since she's granting this interview."

"Absolutely. Absolutely. Ms. Dunnigan will be there Friday night at seven-thirty—with Ace bandage in hand."

Liza put her bag over her shoulder and stepped up to the front desk in the lobby of Jack's posh apartment building. She smiled at the stone-faced uniformed man sitting there and swallowed down her fear. "I'm here to see Jack Graham," she said with as much confidence as she could muster.

"Ms. Dunnigan." A smile softened his features. "He's expecting you—number 2226, go on up." He gestured toward the elevators.

She pressed the button and looked at the dial

above the door. Both elevators were up around the twentieth floor. She closed her eyes and tried to calm her pounding heart.

What did Jack want with her? Was he really going to give her an interview? By now he had to know she hadn't filed the story. Was he still angry about her deception? She would give anything to go back and make different decisions, but life seldom gave you those kinds of second chances. The woman on the airplane had asked her, *if she could change what she'd done, would she?* At the time, she hadn't known how to answer. Now she knew.

She thought of the Ace bandage in her bag and blushed, remembering the last time she had brought up the subject. Maybe Jack had asked her to bring it along as a way of telling her she was forgiven, that they could be friends. It was almost too much to hope for. She mentally rehearsed what she wanted to say to him—how sorry she was for what she'd done, how much she appreciated him giving her this opportunity, how hopeful she was that they could put the past behind them.

The elevator doors opened with a *ding* and she stepped inside. When the doors reopened she headed down the hall, stopping when she reached 2226. Her heart thudded, her palms were damp, and her knees felt like pipe cleaners, ready to bend and collapse at the slightest pressure. She wiped her hands on the front of her wool coat.

Before she could chicken out, she knocked firmly. The door swung open and Jack was before her, smiling one of those smiles that stole all coherent thought from her brain. For a moment she was transported back to the day she'd arrived on his grandmother's front porch.

He was wearing jeans again, and a crewneck sweater over a T-shirt. But he wasn't wearing rag-wool socks this time. Nope, not the same. He was barefoot. She remembered her feet tangling with his that night—

She looked up into his face. "Hi."

"Come on in. I'm glad you could come." He stood back to let her enter.

"Me too," she managed to squeak out, forgetting every other thing she'd planned to say. Well, no one would ever call her too sophisticated, that was for sure. Thank goodness *she* wasn't giving advice to the lovelorn—no one's love affairs would ever last.

Jack hung her coat in the front closet and led

the way to the kitchen. "I opened a bottle of wine—do you want some?"

"Sure." The nearness of him almost made her shiver. She stepped into the living room just to put some distance between them. She looked at the plush navy leather sofa, the Oriental rugs on gleaming hardwood floors, the fire burning in the hearth. At some point, soon, she had to apologize. She wasn't so afraid to do that; it was the conversation afterward that she dreaded.

"This place is gorgeous." She went to the windows facing east, overlooking Lake Michigan. "The view must be incredible during the day."

"Yeah. There are benefits to success, you know." He stood beside her and handed her a glass of wine. "I ordered us Chinese—it should be here soon. You want to get started on the interview? I've got some plans for later."

Liza's heart dropped. Wine and dinner or not, this was business for him, all business. She looked at him. "Why me, Jack? After everything I did to you, why would you give this interview to *me?*"

He paused, considering her question. "Tell you what, I'm going to hold off answering that for a bit."

A few moments later they were seated on opposite ends of the couch. Jack gestured at the fireplace and grinned. "Sorry it's not real logs— not even those fake real logs like the ladies buy," he said. "Gas is the only way to go when you're this many stories in the air."

"Makes sense to me." She bent to dig in her bag for a pencil, pad of paper and the list of questions she and the editor had worked up. Her fingertips touched the Ace bandage and she felt her color rise a bit. If he'd asked her to bring that thing to torture her, he was succeeding wildly.

Leaving the bandage in her bag, she sat up, settled everything into her lap and glanced up at him expectantly. "I've got a list of questions, but we don't have to follow them if you want to go in a different direction. It's mostly just to get us started, or help out if the conversation stalls." She smiled confidently, so he wouldn't know how much her stomach was fluttering.

He just looked at her with those blue eyes, the ones that made her feel as if anything was possible, including love with a man like Jack Graham. He took a sip of his wine. "Questions seem like the best way to go for me," he said.

She nodded and looked down at the page; the questions blurred before her eyes. Maybe she should apologize first, get that out of the way so she could relax. At the thought, her heart pounded harder and she chickened out. She'd work the apology in later.

"I guess the best place to start is at the beginning. What made you start writing Dear Cordelia?"

Jack looked up at the ceiling. "I was in college and broke. So I started moonlighting at a local shopper paper writing classified ads to make a little extra money." He gave a small laugh. "*Little* is the definitive word. Anyway, their advice columnist had retired and I saw the vacancy as a chance to make a few more bucks."

He paused to sip his wine and she took the time to frantically finish writing down his last words.

Jack shifted to face her more directly. "I sent a letter to them, under Cordelia's name, proposing that I take over writing the advice column. I offered to do it free for a while, just as a test. But Dear Cordelia got popular fast and started getting picked up by other papers."

Liza looked up from her note taking. "So the people at that newspaper know you're a man?"

He shook his head. "Nope. As Cordelia, I was never actually an employee of the paper.

All they did was run my column every week. Our interactions were all through the mail."

Liza nodded. "You started this column when you were, what? Twenty? How could a young man, with virtually no life experience, answer all the questions people have about love and relationships?"

He laughed. "It wasn't easy. I based a lot on what I saw around me, families I knew. I'm a good observer—got a lot of experience in it every time I changed foster homes." He drank some more wine. "Anyway, when I got stumped, which happened a lot, I turned to my grandmother. She was an incredible help. And I just learned last week that the ladies next door were helping her when she couldn't come up with the right answer."

He dropped his head back against the couch. "Turns out America's been relying on romantic advice from three old women in Maine and a twenty-something guy who started the whole thing to make some money. How's that for an angle?"

"That's an angle all right." An angle that would pretty much destroy the column. Despite the fact that Jack was telling the truth, that he was handing her a break-out story, Liza wanted no part of it. She looked at him and knew she couldn't do it. "I just don't know. It's a great story about you, Jack Graham. But about Cordelia? She sounds shallow and…unromantic." Liza frowned. "Really, Jack. Cordelia has to say something else. Something more like, *My late husband, Edward, and I had a wonderful marriage and I wanted to help others find the kind of lasting love we had.*"

"Her late husband, Edward?"

"Well, no one knows anything about Cordelia, so she might as well have a late husband. Makes her more real."

Jack frowned. "What are you doing? I'm telling the world that I'm Cordelia."

"And I'm telling you not to. This is your livelihood, Jack."

"Yes. And this is my decision, too," he said, somewhat annoyed. "I've thought this through, Liza. I'm prepared to give an interview to the *Chicago Sentinel.*"

"So give one. I'm here to interview Cordelia—not Jack Graham. This interview should be about who Cordelia is and what she stands for—not how Jack Graham pulled the wool over everyone's eyes."

"Liza—"

"Find someone else to tell your story to then. I won't do it." She set her jaw.

He looked at her for a long moment. "You'll be an accomplice."

"I've called myself worse," she said softly. She turned away and began to speak again. *"We were never blessed with any children, and when Edward died, I found myself alone, remembering the love we'd shared. So, I contacted a local newspaper and offered to provide advice to couples searching for romance in their lives. It has been such a rewarding experience knowing that I can bring people together this way, help them find their soul mates."*

Jack shook his head. "Kind of fluffy, isn't it?"

"Fluffy is what people want to hear," Liza said. "They want to know Cordelia is drawing on personal experience to help them solve their love troubles."

"They do?"

"Imagine what they would think if they found out Cordelia is a single guy who started doing this for the *cash,* who kept doing it for more cash, and has never been in love in his life."

"What makes you think he's never been in love?"

Liza rolled her eyes. "You, Jack. You're a player."

"Point taken. Is there a problem with that?"

She cringed inside. Well, it wasn't as though she didn't deserve it. "No. But Cordelia *can't* be a single guy who's known for great success with the ladies."

"Sounds bad, huh?"

"Beyond bad."

"You're sure about this—me not telling them I'm Cordelia?"

"More sure than I have been about anything in a long time."

He gave her a slight nod. "Okay. What's the next question?"

Liza read off the sheet, "Do people write back and tell you how your advice has helped them?"

"Once in a while. But you know, it's the same as anything else—you usually hear from the complainers not the satisfied customers."

Liza sighed. "Unsatisfactory answer." He just wasn't getting it yet.

"It's the truth."

"Not for Cordelia. I think the answer should be something more like this…" She sat up straight, lifted her chin and splayed one hand across her chest like a prim, older woman. *"I*

often hear back from couples about how I have
helped them improve their relationship, or find
the love of their life. I live vicariously through
each of those letters, reliving the love Edward
and I shared.”

She smiled. “What do you think?”

“Gag me. It’s too much. I don’t think even
Cordelia would be that gushy.”

“Okay, then you fix it. And it better be something more romantic than hearing from unsat-
isfied customers.”

Jack stared at her for a long moment. Finally
he said, “Fine. You win that one.”

“It’s not about winning. It’s about making
sure Cordelia lives up to her reputation. You’ve
been helping people for ten years—don’t pull
the rug out from under them now.” Liza looked
down at the page and read the next question to
herself. “Okay, next. What’s the most romantic
love story you’ve had a hand in?”

“You’ll have to refuse to accept it, you know.”

She gave him a sideways look. “Accept what?”

“The award they’ll want to give you for being
the first reporter to bring in an interview with
Dear Cordelia.”

“What? Oh, because the story’s a bunch of
lies?”

He nodded.

She grinned. "Okay, I'll turn it down. Now, the question? What's the most romantic love story you've had a hand in?" *Say that it's me,* her brain whispered, and she shoved the thought away.

Jack settled into the cushions, one arm up over the back of the couch. His eyes caught hers and he held her gaze for longer than he needed to. By the time she was able to wrench her eyes away, her heart was pounding.

"Let me think on that one," Jack said. "I have a couple of questions I'd like to ask first."

Oh, here it came. The third degree about what she had pulled in Coldwater, questions about her character, her integrity, her deception.

But it was okay—it had to be okay. She could handle it. It was the very least she owed him. This, along with the apology she had yet to make.

She should have apologized right up front the way she'd planned. Then she wouldn't be looking like an ungrateful wretch. "Sure. It's your interview," she said a little too brightly.

"Two questions really," he said. "About Coldwater."

Her stomach churned.

"Why did you make love with me that night? And why didn't you file the story?"

Liza felt like throwing up. This was not the line of questioning she'd expected. Did she tell him? Did she tell him how he'd made her feel, that she'd made love with him because she had been falling in love with him? That she'd probably already been in love with him but had been too dumb to realize it? Oh, brother, she couldn't say that, women probably said that sort of stuff to him all the time.

"Why did I make love with you?" she repeated weakly. "Well, I was caught in your room. I didn't want you to know...the real reason I was there, so at that moment it seemed logical to say I was waiting for you."

He cocked his head, watching her intently.

She faltered under his gaze. "Isn't that a reasonable reason?"

"For a guy. But for Liza Dunnigan, looking for an Ace bandage would have sufficed."

"I didn't think of that until—it was too late."

"So that was your only reason—because you got caught?"

His eyes locked with hers. "No—yes! Isn't that a good enough reason?"

"Sure. Absolutely. And the story? Why didn't

you file the story that would have made your career, that would have gotten you out of the food section?"

Liza tilted her head and sighed. *Because I realized I love you. And even though I know I can never have you, I can't bear to hurt you.* "Oh. Well, I thought, actually, I knew, I'd been totally unfair about it." Weakest answer on earth, but maybe he'd let her slide on this one.

"Unfair? How so?"

She felt a slight blush heat her cheeks. "You know, sneaking into your bedroom, and then telling you I wanted you, using you—"

"You used me?" Jack asked. "Are you saying you really didn't *want* me?" His voice was soft and low and sent tremors through her insides.

"Yes—I mean no—I mean—oh, I don't know what I mean." She turned away, face burning with embarrassment. She refused to be one more woman like so many others who made a fool of themselves over Jack Graham.

"I'm sorry, Jack. I came over here today intending to apologize the minute I came in the door. And I wimped out. I'm so sorry about what I did to you—about what I almost did to you."

His eyes narrowed and he slid across the sofa until his thigh touched hers. "Let me make sure

I have this right. So you made love to me because you didn't want to get caught in my room. And you didn't file the story because you'd made love to me. Is that about right?"

She turned to look at him. God help her, but it took all her willpower not to grab hold of the front of his shirt and drag him close enough to kiss. "Y-yes, that's right."

His eyes bored into hers and she felt a weak defensiveness rise up inside her. "Surely there's not something wrong with that?"

"No. No. It's just I was hoping that…maybe your reasons why you did the one or why you didn't do the other…might have something to do with…me?"

Her heart hammered and the room seemed to buzz around her at the intensity she saw in his expression. "What do you mean?"

He reached a finger up and began to play with the hair by her ear. She couldn't breathe.

"I made love with you that night, Liza, because I wanted to make love with you. And I was hoping…you felt the same."

She looked at his mouth. *Don't kiss him,* her brain screamed. Talk. Talk to him. Make sure you're not just hearing what you want to hear.

"I did want you," she whispered.

"And the story? Why didn't you file the story?" His voice, while still low and soft, was insistent, demanding.

She shook her head.

"At the very least, you owe me the truth on this subject, Liza."

Tears sprang to her eyes. Humiliation stung her soul. "Because I love you." She bent her head and watched as tears dropped from her eyes and landed on her hands, tightly clasped in her lap. Silence hung over them for what seemed like an entire lifetime.

And then his arm was around her shoulders and his mouth was on hers, kissing her gently, so darn gently that she couldn't stand it anymore and had to grab the front of his shirt and pull him up against her hard.

When they broke apart, Jack brought a hand up to caress her cheek. "I've got to tell you. I fell in love with you that first day, when you were sitting all alone at my grandmother's dining-room table trying to find just the right way to sit."

Excuse me. What did he just say? "Could you repeat that, please?"

"What part?"

"The beginning."

"I fell in love with you—"

"You love me?"

He nodded.

"But I'm not beautiful. I'm not tall or fashionable, and I'm—" She couldn't bring herself to say *practical.* "I'm sensible."

"Shh. You're so beautiful I dream of you at night. And you're fashionable in an honest, unpretentious way. And I like sensible—it beats flighty any day."

"But—"

"No more buts. And no more questions. I've made up my mind and nothing you say will change it."

He kissed her ear, her hair, her throat. Liza closed her eyes and let her head drop against the back of the sofa. "What did you want the Ace bandage for?" she asked breathlessly.

"I don't know. I thought maybe you could show me what you had in mind the other night. I was intrigued."

"My ankle—it was for my ankle," she said.

"Bondage?" he murmured against her lips.

She laughed. "No, you goofball. I twisted my ankle."

He kissed her again, hard, as if he couldn't get enough of her. Finally she pushed back just a bit so she could see his face. "What about the rest of the interview?" she asked, only because she thought she should ask and not because she really cared if she asked the guy another question about writing an advice column for the rest of her life.

"You'll get your story," he said, eyes dark and seductive. His hands slid under her sweater around her waist. "Cordelia loves to give interviews."

EPILOGUE

LIZA WALKED across the hardwood floor, her footsteps echoing in the empty room. She opened the sliding door, stepped out onto the patio twenty-two stories in the air and remembered her first time in this apartment—the night she'd come to interview Cordelia. The view of Lake Michigan was breathtaking today, sparkling blue beneath a flawless sky, the water dotted with sailboats as far as she could see. The heat of summer surrounded her and a soft breeze touched her cheek and ruffled her hair.

Behind her she could hear Jack on the cell phone, his voice growing louder as he drew near. "I'm sorry, but she was very adamant about this." He stepped out onto the patio and put his arm around Liza's shoulder as he spoke. "She's chosen to retire in the same manner in which she wrote the column—quietly and privately. No interviews. I'm sorry. Thanks for the call."

He shut off the phone and pressed a kiss to

Liza's forehead. "Two weeks since Cordelia's announced retirement and the calls have dwindled to almost nothing. I feel like a free man. What're you doing out here?"

"Letting the baby enjoy the view one last time."

Jack laughed and set a hand on her very rounded belly. She put her own hand on top of his and looked up into his eyes, this man she loved with all her heart, this man she had married two years ago.

"You still want to do this?" she asked.

"Have a baby?" he teased.

"No, silly. Move to Coldwater."

He looked out over the lake. "Yeah, this is one heck of a lifestyle to give up, isn't it? Gorgeous views. High-class neighbors. Great restaurants. No lawn to mow, no snow to shovel, no gutters to clean out. Always something happening, never a dull moment." He glanced at her. "And, did I mention the gorgeous views?"

Liza nodded.

Jack stepped forward and rested his hands on the railing as he gazed outward. "Yup. No backyard for kids to play in, no driveway for basketball, no garage door to hit a tennis ball against. No front porch for us to sit on after dinner and watch dusk fall and the fireflies come out. No nosy neighbors to treat our kids like they were their own."

Liza caught her breath. "And no gardens to steal tomatoes from to throw at passing cars on hot summer nights."

Jack turned. "Exactly. Any second thoughts for you?"

She shook her head, her emotions welling up inside.

He took her hand and gave it a squeeze. "It's still unanimous. I've had enough of crowds and elevators and smog and rush, rush, rush. Come on." Still holding her hand, he led her through the empty apartment and out into the hall. The door snapped shut behind them and he bent to brush her lips with his own. "Let's go home."

HARLEQUIN SUPERROMANCE
TURNS 25!

You're invited to join in the celebration...

Look for this special anthology
with stories from three
favorite Superromance authors

25 YEARS
(Harlequin Superromance #1297)

Tara Taylor Quinn
Margot Early
Janice Macdonald

*On sale September 2005
wherever Harlequin books are sold.*

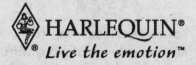

HARLEQUIN®
Live the emotion™

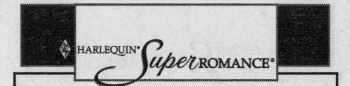

HARLEQUIN *Super***ROMANCE**

is pleased to present a new series by
Darlene Graham

The Baby Diaries
You never know where a new life will lead you.

Born Under The Lone Star
Harlequin Superromance #1299
On sale September 2005

Markie McBride has kept her secret for eighteen years.
But now she has to tell Justin Kilgore, her first love,
the truth. Because their son is returning to Five Points,
Texas—and he's in danger.

Lone Star Rising
Harlequin Superromance #1322
Coming in January 2006

Robbie McBride Tellchick had three growing boys and
a child on the way when her husband died in a fire. No
one knows how she's going to get along now—except
Zack Trueblood, who has secretly vowed to protect the
woman he's always loved.

And watch for the exciting conclusion,
available from Harlequin Signature Saga, July 2006.
Available wherever Harlequin books are sold.

www.eHarlequin.com

HSRTBD0805

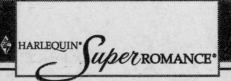

HARLEQUIN *Super*ROMANCE®

Big Girls Don't Cry

by
Brenda Novak

Harlequin Superromance #1296
On sale September 2005

Critically acclaimed novelist
Brenda Novak brings you another
memorable and emotionally engaging
story. Come home to Dundee, Idaho—
or come and visit, if you haven't
been there before!

**On sale in September
wherever Harlequin books are sold.**

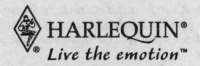

HARLEQUIN®
Live the emotion™